New South ™ Publishing

Raleigh, NC

www.newsouthtm.com

ISBN 13: 978-0-692-92928-5

ISBN 10: 0-692-92928-2

LCCN Library Congress 2017914164

Cover Design: Justin Young

Cover Photo: Tori McKoy

Edited By: LaMia Ashley

Consulting: Kisha Frazier

This book is dedicated to all the women who have been betrayed by loving someone.

First of all, I want to give thanks to God for being a constant factor in my life and letting me be able to continue my journey to write.

To my three KINGS: Shaimek, Shacory and Sharhon Williams. RIP to one and only baby girl Shaquoia Mommy miss you very much.

To my mother, Angela Melvin, you're the epitome of a survivor; one of the strongest and realest women I know. I love you to the moon, Mommy. Thanks for all you do for us and your grandchildren. You are my light when life seems dark.

To my father, Alexander McEachin, I thank God that I found you August 2016. You have helped me close a chapter that I needed to close and a wound I need to heal.

To my step-dad, Derrick Freeman, I love you like you created me. No matter how the chips have fallen, you loved me and my siblings unconditionally.

To my sister, Danielle Melvin, I love you, little mama. You've grown into a great woman and I thank God I have you in my life. You're the greatest mother to my nieces.

To my brothers, Buddy "Jay" Melvin, Deon "KK" Melvin, and Sean McEachin, please continue to live out your dreams and continue being great fathers to my nieces and nephews. Derrick Freeman, you have excelled in all you have done and you're continuing to become a great young man. I love you all more than words can express.

My grandparents, Charles and Virginia Edwards, Lord know I'm blessed to have y'all in my life, because many don't have five generations, so I thank God for you two. Thanks for being the glue to keep our Klan tight. Keep providing us the wisdom and knowledge you always have given us.

To my cousins, Tracey Melvin Maddox and her husband, Joe Maddox, y'all are more like siblings; but I want to thank y'all for the constant support, talks… oh, and definitely the parties and food. LOL. I love y'all to the moon. That's right,

Tracey, Fuck Cancer! You beat the hell out of that shit. I love your strength and nurturing spirit.

My besties, Shauna AKA Shon Juan the Streets, Preston Hylton, Erica Mitchell, and Tara Miller, thanks so much for your continued support and push for me to continue this journey and telling me to never give up on my dreams of writing and starting my own publishing company. New South™ Publishing is coming through. Y'all are my strength when I'm down.

My aunt, Pamela Williams, I love you for all you do for me and the boys. I thank you for showing me what being a woman is all about, knowing my worth and to not take no shit from no man. I will forever be grateful for your wisdom and talks with me during really tough times.

To my uncle, Mickey, I don't see much of you but I do love you very much and nothing will ever change that. You are the rock of the family, no matter what you may think, or how much you fuss with us. We all love you, ANIMAL! LOL (insider). I love you, *my still fine as wine*, Uncle Mick.

My 1st cousins:

Keir Melvin, my brother/cousin, you've always been a go-getter and worked hard. Even though we don't talk every day, just know the love is still the same.

Billy "Blast" Mosley, thank you for supporting me, being there when I need you, and the father I know you will always be to your children. No matter what no one says, we know, and God knows your love and heart are genuine

Randy "Rude" Lyons, I love you so much. You came home and did what most niggas wouldn't do when they come home, and I'm so proud of you for that. You and Blast never let the system deter y'all from making moves. Keep doing that ish, cousins.

James Melvin, Jr., Vonetta Melvin, Justice Lyons Melvin, Nina Austin, and Donelda Austin, I love you all so much. Even though we are not close as we should be, my love for y'all is the same as all my cousins. We have the same blood running in our veins, so know that no matter how long or how far, I love y'all and I'm here if y'all need me.

Monna Sidney, I am very proud of you, baby girl, and the woman you have become. I thank God that we have grown a great relationship and I love how you love your family. No matter what no one says, you are going to be great in all you do, baby girl. Hugs and kisses.

Torraine Melvin, Marquis, Miracle and

Jovon Maddox, I love y'all like my own. Keep

reaching for your goals. Don't let nothing or

anyone stop you from doing so. I believe in each

of you and I will stand behind y'all 100%, with

whatever; whether right, wrong, or indifferent.

Keep striving for the stars, babies.

To my nieces and nephews: I love all of

you so very much. Keep making Auntie proud and

be all that y'all can be in life. Don't ever give up

on y'all dreams.

To my sister-in-law, Hwan Puih-Melvin,

you have grown into a beautiful soul. I've seen

you grow from a girl to a woman. I can say you

have done your thing as a woman, wife and

mother. I love you to infinity, baby.

To all my people in the places I've called

home: Brooklyn, I'm coming back and I'm

networking very soon! What better way to do it than to go back home? To all my people in Ruff Raleigh and Chapel Hill, y'all know how we rocking. Brooklyn Bred, Southern Fed.

My business connects and the people who made this all possible: My editor, LaMia Ashley; My consultant, Kisha Frazier; thanks for keeping it real and guiding me. My proofreader, Kionne Reeves; My book cover designer, Justin Young, you the best! My photographer, Tori McKoy, videographer.

My *Glam Squad that* made my cover come to life: Thanks to Charisma Brockington for my hair. Makeup by Tori McKoy and Styling by Tina B. Kontroversi. Thanks to you all for doing exactly what I asked for. ***My black girls' rock.***

To all my family and friends in New York, New Jersey, Philadelphia, North Carolina,

Virginia, DC, Maryland, Florida, Atlanta, New Orleans, and everywhere you all are, I love y'all! It's too many to name; but just know, if y'all rocking I'm rolling…Thanks for all the support. I'm so humbled at this point in my life.

Always make sure that you give up the things you want for the things that you need.

POEM: BETRAYAL OF TRUST

I believed in you until my faith in you grew religious,

Prayed you'll forever be solid when others folded,

I was invested in you and gave you my all

I was all in with my love for you,

But you played to another team tunes,

I caught you slipping and called you offside,

My star player, my champion,

I never dreamed you would one day lose me,

Abandoned me when it was overtime,

My university of home taught me,

I would win some and lose,

With that understanding and my trust in God I refuse,

To let betrayal of others to cause me to live less passionate,

About anything I choose,

I trust in happiness while you frown upon
my faith,

At the end of the day I keep my head up
with ten toes down

It's me against the world now

And I won't lay down,

Trust

Kionne Reeves AKA Amayson Keys

Betrayal of Trust

By Tamika Melvin

Chapter 1

Why can't he love me and only me? What is it that he's looking for out here in these streets that he doesn't have at home? I been holding him down since I was 15, and it's still not enough. He still screws around with this and that, Keosha behind my back, and doesn't care if he gets caught.

◆◆◆NewSouth™◆◆◆

Crying, Niema thought to herself, while waiting for her best friend, Endy, to come comfort her - as always. Niema was a beautiful, 28-year-old, educated woman who doesn't know her worth. She has the most beautiful caramel skin tone, long, jet black hair, hourglass shape, and owns her own modeling agency named Beauty of NY, which stands for her name and her home -

New York. She owns a beautiful, three-bedroom house and a S600 Mercedes Benz, due to her mother passing two years prior from Cancer. That's how she inherited the money to start her own business. Like her mommy, she had always been determined to become an entrepreneur, so she could live comfortable and happy. Which you would think she would be, considering all she has accomplished. However, she is still unhappy, due to the constant encounters with her man, Caine, who some called CJ, being unfaithful.

"Hello! Earth to Ny. Where you at right now?" Endy laughed, waving her hand side to side, in front of her best friend's face. Niema sat on the couch, still pissed with Caine for betraying her - once again. "Endy, leave me alone. It's not funny. I'm so sick of Caine's bitch-ass" Niema groaned. Her legs were shaking uncontrollably, up and down.

Laughing, Endy said, "Girl, you whipped Keosha's ass though. And I can say I don't feel bad for her at all. I'm sick of that bitch doing that bullshit all the damn time. I mean, damn, she didn't learn anything when Ari whipped her ass three years ago over Ty?" Endy hyped.

"No, her and that black ass Tiffany Harris love messing with other people men. It makes them feel like they're doing something big by fucking other chic's men, when they are nothing but Jump-offs!" Niema spat, with a disgusted look on her face.

"Ny! Now bitch you know Tiffany and Keosha are known strippers around Brooklyn. Because they're cute, with nice, plump asses and voluptuous tits they purchased, they use it to their advantage. Those chic's are ratchet as hell, but dudes like that type of shit these days. Like, bitch, really? They still living in the projects but spend their money on bullshit. They're not even trying to get their money up to live better. All they do is strip, shop, and fuck different dudes with money 24/7. Why wouldn't they fuck your man without a question, girl?" Endy couldn't help but keep it 100 with her friend.

Niema couldn't help but laugh "Bitch, you are silly, but I feel you though. I just can't even process that he was at the hotel with that nasty-ass trick, and really thought Chynna wasn't gonna tell me she seen his ass. Like, dude we are friends.

Is this dude really serious, Endy? I mean, for real. Come on; what she got on me? Then, he thought he was gonna get away with it." Niema's voice trembled; making herself upset all over again. Crying, again, this time loudly, she continued "Why? Why does he keep doing me like this, Endy? That's why I whipped him and that little bitch ass. I'm so sick of playing the fool."

"Well, Niema, you have to do something about it. You can't keep getting mad with Keosha because you don't know what he's saying to her."

"Endy, are you for real? Are you defending that nasty bitch?" Niema was starting to turn up.

Endy walked over to hug her friend. "No, girl, I'm not defending her but you have to be logical, Ny." She hated to see her friend go through this over and over again.

Although this was a constant thing with Caine cheating, Niema wouldn't leave him alone. Endy or no one else could make her leave him. She had to want better… to get better… and that's what Endy always told her. Through it all, she never turned her back on her. Even if their other friends, Ari and Chynna, thought Niema was a damn fool, Endy knew that Caine loved Niema very much. But she also knew that he took advantage of her kindness. He's just too damn comfortable; and when a man gets comfortable, shit gets dangerous.

No matter how many times Niema told herself to leave him, she knew he would come with some lame-ass excuse of why he did what he did, just to keep her there with him. In the end, it worked out for him and she was like putty in his hands again. Caine would buy her expensive things, from diamonds to cars, trying to replace the pain and everyone knew it but Niema. He helped pay her house off, after he gave her a STD and stayed gone for two weeks with another stripper named Cookie.

"Endy! What is it about me that make him cheat? I mean, I know he loves me, and I know the sex is the bomb. So what am I doing wrong?" She asked, confused.

"Nothing, honey, that's just Caine. He loves sex all the time. He wants a freak that does what he wants when he wants. You feel me?" Endy explained. "You don't like giving head and a man likes that. They want that. Hell, they need that!!! You feel me, girl?" Endy laughed, trying to cheer her up. Although Endy knew Niema was still pissed, she tried to get her out the house, thinking that maybe that would take her mind off the situation.

"Look, girl, let's go somewhere. You know it's some pre-Thanksgiving parties going on in the city. We need to get out of Brooklyn for a while and have some fun." She tried to persuade her.

"I don't know, Endy, I'm not in the clubbing mood tonight." Niema declined.

"Well, bitch, you going. That's just that. I'm calling Ari and Chynna and, bitch, we're hitting the City.

"I guess I have no say so in this, huh?" Niema threw her hands up, surrendering.

"Nope, you sure don't! You're not getting ready to sit here and stress yourself. You're too young and beautiful for this mess. I used to do the same damn thing with Jasean, until I turned the tables on that ass. I saw I was worth more than what he was dishing out. Until you realize that, you will never leave him. You're 28yearsold and you're going to start acting like it and have fun.

Enjoy life; stop being the old hag all the time. Fuck that!!! Life is too damn short." Endy shot Niema some real shit.

Endy has been friends with Niema since Junior High School. Now that they're in their 20s, she hates to see anyone including Caine continuously hurt her with his cheating nasty ass and being open about it. Especially, since he's Endy love of her life Jasean's first cousin. Jasean is Endy's heart and soul who was once just like Caine to a certain instinct. She showed his ass a lesson and his ass got it together. It's nothing like giving a fuck boy a taste of his own medicine. "Girl come the hell on now and get ready we are going to this bash uptown and have some damn fun. I just spoke to Chynna and Ari too and they're going to meet us there." "Endy thanks for doing this for me sis. You always got my back"

Niema hugs her friend. "Okay enough of this mushy shit let's turn up for the night."

The girls decided to go to club Amnesia, Uptown, since they were having a promotional party for Nicki Minaj's *Pink Print* album. The club was packed and all the ladies were looking right, in their body-hugging dresses. All, except Niema, who still looked cute in some fitted, white pants with a green, knit sweater and pumps to match from Nine West. She was always the odd ball, so she doesn't offend or disrespect Caine by showing some skin. The girls always wished she would loosen up, but it never happens. She hated to wear sexy clothing, so they called her *The Grandma*.

"Hey, y'all, I needed this night out. Reeko won't let a bitch breathe, since I gained this weight after the baby. He's like a dog in heat every damn night. That damn Cuban side is showing more. But can you blame him?" Chynna twirled, showing off her figure.

Chynna was the spitting image of Endy. Both were light skin with hazel eyes and black, long hair. They all burst out laughing.

"Chynna, you and Reeko always been the freak couple," Ari said.

"No, girl, I'm telling you, that dude has really turned into a controlling-ass nympho." Chynna shook her head.

But Chynna was absolutely right. Since she had her son, Enrique, eight months ago, her fiancé, Reeko, had been in her ass. She went from wearing a size three to a size eight. He was already the jealous type, as most Hispanic men are.

"I know, girl! Tylon came asking me all these questions before I left. I'm like, dude, I'm gone. Now, go get the twins, please." Ari added to the story.

"This is our night to get twirled and have fun. Mommy and Nana are cooking Thanksgiving dinner tomorrow, so we can really enjoy ourselves tonight, because tomorrow… it's straight family time." Endy said, walking toward the door.

The line was long, but Caine and Jasean's uncle, Jack, was the promoter. The girls went straight in to the VIP section. When they got to their section, it had a plush, white, leather couch with a nice, round table that already had a bottle of champagne, chilling on ice. Niema was the most quiet out the bunch. Her mind was on Caine and what he was doing. Who he was doing it with, and if he was with Keosha or not. She couldn't fight it; he was on her mind all the time.

"Girl, this is nice. Y'all future uncle-in-law has some major pull!" Ari threw Endy a high five.

"Look, Niema, we're going to have fun tonight," Chynna shouted at her, drawing her from her trance.

"Girl, I'm good. I'm enjoying my bubbly right now. Damn!" Niema snapped.

"I see your ass over there staring off in space, thinking about that sorry-ass Caine, and his tail out doing God knows what, with God knows who. Girl, I keep telling your ass to find a new man, a friend, or something." Chynna laughed, giving Ari a high five.

"Y'all know that's not me. I'd just rather leave Caine alone than cheat on him," she said, sadly.

"Well, honey, that is your dumbass, but you'll learn one day," Ari added

"Look, y'all don't start that bullshit! If Ny said she good, she good, damn it!" Now, it was Endy who snapped.

"Okay, Endy, damn; we were just joking." Chynna cut her eyes at Niema. All the girls meant well, but they were fucking pissed with her ass because she wouldn't even try to find her a nice sidepiece, guy friend, or something.

About an hour later, Lil' Kim's old school jam, "Crush on you", began blasting through the speakers and the ladies, immediately, hit the dance floor. They were bombarded by men who had been eyeing the *sexy squad* from afar. Niema had gotten a little looser, since she'd been hitting that champagne and had a Screaming Orgasm, which was her favorite drink. The girls were having themselves a good time, dancing to 90's hits, and just enjoying being out with each other. Niema even backed it up and dropped it low on a few dudes at the club. The girls were getting loose and having fun, with the eye candy full of men at the club.

♦♦♦**NewSouth™**♦♦♦

About five o'clock in the morning, the girls hopped in Endy's black 740 BMW to go home. The speakers in the car were blaring Nas's "Ether". Endy's cell phone rang, and it was none other than her baby, Jasean. Everyone envied their relationship - even her girls. Jasean and Endy were what you called *in love*. No matter what they went through, Jasean showed Endy the most unconditional, love and respect she could ever ask for.

"What's up, baby?" she said, with a big smile across her face, showing her beautiful dimples.

"What up, boo? I miss you. When you coming home? Me and CJ just left the pool spot over here on E. 98 Street in Brownsville," Jasean told her, hoping she was close by.

"I'm dropping these bitches off and then I'm heading home, baby", she said, blushing.

"Okay; hurry up, boo. I miss you" He whined, playfully, like little kid.

"Alright, Jay, I'll be home in a minute," she said all sexy and exotic.

"Aight, babe. Be careful. I love you" he conveyed, before hanging up.

"Awe, y'all are too damn cute!" a slurring Chynna shouted from the back.

Niema gave a little smirk and said, "Yeah, you see that sorry bastard didn't even call me."

"Girl, I told you to leave that damn loser alone. You are too beautiful for that jerk!" Chynna rolled her eyes.

"Stop it, Chynna! When Ny is ready, she will leave his ass alone; just watch!" Endy had confidence in her friend.

"Endy, you just don't know how lucky you are. Yeah, y'all can laugh and joke about my relationship, but one thing about it: we all have been through it. It's just Endy didn't put up with

Jasean's shit and gave him the fucking business. That shit made him straighten up real fast. Y'all know that Caine is one of the oldest out of the men and acts like the youngest." Niema spoke up, trying to excuse his actions. "He just really doesn't give a fuck if I'm there or not."

"And you really need to stop giving a fuck if he's there or not, Ny. I only bitch about it because I love your little, herb-ass" Chynna's voice cracked.

"I know, boo." Niema grinned. She knew Chynna meant no harm.

Endy felt the need to correct her crew. "Hold up, y'all, don't get it twisted. We fuss and fight, just like the next couple. He had his times when he was a sorry bastard too. I just wasn't putting up with that shit. I gave his ass a taste of his own medicine and that's that. Until Niema does the same, Caine is going to keep running like a stray dog." Endy broke it down, clearing up any mishaps that she had a perfect relationship with Jasean.

"Yeah, but he still respects you and don't treat you like dirt." Ari put her two cents in, glancing up front at Niema.

"Fuck you, Ari! Hell, Tylon is no better than Caine. Hell, he fucks over you and whips your ass. So what you got to say now?" Niema barked at her, which shocked everyone. Niema didn't like confrontations, but she would get in your ass, if pushed to the limit.

"LOOK!!! We're like sisters; dead this shit now! It's Thanksgiving tomorrow, for God's sake!" Endy yelled, pissed the hell off at their drunken asses.

Everyone was quiet for about five minutes, until Ari blurted out, "Damn...Grandma acting like she wants to take it there with me!" They all laughed.

"I wasn't trying to go there, but you pushed me, bitch." Niema smiled.

The girls started apologizing to Niema, and told her how much they loved her and genuinely wanted to see her happy. By the end of the night, they were all crying and hugging.

When Endy finally arrived at her condo, after dropping off the girls, she saw that Caine's car was parked in the garage. She became suspicious, as to why he was over there with the spare bedroom door closed and music playing. She stormed straight to her room to find Jasean lying on his back, halfway on the bed, in his boxers. She walked up to him and stroked his manhood, slowly, which immediately put it at attention. She looked at it and licked her lips, but still couldn't fight the feeling that something funny was going on.

"Baaaa...by," she whispered, cradling on top of him.

Jasean woke up and smiled. "Damn, baby, I thought you would never get here. I'm horny as hell." He cupped her ass, while grinding his tool against her moist treasure that awaited his entrance. Endy was no slacker, by no means. She had nice-sized, beautiful, bow legs, size D-cup tits, and a round, plump booty. She was beyond a bad bitch, because she had brains too.

She quickly undressed and whispered, "So you want some of this good, good, baby?"

She sat on his erect penis, backwards, and let him see how wet and creamy her pussy was by grinding on him. He cuffed her ass even more, pushing her down on him so he could feel her warmness.

"No, are you ready for me to fill that pussy up with this dick? Ugh." He moaned and grabbed her hips, pushing his dick deep in her dripping, wet pussy.

"Jay, baby, you better stop. I have been drinking. I don't think you're ready for this. Ooh..." Endy moaned, as she rode his dick nice and slow, backwards, where he was now hitting her spot.

"Yeah, baby, I have been thinking about this good pussy all damn day. Ughh...Shit, Endy, this pussy good!" Jasean moaned, grinding in rhythm with her. Their love making was always connected. She scooted up, with her ass in his face, and grabbed his manhood. She deep-throated it, while he sucked her warm, creamy pussy backwards.

"Baby, this pussy runs like a faucet, every time we make love." Jasean was lost in her essence for about 20 minutes. She scooted up and began to ride him again, with pure bliss; as his manhood was glazed with her juices, she bounced up and down. He could feel her juices running, steadily, down his dick and the warmness of her pussy drove him crazy. He couldn't take any more.

"Damn, baby! Ooh…I can't leave this pussy…shit…it's just so…fucking…good. I love you, Endy. I love you so much, baby…Damn, baby! Damn, baby! DAMN, BABY!!!" He moaned, grabbing her by the waist, going deeper

inside her pussy.

"I love you too, BABY!!! DAMN,

BABY!!! This shit feels so good!" She screamed

out with pleasure, as her pussy tightened and she

came.

He could feel her walls contracting and

squeezing on his dick, and she could feel him

hitting her spot. "Ugh, ugh, Ugh!"They both came

at the same time. Too weak to even move, she lay

right on his chest. Both of them panting, trying to

catch their breath. "It's not over, baby. I got even

more." She told him.

It amazed them how in-sync they were

with each other, sexually. They knew each other's

every want and need.

Endy stopped and scooted back, with her ass right in his face. She bent down and took all of him in her mouth, again. She loved giving him head until he came because she knew she had his ass stuck.

"Damn, girl! SHIT!!! I don't know what I would do without you," Jasean moaned, grabbing his head, looking down at her sucking his dick like a vacuum. Even though he enjoyed it, he knew this was the perfect time to torture that pussy like he had planned to all day. While she was sucking his dick, he took his tongue and stuck it straight in her already-dripping, wet pussy, which almost startled her.

"DAMN! Jay…Sean…what the fuck? Ooh… uh oh… damn, baby. I love you, Jasean. I can't wait to be your wife, baby, so this dick can be all mine" she moaned, as she sat on his face.

"This dick already yours, baby. Nobody get this dick but you. Oh shit, baby. Let me hit that pussy again, so I can cum inside you. I want my baby now." He flipped her over on her back and pushed her legs up on his shoulders.

"I want to have your baby, Jasean." He entered that place he knew all too well, and pumped at a steady rhythm. Endy moaned with pure ecstasy, ready to cum for the third time, and he was ready to deliver. Each stoke became stronger and deeper.

"Uh, uh, uh… I'm Cumming, baby" Jasean moaned.

"Come on, baby. Cum inside your pussy, baby. Uh, uh, uh..." Endy moaned, letting him go deep inside her, by opening her legs as wide as she could.

"Here I come, baby. Here I come. DAMN, girl! I can't hold it, baby. Ugh…shit, Endy. Damn, baby. I'm cumming… I'm cumming. SHIT!!!" He yelled and his body jerked and twitched out of control, like he was possessed. He'd wanted his baby all day, and he finally got his fix. After their sexcapade, he watched her sleep. He was whipped and didn't care who knew it, because he loved her.

Chapter 2

The next morning, in the kitchen with his boys making breakfast for Endy, Jasean bragged about Endy - as always - and how he didn't know what it was about her, but the thought of him losing her again scared the hell out of him. Caine and Ty clowned him, saying that he was pussy-whipped. But he didn't care.

Making love to her was all he wanted and needed. It used to bother him, so he would try to prove a point and deal with other chic's, but their sex game just couldn't compare to what Endy's double-jointed-ass was putting down. He especially learned his lesson, when Endy found out about his unfaithful acts and gave him a run for his money, when she met this cat named Sincere from Harlem. Jasean stopped his shit, immediately. He was sick without her. He didn't care what they had to say now because he loved Endyia Hinton.

"Y'all can clown all y'all want to I love my baby too death and she is going to be my wife soon" Jasean spat back. "We only joking with you man we know you're a lover boy" Ty said. "Yep and so are you because Ari got that ass on a tight ass leash" Caine laughs. "Y'all dudes are deadass crazy but I'm about to go back here and eat with my queen. I'm not about to keep messing with y'all clowns" Jasean grabs the plate of eggs, bacon, grits, and toast he made for her and head back to the bedroom. I'm about to head out too I'll hit y'all up later" Tylon heads to the door.

Jasean tried easing back in the bedroom but Endy woke up anyway because she hears the door open. "I hope you're hungry baby" he sits the food on the night stand and gives her a kiss.

"Yes I am let me get myself together bae it smells good too" she says putting on a pair of shorts and a t-shirt of his. "Okay baby hurry before the food gets cold" he said. "Okay baby let me wash my face and brush my teeth" she walks out the room and goes to the bathroom. She starts to wash her face and brush her teeth but she thought she heard something so she turns off the water. She quickly ignores it. When she got back in the room, she heard talking.   An eerie feeling came over her.

"Baby, who's in the spare bedroom?" Endy Questioned, as she overheard Caine's voice.

"Come on, babe, that's CJ's business," Jasean replied, pulling her close to get a kiss.

"NO! Who the hell is in there?" She yelled, snatching away.

"Lord, Endy, it's Keosha. DAMN!" Jasean yelled.

"Who the hell are you yelling at? Y'all the ones doing grimy shit! Who the hell did you have here? Tiffany nasty-ass?" Endy was now furious, storming back to the bedroom.

"What? Are you kidding me, E? For real, ma, you acting real fucking stupid right now!" he said, upset that he was in the middle of Caine's mess - yet again.

"You know what, Jasean; fuck you and your sorry-ass cousin. I'M DONE WITH Y'ALL FUCKING JERKS!" She yelled, hurrying towards the door, but he stopped her.

"E!!! Are you serious? Do you really think I'm that damn stupid to have a chic here?" Jasean asked, with a sincere look in his eyes.

"I don't know, Jay. I don't have time for these games no more."

"E, I would never hurt you like that ever again. I promised you that, and I meant it, okay? I can't help what Caine does. Niema just needs to leave his ass alone and let him realize what he has." Jasean said honestly. He really loved Endy, but he messed up so much in the past, she didn't know how to fully give her all to him anymore.

"Okay, baby; I'm sorry. I just hate how Caine is. I guess I'm just scared it's going to rub off on you. But I also know I have to trust you," Endy said, apologetically.

"Girl, you know I can't lose this good stuff." He embraced her and cupped both of her butt cheeks.

"Why are you always messing with my ass?" she groaned.

"Because it's so fat," he laughed, and they kissed passionately.

"Okay, let's go for round two." Endy suggested, and they headed towards the bedroom to have makeup sex. Endy loved her man and he loved her, so that was all that really mattered.

Meanwhile, while Caine was at Jasean's house with Keosha, Niema was at home, wondering where Caine could be. It was the next morning, and he still had not been home. Worried sick, Niema had been up and down all morning, with no real sleep. It was now a little before 9 a.m. Endy's mom and grandma were expecting them for Thanksgiving dinner at 2 p.m.

"Where the hell is he at? I know this bastard is not going to stay out all night again, knowing what he just did, and it's Thanksgiving on top of it," she mumbled. Tears began to stream down her face and she yelled, "Why do I keep doing this shit to myself?" She called him again, but as usual, she went straight to voicemail. Then, she called Jasean and Endy, over and over, until she had called them over a dozen times. "That ass got to come home sometime, and I'll be right here waiting on his sorry-ass!" She said, pacing the floor, as she continued calling him, back-to-back.

♦♦♦NewSouth™♦♦♦

"Baby, you know that's your girl blowing up your phone. You better call her back before she comes, kicking our asses again." Keosha laughed, standing up, twerking for Caine. Keosha was one of those chic's, who grew up with nothing in the projects, and had to take care of herself. She was a very pretty, high yellow, with shoulder-length, brown hair cut into a bob. She stood about 5'2, was thick, and had the biggest ass a man had ever seen.

"I will see her ass when I get home. I'm with you right now, so let's focus on that," he told Keosha, smacking her butt cheeks.

"You haven't had enough yet, baby? Are you ready for round three?" she squirmed. Standing in front of him, with her apple-shaped, round ass right in his face, she bent over and, immediately, he starts plunging her from the back.

"Oh, Oh, Oh, Caine! Damn, Caine, your dick is so big!" Keosha moaned, loudly.

"Damn, ma, this shit good as hell. I don't know what you're doing to me, but you're gonna make me leave my girl … Damn, Keosha!" his

moaned. His eyes were rolling to the back of his

head because he could feel himself about to cum

quicker than he thought.

"Baby, you about to cum already? No,

baby; not yet, come on," she moaned, throwing

her ass up harder against his dick. "Okay, baby,

I'm about to cum with you. I'm about to cum with

you, Caine; damn."

When she threw it back, one good time

while tightening her goods around his, he couldn't

hold on any longer. He grabs her tightly by both

hips, and pumped faster, until him and her were

both shaking.

"Oh, uhhh, ooh, ooh, ooh, damn,

Ki...Ki... Shit! I'm cumming!" Caine yelled out.

He then squirted hot, thick, white cum all over her

ass cheeks and rub it in. He started kissing her on

her back, which was lined with butterflies from the nape of her neck, down to the top of her ass.

"Damn, girl, you really don't know what you doing to me."

"Yeah, I do know. I'm doing just what I came here to do, sweetie." Keosha smiled. She pushed him down on the bed, jumped on his dick, and began to ride him until he came again.

"Damn, what the hell am I going to do with her?" He asked, aloud, grabbing his head, confused but enjoying the ride.

♦♦♦NewSouth™♦♦♦

The Thanksgiving celebration had begun, and everyone was meeting up at Luella's, or as the family called her, Nana's house. She had a two-story brownstone in the Bedford-Stuyvesant area, on Lexington Ave. All of Nana's kids, grandkids, and friends were in attendance, and she couldn't be happier. She loved to see her family come together, but she knew something was bound to go wrong. The family was at the table, seated with everything from turkey, ham, stuffing, baked macaroni and cheese, collards, yams, potato salad, Spanish rice and beans, cabbage, fried chicken, and about three different cakes. Pablo, Nana's man, blessed the food and everyone dug in.

After finishing up dinner, everyone had the itis.

"Nana, that food was banging!" Chynna said, rubbing her belly.

"I know, girl, that just made me lazy," Egypt said, giggling. Egypt was Chynna and Endy's first cousin, who was more settled than they were. She wasn't as close with them, as they would like, but when something went down, she was right there along with their other cousins, J.J., Rocko, Asia, and Karishma.

"What happened to Niema and Caine coming?" Endy's mother, Tanya, asked. Tanya and Endy looked more like sisters.

"I don't know; it's after five now. She said she would be here around four o'clock" Endy shrugged.

"I bet that sorry-ass Caine has something to do with it." Chynna shot Endy and Jasean a look.

"Anyway… that's their business," Egypt interrupted, shaking her head at her cousin. She always wondered how they hang so tight but bickered so much.

"Game time!" Reeko shouted, heading toward the family room, where the television was.

"No, don't start that game shit. We want to hear some music," Asia shouted, rudely.

"Anyway… Come on, fellas, it's game time; like I said" Reeko ignored her.

"Girl, leave them men alone. That is a Thanksgiving tradition. The men watch football, after eating dinner, while the women clean up and talk" Luella informed her granddaughter.

"Nana, this is not the olden days" Asia laughed.

"Well, you keep thinking like that, you will never have a husband; or even a damn man, for that matter" Luella frowned.

"I don't want one, Nana. All they do is control what you do and where you go. Then cheat when they feel like it. I never want to get married" Asia laughed and shook her head.

"Well, when you do find the man of your dreams that you really love, it's going to hit you so hard, you're not going to know what to do." Nana laughed, and so does everybody else.

"Well, we will see about that, but I doubt it very seriously. Look at all the shit Endy, Chynna, Egypt, Ny, and Ari go through with men. I don't want a steady boyfriend right now, more or less, get married Nana. I'm mingling; it's easier."

"Fuck you, Asia," Chynna shouted.

"Fuck you, Chynna. Don't get mad because I'm telling the damn truth." Asia stood up.

"Chynna! Asia! STOP IT NOW! Y'all disrespecting your Nana" Lisa, Chynna's mother, yelled.

"Nah, Mommy! She is always minding someone else's business." Chynna said, annoyed by her cousin's constant remarks about her and others' relationships.

"Nana, I'm getting ready to go, before your granddaughter gets all ghetto on me," Asia said, kissing her grandmother on the cheek.

As she was about to put on her coat, Tanya, and her cousin, Karishma, catch her at the door. "Asia, please don't leave now. Y'all are family and need to start acting like it." Tanya begged of her niece.

"This is the first Thanksgiving we've all been together, in the same house, at the same time in a while" Karishma plead with her cousin.

"Damn, okay, I will sit a little longer for the family." She hung her coat back up and shook her head. She was surprised they went through all that for her to stay, since Endy and Chynna was everyone's favorites. The women all crowded the den and began playing oldies. "Outstanding" by The Gap Band, poured through the speakers. It was a family favorite, and they were all getting crunk - even the small children. They were having a good time. It felt more like the old days for Nana again.

♦♦♦NewSouth™♦♦♦

About six o'clock, the phone rang. Niema leaped to the dresser to see who it was, and if Caine was finally calling her back.

"HELLO!"

"Look, Ny, I don't have time for no damn fussing. Where Jay at?" Caine quickly blurted out, like something was wrong.

"Are you really serious right now, CJ? You stayed out all night and all day. Then your ass is going to tell me YOU DON"T GOT TIME FOR NO FUSSING! " Niema was fuming. Her nose flared and all. Her breathing was heavy, like she just got through running a five mile race and her eyes were bloodshot red from crying and smoking. She had been smoking blunts all day, to calm her nerves.

"Look, if you're getting ready to act all damn stupid, I'm not coming there at all."

"NO, CJ! Okay, please don't do this, baby. Just come home, okay? I promise; no, I swear, I won't fuss, baby. I just miss you so much. Please, just come on. It's Thanksgiving, Caine. I want to spend it with you" Niema begged.

"Well, I'll come, but you need to be ready because Nana going to flip. We already late."

"Okay, CJ, whatever. Just come on, please."

"I'm on the way now." He hung up. Niema jumped up to spruce up, because she had been crying all day, and hadn't done anything to herself. She jumped in the shower, threw on her beige, Ralph Lauren, sweater dress, black tights, and beige wedged UGG boots. She quickly flat ironed her hair and threw on her beige hat to match her boots and Louis Vuitton purse. Now, she was just waiting on Caine, so they could get to Luella's.

"Look, let me get on before this girl commit suicide or something" Caine laughed, as Keosha walked out the building with him.

"That girl is crazy to keep putting up with you" she laughed.

"She's not going nowhere, and you about to be the same way," he said, all cocky.

"Yeah, we'll see about that." Keosha walked to her Infiniti, while Caine just watched, reluctant to let her go. He didn't know what it was about her, but he did know that he would be seeing her again.

"Yo, call me, ma." He held his hand up to his ear.

"Yeah, C.J, I will call you later." She got in the driver's seat of her car, smiling as she bumped "Neva End" by Future and Kelly Rowland and skidded off.

"Damn that bitch make a brother weak in the knees." Caine whispered to himself, as he walked toward his BMW. He knew it was best to nip the situation in the bud now, so he stopped at Avenue J Florist in Brooklyn and pick up some roses. He had to make a pickup in the neighborhood, so why not?

Buzz Buzz...His phone vibrated. He looked and it was Jasean. He already knew Jasean was going to have something to say, because he told him he would be at Luella's by six. He didn't even answer the call.

When Niema and Caine finally arrived at Ma Luella's house, it was about 7:30.

"What's up, everybody?" Niema shouted, as they entered the house.

Seeing that it was her, and that Caine was with her, Endy sighed; a sense of relief came over her. She knew Caine had been with Keosha, so she didn't know if he was coming or not.

"Hi, Ny. We thought you weren't coming" Tanya said, giving her a tight hug.

"I had to stop by my aunt, Sally's, and then I came on over" she lied.

"Ny!" all the kids came running. They loved her.

"Y'all let her breathe" Karishma laughed.

"Are y'all hungry, baby?" Luella asked.

"Yes, Nana but let me go speak to the fellas first" Niema replied. As she heads to the family room, she overhears Rocko's baby's mother, Taiya, say, "Y'all, the odd couple is here." Everyone started laughing. Now, Taiya was an ex-stripper turned housewife. She was hi yellow, with light brown eyes and a banging, Coca Cola-shaped body. She and Keosha are friends, and she has cheated on Rocko their whole relationship. The family can't stand her, but they deal with her on the account of him and their daughter, Rachelle.

"Yeah, we here, in full effect" Niema joined in the joke and gave Taiya a dirty look.

"Hi, baby, how have you been doing? You know I'm going to steal you from Caine," Endy's uncle, James, said.

"Okay, Uncle James, I'm ready" she giggled.

"You know that's my baby, Uncle James." Rocko said, standing up, and hugging Niema tightly.

Rocko was sexy as hell. He stood at 6'2, had curly, jet black hair, light brown, slanted eyes, almond-colored skin, and was just rugged as hell. Niema always thought he was fine as hell, but wouldn't cross that boundary, on account of Endy. They had a few encounters when they were young, but nothing serious.

"Y'all are a mess. I love y'all too. I'm about to get me something to eat. I'm starving." Niema rubbed her belly.

Rocko openly flirted with Niema, and Taiya didn't like it, but she knew he was in love with Niema and he always had been. As Niema walked out, Rocko's eyes were planted on her ass. Taiya was enraged but she didn't want to mess up the happy occasion. Niema giggled to herself. She knew that Rocko had always been in love with her - since they were younger. She also knew that Taiya was close with the thots Caine fucked around with, so that was her revenge. Niema loved to get under her skin with Rocko.

Meanwhile, in the kitchen, Endy confronted Caine. "Look, motherfucker, don't you ever do no shit like that again and have me in the middle” Endy groaned at Caine, while he fixed his plate.

“Look, I’m a grown-ass man. You don’t tell me what to do, Endy. I’m not Jay” Caine barked back.

“Yeah, thank goodness you’re not, because I would have been cut your sorry-ass off. Like I said, don’t ever put me in another compromising position again or else.” She assured him; she was not playing.

“What compromising position, Endy? What the hell is going on?” Niema entered the kitchen, confused.

“Ask your friend” Caine smirked and walked out the kitchen.

Niema turned to Endy. "Look, Ny" Endy told her. "You better get rid of that sorry-ass Negro real soon, or you're asking for a world of trouble." Endy also walked off, leaving Niema hurt and confused.

"What the fuck is really going on?" Niema mumbled to herself.

Chapter 3

It was a week before Christmas, and everyone's spirits had been really high, as of late. Chynna and Reeko were planning their wedding for the spring. Niema had been dating, hard, and had cut Caine's ass off - completely. Endy and Jasean were happier and trying to have a baby. Ari and Tylon were giving a big Christmas party, and everyone was invited, including Caine. Endy let Niema know that if she didn't come, they all understood, but Niema refused to hide from him.

"What's up girl? You ready to go to Kings Plaza to do this last minute shopping?" Endy asked Niema, over the phone.

"Yeah, I guess so, but I had a long night" she giggled.

"Well, you better start learning how to get some rest?" Endy laughed. "Jay is so much of a Grinch around Christmastime, he didn't even want me to decorate the house or put up a tree. I told him Christmas is the day Jesus was born and this negro had the nerve to say 'do you know Jesus? How do you know that to be true?' Come on, Ny, how hateful is that?" Endy began to giggle.

"Endy, why are you laughing? It's not funny what your man does." Niema said, annoyed.

"Ny, it's okay, sweetie, you got to stop being so sensitive about Christmas."

"You know that's my favorite holiday, bitch" Niema said, jokingly.

"Well, get ready. Since you're so tired, I'm going to drive. I'm on my way, bitch; be ready" Endy told her, before hanging up the phone.

This bitch crazy; no bye or nothing. She thought, looking at the phone.

When the girls finally get to Kings Plaza, it was packed with last minute shoppers. Endy made sure Jasean's Lexus Coup was secured with the snake lock around the wheel, and then they headed inside the mall.

"Girl we're not going to be in here that long" Niema shook her head.

"You know how my baby is about that damn car" Endy laughed.

They started on the second floor of the mall, at Frederick's, and meet up with the rest of the girls.

"What up, slut buckets? What in the hell took y'all so long?" Chynna asked.

"I was waiting on this one. I had to go get her, y'all .She's been having long nights," Endy said.

"Well, y'all, fuck all this. I need to be a bad bitch at the party" Niema blabbed out. She knew Caine was going to be in attendance, and she wanted to look flawless. "I need to get some nice pumps to go with my dress, y'all. All y'all need to know is that it is form-fitting and red" Niema said, giving them a little idea of her outfit. She wanted her friends to be surprised, because she had something in store for them, since they called her the grandma of the crew.

"I see you wearing more fitting clothes and not looking like somebody's mommy no more" Ari laughs.

The girls all got some soup and sandwiches from Quiznos to fill their bellies.

"Well, Ny, how you feel about Caine getting that bitch pregnant?" Ari blurted out. Awkwardness filled the air, instantly.

"GOT WHAT BITCH PREGNANT?!" Niema shouted, as others in the restaurant look stunned.

"ARI!" Endy yelled, kicking her under the table.

"What? Shit, she needs to know what the hell is going on with that treacherous-ass man" Ari yelled back at Endy.

"So, when the fuck was everyone going to tell me?" Niema's emotions were growing by the minute.

"Look, Ny, I was hoping his ass would say something himself. I would never compromise our friendship, but Jasean asked me to keep my mouth shut this time," Endy tried to explain.

"So you bitches thought it was better to keep it from me? And since when you listen to everything Jasean tells your ass?" She shot to Endy.

"Ny, don't do this. He's not worth it. He is a whore and always will be," Chynna added.

Niema jumped up and yelled, "WELL, YOU KNOW WHAT? I'm not even fucking surprised, because he said y'all know what he does and how y'all not any real friends to me...

How y'all say I'm stupid for being with him and shit."

"Are you fucking serious, Niema Mason?" Endy stood.

"YES!!! I'm serious. Y'all bitches are not my got damn friends" She cried.

"Bitch, you done lost it for real now. Are you going to stand the fuck up here and blame us?" Endy was furious at this point.

"I'm going to have to ask y'all to keep it down, please," A little, Arabic woman, who was the store manager, advised the girls nicely.

"I can do one better, I can get the fuck out of here now!" Niema shouted, again, throwing a twenty dollar bill on the table and walked out.

"I know this bitch done lost her mind, Endy. You better be glad I didn't snuff that bitch. How the fuck is she going to blame us for that sorry motherfucker's actions?" Ari asked, pissed. She felt like she should have gotten in Niema's ass. Endy, however, was hurt because she and Niema hadn't argued like that in years.

"Fuck it! I will deal with Ny later because her ass is really bugging," Endy muttered.

◆◆◆NewSouth™◆◆◆

The night of the Christmas Eve party, the girls were worried because they hadn't spoken to Niema since the mall incident.

"Yo, Endy, have you talked to Ny?" Egypt asked.

74

"Nope, I tried calling her and even went by the house. Girl, when she's ready to talk to me, she will." Endy sighed.

"Well, Ny can't blame anybody but her damn self. When you let a cat like Caine get away with shit like she does, he's bound to stray," Jasean butted in about the situation.

"Well, I don't think she should blame you for not telling her every, little thing, because she knows that will put you and Jay at odds. I would think she would understand that." Egypt said.

"Well, I'm not going to let that shit ruin my holiday. If Ny wants to act stupid as fuck right now, then that's on her stupid-ass. I'm not up for that shit with her and Caine tonight. I'm going to enjoy myself, whether she talks to me or not. Fuck that!" Endy responded.

Egypt and Jasean burst out laughing because Endy was always team Niema.

"THAT'S MY BABY! Fuck these motherfuckers! It's about us," he said, walking up and giving her a sloppy kiss. Jasean loved her so much and didn't like seeing her stressed over other people's bullshit.

"Look, y'all, let's go; nobody want to see all that." Egypt smiled at the cute couple.

The party started and was live as hell. Ari had outdone herself, as usual. The house was decorated in red and white decorations, balloons, and party favors. She had soul food and seafood laid out on two, long tables in the dining room. The family room was set up with disco lights, had a bar and music. The living room had several people mingling and enjoying each other's company.

"Girl, you threw down on the food. I'm stuffed," Chynna complimented Ari.

"Yes, I almost killed myself eating, and you know I put me some food up," Endy added.

"Y'all know how I do around Christmastime. I love the holidays.

"What up, mommies?" a loud voice said. The girls looked up to see their cousin, Rocko, with his baby's mother and J.J.'s girl, Lynasia, looking sexy as ever, following behind.

"It's the Roc and his hoes" Chynna blurted out.

"Girl, would you stop it?" Endy giggled.

"What up, y'all?" Ari spoke because it was awkward.

"Umm… hi to y'all too," Taiya said, dryly.

Endy gave them the *bitch better get on* look.

"Well, y'all go to the dining room and get something to eat before it's all gone." Ari defused the situation.

"Yeah, y'all do that." Endy butted in.

Taiya cuts her eyes at Chynna and Endy and grabbed Rocko so he'd follow her to the dining room.

"I'm gon' see y'all in minute," Rocko said, before being yanked away by Taiya.

"I can't stand that bitch," Endy groaned.

"Y'all leave that girl alone, Endy. You know her ass is mental as hell. Plus, I don't feel like fucking her up tonight." Chynna laughed, slapping Ari five.

"That's y'all cousin, with her slut-bucket-ass," Ari added on.

"Whatever! She's in the family by default - that's all," Chynna said, making everyone laugh. *I got some good Kush and alcohol.*

"Aye yo, come on, that Lil Wayne shit on." Asia motioned her cousins to go dance. Almost the whole party raced to the floor, crunk as ever. The crowd was going crazy, yelling the words. Even the DJ was hyped. All the women were dropping it low, and everybody was having a good time, until Niema walked in. Rocko was especially mesmerized because she had on a red Versace dress with the front open, all the way to her belly button, and some black, satin, Jimmy Choo pumps. Her hair was pulled up, curly and hanging to the right side. She looked absolutely gorgeous.

"Girl, what's going on with you? I haven't seen you dressed this sexy ever," Ari said, in amazement.

"It's a new day; a new me, girl. You like?" She twirled around, smiling from ear to ear.

"Girl, you look so fucking pretty. What in the world has gotten into you – literally?" Chynna was surprised at how Niema was dressed.

"That's for me to know and y'all to find out." She laughed.

"Hi, Endy, you look so beautiful, hun."

Niema hugged Endy but you could feel the

tension between them.

"You know I got to give this bad-ass chic

some love." Rocko playfully pushed Endy and

Chynna out the way.

"Merry Christmas, Rocko." Niema

grinned.

"No, ma, Merry Christmas too you...woo!"

He undressed her with his eyes.

"Boy, you crazy as hell; get the hell on. I

don't feel like beating Taiga's ass tonight," She

joked with him.

He embraced her soft, warm body in his

arms and the smell of her fragrance: Love Spell

from Victoria's Secret drove him wild. His peter

stands straight up, immediately. He wanted to knock her down right then.

"Rocko, can you come here a second?" His thought was interrupted by Taiya's voice. "ROCKO!" she yelled again.

"Ny, you pretty as fuck," he whispered to her, looking straight in her eyes, before walking away. Niema was now hot but shook it off because she knew it could never be.

"Girl, your cousin better stop it now…" Niema told Endy, who was barely smiling.

The party was still going about 20 minutes before midnight. Niema and Endy were at the bar, getting champagne to toast with. When Niema glanced to her left, she saw Caine and Keosha entering the room .Her stomach was in knots and her palms became sweaty. Keosha was looking sexy, as usual, with a black, satin, Gucci dress and leopard print, Chanel heels. Her Chinese bangs and long pony tail accentuated her chinky eyes.

"Be good, Ny. You're so over this bullshit," Niema mumbled to herself.

"Girl, you sure you're okay, because you are scaring the hell out of me?" Endy asked.

"Girl, I'm so beyond this bullshit. I didn't lose; he did. He will realize it soon enough." Niema smiled with confidence.

"Ny, are you okay? I see Caine is here with that whore." Chynna groaned.

While Keosha linked up with her girls, Taiya and Lynasia, Caine slid his way over to Niema and her girls.

"Caine, what's up? How you been doing?" Chynna said, giving him a hug.

"I'm good, ma. How y'all doing?" he replied.

"We all good," Chynna responded for everyone, but Caine could feel the tension in the air.

"What's up, Ny? How you been?" He missed her like crazy but he was too stubborn to show it.

"I'm just wonderful, CJ. Just trying to enjoy my night," She replied.

"Everybody get with your boo. Merry Christmas!" the DJ shouted in the microphone.

"Merry Christmas, baby!" Keosha appeared out of nowhere, kissing Caine in front of everyone. Niema downed her champagne,

slammed her glass on the bar, and briskly walked

away.

"Hehehe..." Keosha laughed.

"What the fuck is this bitch doing here

anyway?" Endy snapped.

"Who you calling a bitch?" Keosha shot

back.

"Look, y'all stop it, now! This is not the

time." Chynna grabbed Endy while Caine grabbed

Keosha.

"I'ma say okay for now, bitch. Caine,

check your bitch– now! That's why both my

bitches tapped that ass. You want another ass

whipping?" Endy yelled, as Keosha and Taiya

walked away. Keosha was so mad Caine didn't

defend her, she could've spit fire.

"I'm about to skate on out of here because

I don't feel like seeing no brawls tonight," Caine

said, giving the girls a hug, before walking away.

"Where's Ny at?" Endy asked her cousin.

"I don't know, but go find Jay and calm

the fuck down," Chynna told her.

"Well, hello to you too" Niema shot to

Jasean, who was in the kitchen alone.

"Hi, Ny. What's up with you?"

"Nothing much. Just had to get away from

your boy and that wannabe Barbie bitch." Niema

laughed.

"Girl, you a trip. You look really nice tonight," Jasean said, admiring how beautiful Niema looked, since she left Caine's sorry-ass alone. He knew his cousin was sorry, but he couldn't make him do shit he didn't want to do.

"Thanks; and I'm sorry for how I been acting, but that jerk had me twisted for a minute," Niema said, apologetically.

"It's all good. I'm here if you need me!" They hugged.

"So, y'all friends again?" Endy startled the two.

"Yes, we are, and I thank y'all both for everything." Niema started to tear up.

"Don't start, Ny. Let's get some more champagne and enjoy the night. It's Christmas, bitch!" Endy slurred, tipsy as ever. They headed to the bar, so they could enjoy the rest of the party.

By the end of the night, Niema was drunk and realized that this would be her first Christmas, in years, that she would be without Caine.

"What up, ma? You good?" Rocko noticed Niema looking sad.

"Yes, boy. Get on before I have to smack your girl."

"She gone with Lynasia and Keosha, so there's no need for that." Rocko threw her that sexy grin that always made Niema's pussy instantly throb.

"How the hell you leave your man on Christmas?" Niema mumbled and stumbled in her heels.

"Whoa...You okay? You can't drive like this." He caught her.

"I'm okay, dude. I'm about to go home."

"No, I'm going to take you home, girl. You tripping, and that's that!" Rocko exclaimed.

"Okay, Daddy, I hear you." Niema held up her arms, surrendering. He escorted her to his silver Jaguar, opened the door for her, and fastened her in tightly.

They pulled up to their destination, and Niema noticed she wasn't home. They were at a hotel.

"Where the hell you taking me to?"

"Ny, I just feel like our time has come."
He gently rubbed her cheek with the back of his
hand. He had her face to face, and she couldn't
fight the temptation.

"Rocko, you have someone already and
I'm not anybody's jump-off." She hopped out his
car.

"I know that, but I've been so in love with
you for years. You just couldn't see it. I love you,
Ny, real talk" Rocko told her. They started
kissing, and when they parted lips, he asked, "so,
is this really about to go down, Ny?"

"I think it already has." She grabbed him,
kissing him again, more intensely. They went into
the hotel and had a full night of intense, great sex.
Neither knew what tomorrow would bring, but
they both would see.

Chapter 4

Niema woke to Rocko slurping up her goodies. "Just lay there, baby. I'm gonna show you how a real man appreciates good pussy."

Niema was still a little tipsy and daylight was peeking through the windows. "Umm… what time is it, Rocko?" she moaned.

"About six in the morning, but just relax," he commanded her.

Although she knew she needed to stop him, all she could do was moan from the way he had her pussy tightening. After a while, she couldn't take any more, and let out a loud moan.

"Ahhh... Roc...Roc...Rocko."

"Shhh... just relax and let me take care of this beautiful body, baby." He looked at her and

dove in again. His tongue was so mesmerizing.
With each slurp, Niema couldn't stop her legs
from shaking. He finally let up, once her cream
filled his mouth.

"Are you okay, sweetheart?"

"Dam-m-n, Rocko. I didn't know you had
it in you." She was stunned at how good he was.
Then, he started sucking on her nipples, licking
and sucking each at a time, getting her even
wetter.

"I've dreamed about this over and over
again, Ny." He sat up, while she laid still.

"What you doing?" Niema asked him,
ready to feel what she came there for.

"I'm getting ready to show you right now.
Are you ready for it" he asked, sliding on a
condom.

"I was born ready," she replied. He
pushed her legs up, as far as they could go, and
slid his tool in her moistness.

"Ahhh!!!"Niema yelled out. Rocko's
penis was nothing like she thought. He filled her
walls completely.

"Damn, baby, this pussy is s-o-o good," he
grunted. With each stroke, their bodies became
one, and he made her cum back-to-back. By the
time they finished, it was eight in the morning.

"Oh shit; we gotta go!" Niema jumped up,
grabbing her clothes to get dressed. Before she
left out, she looked over her shoulder, smiling at

him laying on the bed, and said, "But we must do this again."

She went to the lobby of the hotel to catch a cab, but Rocko laid there in amazement. He finally got her and now he was feeling all fucked up about going home to Taiya. "Damn, Ny!" He grinned hard as hell.

♦♦♦NewSouth™♦♦♦

After Niema took a short nap, she got up and took a nice, hot shower. Suddenly; there was a knock at her door. The knock startled her.

"Who is it!" she yelled.

"It's Endy. Girl, open this door."

Why is Endy at my house instead of home? Did she see me come home? Did Taiya find out?

94

She thought, but decided she may as well open the door.

"Coming!" she yelled, again, grabbing her robe. Her mind was going like hell, as she raced to open the door.

"What up, chic? Merry Christmas." She smiled.

"I was worried sick, Ny! Why you not answering the phone?" Endy asked, with a sigh of relief.

"Girl, I was twirled last night. I fell straight to sleep." She gave her friend a hug.

"I was just getting dressed to head over there. I'm good though. I'm coming over your house." Niema was kind of nervous.

"What's wrong with you? Why you acting all funny and shit?" Endy asked.

"Girl, I'm fine, just a little tired; that's all." Niema put on a fake smile.

"Ok, well, hurry up. We're eating at four o'clock, okay?" Endy said, grabbing her Dooley and Bourke bag.

"Okay, sis. I'll be right over there when I finish getting dressed."

Endy left and Niema breathed a sigh of relief. "Damn, how am I gonna get through the rest of the day?" She sighed.

♦♦♦NewSouth™♦♦♦

Everybody was at the community center, where the dinner was being held, laughing, dancing, drinking, and eating - having a good time. Rocko had been watching Niema from across the room, the whole evening. She'd been avoiding contact with him all night.

"Babe, you ready to go yet? Taiya asked, breaking Rocko's concentration on Niema.

"Hell no, I'm not ready to go yet," Rocko snapped.

"Well, I'm about to go, because this family shit is overrated with y'all." She rolls her eyes.

"Taiya, if you want to go, take your ass on but leave Rachelle here!" He yelled because she was trying to take his daughter. Everybody looked, and Taiya immediately gets pissed.

"Fuck you. I'm gone!" She stormed out the center. Rocko sipped his drink, as if he was unbothered by her reaction.

"Rocko, what the hell?"Ms. Luella shouted at her grandson.

"Sorry, Nana, damn!" He jumped up, walking out too.

"What the hell is wrong with these damn kids today?" Luella shook her head. Niema felt awkward because she wanted to check on Rocko, but she knew that was a bad idea.

"Rocko better get his bitch in check. I don't like seeing Nana upset like that," Endy groaned, pissed as fuck.

"E, calm down. Don't trip with that bitch. She's psycho as hell" Egypt threw her arm around her cousin's shoulder, giving her a hug.

"I know, but that bitch is disrespectful to the family," Asia added.

"Well, we're not letting that bitch ruin our holiday because I'm trying to get tipsy," Egypt said, holding up her glass.

"Girl, please drink some, shit!" Asia teased Egypt, which got Endy laughing.

Niema went outside to check on Rocko, when she realized it had been almost 30 minutes that he'd been gone. She looked around and didn't see him. Just as she was about to re-enter the building, she heard a horn. Rocko was sitting in his Jaguar a few steps away.

"Come here, ma," he yelled to Niema.

"I was just making sure you were good. It's cold out here; hell no." Niema shot him a quick excuse.

"That's why I said come here. You can get in the car, ma." He threw her that sexy-ass smile that always made her panties moist.

"No, Roc, I'm not getting in your ho mobile. I already feel freaking crazy." She giggled.

"I can still taste your pussy on my tongue, Ny."

"Okay, that's my cue." She giggled again.

"Okay, at least stand out here with me for a little bit." Rocko got out the car. Just as he walked up on Niema, the sound of some bass was blasting, and who pulled up but Caine in a new, black on grey, MercedesS500. Niema quickly backed away from Rocko. Caine didn't like what he saw because he knew that Rocko had been after Niema for a while.

"What's up, Caine? I didn't know you were coming through. Where Ki Ki at?" Niema asked him, being funny, as he exited the car.

"She at where she at. What's up with you?" He said, sarcastically.

"I'm good and blessed; just enjoying this holiday with family and friends. Well, let me get my tail back in here where it's warm," she said, walking away, in a nice, form-fitting, BCBG dress that showed all her curves. The dress was the whole reason why Rocko couldn't keep his eyes off her ass, and Caine was looking right along with him.

"Man, how the hell you mess that shit up?" Rocko shook his head and smiled.

"Don't worry, my dude, she'll be back. I ain't worried about it," Caine stated, feeling real cocky-like.

"Oh, really I don't know about that, Caine. You been pulling some over-the-top shit, my dude." Rocko said, disgusted.

"Whatever! Ny can't be away from this dick too long. She'll always come back to me." Caine grilled him.

"Okay, dude, whatever you say" Rocko walked away, laughing.

♦♦♦NewSouth™♦♦♦

In the wee hours of the morning, while Niema was in a deep sleep, Niema heard a loud knock at her door. She jumped up, startled and looked at the time. It was 3:48 am on her alarm clock.

"Who the fuck is knocking on my door this time of morning?" She jumped up. The knock came again, even louder. "Who the hell is it?" she shouted. When she looked through the peephole, it was Caine. She was stunned and mad at the same time.

"What do you want, Caine? Go with your pregnant bitch!" she yelled through the door.

"Ny, baby, please let me talk to you. It's a lie. Open the door, baby, please. Let's talk," he pled.

"Caine, I'm tired. I'm not up for your shit tonight."

"Ny, just talk to me; that's all. I want to talk to you for a few minutes. I promise." His pleading must have worked, because she began to unlock the door.

"What is it, Caine?" She folded her arms, with the door still open.

"Damn, can I at least come in, Ny?"

"Caine, you got five minutes. I'm tired and I got to get up early to go shopping." He entered the house and went to sit on the couch.

"Ny, I just want to say I'm sorry and I know this is a repetitive thing with me, but I really never wanted to hurt you. I just got caught up in the life."

"The life? Really, CJ? If you didn't notice, you really don't have shit but your cars and clothes. Like, you got to be fucking kidding me!" She started pacing back and forth.

"Ny, calm down, yo! I told you I know I fucked up" Caine painfully pled.

"YOU FUCKED UP?!? You fucked up? Yeah, motherfucker, you did fuck up! It's too late for apologies now and shit. I'm good, hun know that!" Niema turnt her head.

All Caine could do was hold his head down. "Ny, I don't know what else to say."

"It's nothing to say but goodbye. Take care of your baby mother and miss me with the bullshit." She started crying.

"Niema, please don't cry." Caine tried to hug her. **Whumph**...Niema slapped him.

"Get the hell out of my house…NOW!"
She was now crying and screaming.

"Okay, Ny, I'm gone. I hope you find it in
your heart to forgive me," Caine muttered, before
walking away.

♦♦♦NewSouth™♦♦♦

About eight that morning, Ari called
Niema to see if she was still going to meet them
for shopping and brunch.

"Hello," Niema said, all groggy.

"Ewe... Why you sound like that?" Ari
asked.

"I had a long night and I don't want to talk
about it."

"Well, are you going to meet us Downtown?"

"Damn, I forgot we were supposed to grab lunch and go shopping. Okay, let me throw something on and meet y'all at Macy's." Niema jumped up out of bed. She threw on a beige, BCBG, velour jogging suit with her beige Adidas Samoa's. Her hair was pulled up in a messy bun because she had no time to flat iron it, since she was in a rush.

When the girls spot Niema walking into Macy's, they're stunned that she's so dressed down out in public. Even though she's not in heels like she usually would be, she still looked cute and comfortable.

"What's up, Ny? It took you long enough." Endy smiled, noticing a glow about her friend.

"I know, I know, but a sista had a long night. So, please spare me the cursing out," she pled with her friends.

"Bitch, we will let you slide this time, but you know my greedy-ass is hungry as hell." Ari groaned.

"Okay, well… since I'm late, I got lunch today." Niema tried to compromise.

"Oh, well… in that case, then we going to Five Spot Soul Food," Chynna advised.

"Ok then, let's go because I'm starving." Endy rubbed her belly.

"Well ladies, I got something to tell y'all," Endy said, anxiously.

"What is it, and can you tell me while I smash this food?" Ari asked.

"Yes, bitch, you can go ahead and eat but listen, ok? Well... I want to tell y'all…" Endy whipped out a piece of paper. "BOW! Y'all are going to be aunties," she shouted.

"Endy, why you just telling us this shit? Congratulations, cuzzo." Chynna got up and gave her a big hug.

"I just found out, but I haven't told Jay yet. I'm going to tell him at the New Year's Eve bash. I'm excited and nervous. This is the best present God could have given me. Niema, what's up? You haven't said anything."

"E, you know I'm happy as hell; just still in shock, girl. Congratulations" she put on a smile and gave her friend a hug. Deep down inside, she wished it was her though.

"Well, I tell you what… next year is going to be full of blessings, y'all." Chynna was so happy for her cousin because E had a miscarriage a year prior.

"Well, I want to toast to a better new year for us all," Ari said, holding up her glass.

"Cheers!" the girls toasted with their drinks and continued on with their afternoon, ecstatic over the great news.

♦♦♦NewSouth™♦♦♦

The night of the New Year's Eve bash, Endy was nervous as ever.
"Baby, I'm gonna head over to the club with Uncle Jack." Jasean said, walking up behind her and giving her a soft kiss on her neck.

110

"Okay bae, Ny is gonna pick me up and we'll be out there."

"Okay, ma. I love you." He cupped her face, giving her a wet kiss.

"You better stop before you start something, Mister." she warned.

"Yeah, because you know if we hit that bed, Uncle Jack gonna curse my ass out" he laughed.

"Exactly, so take your ass on!" she playfully pushed him away.

"Okay, I'm out, but you owe me big time. Y'all hurry up too." He grabbed his keys and headed out the bedroom.

"We'll be there as soon as she gets here, baby."

About an hour later Ari and Chynna arrive at Endy's house. "Yo where Ny at it's almost 10:30" Ari checks her gold diamond studded Rolex watch Tylon gave her as one of her Christmas gifts.

"I see you shining baby girl" Endy calls her out.

"You know I'm spoiled bitch don't hate" Ari says flashing the watch.

"Look call up your little hating ass friend so we can go" Chynna's growing impatient now.

"Why you say that?" Endy gives her a disapproving look.

"Girl I felt the hate as soon as you said you are pregnant. You know that's the last thing she wanted to hear right then, especially with

what Caine and Keosha did to her" Chynna said.

"Chynna I doubt if she hating on me, but I

can understand it bothering her a little. You know

she has wanted kids more than all of us and now

we all will be mothers and she's not."

"Whatever Endy keep being naïve to the

shit Ny does. You're in for a world of

heartbreak" Ari warns her.

"I'm not naïve to shit, Niema's my friend

and she will accept it if she really loves me."

"Y'all I finally made it" they heard Niema

yell as she came down the hall to the bedroom

where the girls were freshening up their makeup.

When she enters the room they're shock to see Niema has a hot ass see thru tight little black dress on from Endy's boutique named E-Class.

"Umm bitch you know we can see your underwear right" Ari asked her.

"Umm yeah that's the idea. How I look y'all? Endy said she had something for me but damn" Niema responds boldly.

"Girl I don't know what got into your grandma acting ass but I must say I like this new and improved Niema" Endy said and gave her a hug and Chynna shoots Ari a funny look.

"Well Ny I must say you're coming out your shell pretty well" Ari adds.

"Yep I'm all about living life and enjoying it along the way" she struts across the room with confidence.

"Well let's go I'm ready to drink and party" Chynna jumps up.

♦♦♦NewSouth™♦♦♦

They get to the club and it is jumping. Everyone is having a good time. Niema's been on the floor most of the night. The girls are worried because Jasean just warned them that Caine and Keosha were on the way inside. Before Endy can get to Niema, in walked Caine and Keosha, right beside him, hanging on his arm. Niema spots them and race across the club to the bar and Endy follows her.

"Girl I know this some bullshit but don't let that shit bother you. We here to have a good time but if some shit pops off you know we got

your back" Endy let her know she got her.

"Endy I'm good boo, believe me he will

act up before I do" She holds her glass up, smile,

and walks away.

"Okay Ms. Thing I see you that's what I'm

talking about real boss women don't need to act

up" Endy says feeling relieved.

Everybody is dancing and having a good

time. It's about time for the countdown and the DJ

asked everybody to grab a glass of champagne

and gather around. Caine finally spots Niema and

couldn't help but lust for her. He had never seen

her look sexier to him then he see tonight. She

catches him lurking but she plays it off like she

doesn't.

"7, 6, 5, 4, 3, 2, 1…Happy New Year!"

the DJ yells with everybody yelling along.

Keosha grabs Caine and kiss him and

when he looks up Niema had disappeared. He's

looking all around and can't find her in the crowd.

He is bothered that she hasn't said anything to

him but who could blame her. He needed to see

her in this new element enjoying life without him.

He still didn't understand the extent of hurt and

disrespect she felt. Not to mention she done

procured some new pipe from Rocky.

"Hi beautiful" Niema hears a familiar

voice.

"Rocko you scared the shit out of me"

Niema says giving him a sensually tight hug with

Caine watching from across the club boiling mad.

"Yo you look sexy as hell Ny" Rocko couldn't believe his eyes. "Thanks baby but where can we puff this at" Niema says pulling a blunt out her clutch. "I know exactly where we can go come on with yo sexy ass" he grabs her hand. She shoots Caine a smirk and they head outside.

They go to Rocko's truck which is parked right in the back of the club. He turns on some music and the atmosphere just seem so right so relaxed. Yo I saw you run off so I figured why not check on my baby" he moves closer rubbing her left thigh.

"Roc stop it please I don't need no shit tonight with Taiya" she pushes him away.

"Man fuck Taiya I want you Ny. I always have and I think this is our chance to try to make it work. I don't give a fuck about Caine ass either.

Taiya has stepped out on me so much I'm only there for my daughter" He pleads with her.

"Roc we can't do that I won't be the cause of your family breaking up. It just won't work we had what we had and that's that. I love you Roc but as a friend and I thank you for being there for me" Niema blows him off.

"You still stuck on that dude Ny! He doesn't give a fuck about you. Come on bringing a stripper bitch he cheated with and got pregnant to a spot he know you're gonna be at" He snaps.

"Rocko look chill before somebody hears you come on we are grown don't do this" she begs him.

He calms down because he knows he been drinking and he don't want to bring her no more drama then she already has.

"Okay I will be patient Ny but at the end of the day you will be mine. Mark my words" he gently kiss her lips.

Niema see he is serious and she doesn't want to say the wrong thing to piss him off so she just doesn't say shit.

"Well I'm gonna go back in here. You need to get in here too it's cold" he tells her.

"I'm coming you go ahead we don't need to go in together" she said and he does just that.

When they get back to the party Endy is on stage about to make her announcement. That was the last thing Niema wanted to see but she couldn't blame her friend for how her life turned out.

"Hi everybody Happy New Year! Well I need my soul mate to come to the front Jasean please come up here baby" Endy signals him up to toward the stage.

Jasean is a bit confused on what she's about to do but he goes anyway. As he walks to the stage he is looking at his boys like what the hell is going on? He gets on the stage with her and she grabs his hand.

"Baby you know I love and you know we been through some rough times but we manage to still pull thru. Well I wanted to tell you along with our family and friends. CONGRATULATIONS!!! YOUR GONNA BE A DADDY!" Endy yelled.

Jasean jump up and scream "Yeah, Yeah!" he kiss the love of his life long and hard. You can see the excitement on his face. Everybody is clapping and trying to give them hugs.

"Wow Endy having a baby huh." Niema turns around and who is it standing behind her…Caine. "Oh hi Caine Happy New Year" She quickly says and tries to walk away but he grabs her arm. She snatch her arm away "What?" "I just want to say you look good as hell tonight and I miss you." "Boy please get the hell out my face. I told you we are done go with your little thot baby mama and spare me the lies" she storms off so she can get to Endy and Jasean.

"Yo Caine you fucked that up" Reeko walks up to him shaking his head.

"Niema can play these games all she wants that pussy is still mine until I say so" Caine boastfully states.

"Oh really you that cocky" Reeko laughs.

"B she not going nowhere believe that"

Caine says really unsure.

"Okay motherfucker if you say so" Reeko

laughs walking away laughing shaking his head.

Caine gives him a look and finish up his drink.

It's about five in the mooring and the party

is over. Everyone is heading home. "Ny you

gonna be alright getting home" Endy asked

because Ny was putting some drinks down.

"Girl I'm good. I'm just gonna go straight

home and get me some sleep" she hugs her

goodbye.

"Okay boo I saw how Caine was looking

at that ass all night. He missing his poo poo" Endy

laughs.

"Girl, you stupid, he know I got that good, good" Niema chuckles.

"Bye girl talk to your crazy ass tomorrow." Endy walks off as she watches Niema's cab pull up.

"Okay boo talk to you later" Niema said and get in cab trying to get warm it because it's cold in New York right. (ding, ding) Her phone rings. When she looks at the caller ID she shakes her head "Damn I can't believe I'm about to do this shit again."

Chapter 5

The couples have set up a getaway to Atlantic City for Valentines weekend. Endy is skeptical about going because she's been spotting and only four months into her pregnancy. They all been so busy with their personal lives they've hardly been able really spend together. Niema been M.I.A. and Endy's missing her friend right now especially since her and Jasean been at it a whole lot lately.

"Are you going to be back in time for us to hit the highway?" Endy questions Jasean with her arms folded.

"Look I said I will be back in time so stop bugging me about it damn. You been tripping ever since you been pregnant E. You know I got to make this cash before this baby is born" he snaps back.

"Jay that's an excuse you can at least try to make it home after the club closes. You're damn near coming in at daylight six days a week now Jay. Damn I want to fall asleep with you more than Monday nights and even then you're up doing shit for the club" she barks back.

"I'm out E you tripping and I don't have time for this shit today."

"Jasean Newman I know you did not just walk out while I'm talking." Jasean rush out and left Endy standing there teary eyed and emotional.

Jasean get in the car and sighs. He pulls out his phone "Yo, Chynna wat up? Where Reeko at?" Jasean speaks into his cell.

"Hello to you too Jay damn hold on" Chynna replied.

A moment later, Reeko's on the phone. "What's good, my dude?" he speaks.

"Man I can't take this shit. I'm trying to get shit done and she bugging. I'm happy about the baby but I just don't want to get my hopes up again. I hate to see her cry but it's like pushing her away seems easier. I know it's wrong but I just got mad shit going on. You know I'm trying to get this surprise together and her bitching all the time is not helping" Jasean vents to Reeko.

He's feeling the pressure of the pregnancy and he's lashing out at Endy.

"Yo man, you gots to chill with that bullshit. You know women emotions be high as hell when they pregnant just stick to the plan man. Endy loves your ass but you know she will cut your ass loose if she needs to. So you better tighten up!" Reeko warns his ass

Jasean reflect on her last encounter with the dude Sincere. He knows if he lose her somebody gonna snatch her up with the quickness.

"I know man I don't know what the fuck is going on with me. I love that girl to death but I want to make sure we got financial security when this baby comes. I want her to know I'm all in for the long haul" Jasean said with a sense of panic in his voice.

"Jay, y'all will be good. Just relax and stick to the plan man. Just be there for Endy, bruh.

We're gonna enjoy this weekend and some quality time with our ladies" Reeko assures him.

"Okay bet B" Let me get back here and do some serious apologizing. "Okay see you in A C" Reeko hangs up.

Endy and Jasean arrive at the Caesars Hotel in Atlantic City and it's a pretty day out for February weather.

"Ma, don't it feels good to be out of New York for a few days on vacation and not business" Jasean kiss her cheek.

"Yeah it does" Endy dryly replies. "Come on Ma, I apologized let's enjoy ourselves please." Jasean begs her gently kissing her hand.

"Okay Jay your right we need this because we have been going in on each other lately." Endy softens up and give him a kiss.

"Yes your ass really been turnt up on me" he laughs and gives his baby a big hug.

That's one thing he knows for sure he loves her more than words can explain. As Jasean is getting their bags out the trunk a voice appears.

"What up son? Give it up?" He spins around and sees Niema's and some slim dark skin chic.

"Ny, stop playing so damn much." Jasean said jumping at her.

"Yo don't tell me I had that ass shook?" Niema laughs.

"Who's your friend Ny?" Jasean questions as Endy gets back out the car.

"This is Ni'Yana, my cousin from New Orleans. You can call her YaYa. She used to come up back in the day, when we were younger. She didn't come to Brooklyn much after we became teenagers though. She got too grown" Niema jokes.

"Stop it Ny! Hey how y'all doing" she smiles shaking Jasean hand as Endy walks up.

"Oh Ny glad you could make it I didn't think your ass was coming" Endy eyes Niema and her all so familiar looking cousin.

"Girl I been so busy working and partying I just have been neglecting my baby mama" Niema rubs Endy belly.

"Hi girl I haven't seen you in years?"
Endy puts on a fake smile.

"Yes, it has. I remember y'all coming to Mardi Gras a few years back. I mostly remember you at Aunt Sally's fortieth birthday party though when we got tore up. You look so cute Prego Endy" she giggles giving Endy a hug.

"Girl you look great too what brings you here" Endy asks confused since this was supposed to be a couples trip. She hadn't heard from Niema like that so she assumed she wasn't coming.

"Girl when I was here for New Year's I told Ny I would be in New York to look for a place. I'm so ready to be closer to my family and start a new beginning" YaYa sighs.

"Well New York is a great place to do it" Endy said who is still agitated that Niema didn't mention anything to her at all about her cousin moving New York.

YaYa was very beautiful chocolate babe with curly hair down her back almost to her butt that accentuates her small waist and big ole country booty. You couldn't help but see it.

"Well babe let's get to our room so we can get ready for dinner. Everyone will be here soon" Jasean interrupts. Endy have this vicious stare. He knew she was pissed.

"Yeah Jay let's do that I guess we will be seeing y'all later" Endy rush off.

Niema can sense Endy's coldness but she ignores it as she's been doing a lot towards her lately. "Yeah YaYa let's get settle in our room because I'm ready to see what Atlantic City has going on" she shouts all excited getting her bags out the car.

"This gonna be a long weekend I see" Endy grunts as her and Jasean head in the hotel.

♦♦♦NewSouth™♦♦♦

"Why Endy just text me saying that Niema is there with her cousin YaYa from New Orleans" Ari shakes her head.

"So what?" Tylon replies. He is confused about why that's a problem.

"What you mean so what? This is a couple's trip and besides she has been acting like a jealous envious bitch since Endy told us she's pregnant" Ari shouts.

"Okay babe you gots to chill don't start acting up this weekend. I know you and Ny have

y'all issues but please let's just enjoy ourselves"
Tylon pleads with his wife.

"I'm not Ty but if that bitch pulls one stunt
this weekend it's off with her head for real" Ari's
turnt to the max now.

Tylon laughed. "Babe, you super-hyped
right now, yo; just chill and let's enjoy this kid-
free weekend alone" He says, giving her this sexy
look.

"Yeah baby you right and we can do it all
night without worrying if the kids gonna knock at
the door" she gives him this seductive smile
sticking out her tongue.

"You so nasty Ari" he laughs.

"And you love it too" she laughs too.

"E, come on what you doing now? Everybody waiting on us downstairs" Jasean yelled through the bathroom door.

"I'm coming but my outfit looks kind of tight baby."

"Let me see babe "he tells her.

When she walks out with her little bump Jasean smiles at how beautiful she looks. She's wearing a baby doll type dress that shows off her bump. Her pregnancy glow just makes him forget about all the troubles life brings.

"You look so beautiful my baby got you glowing" he grabs her close to him rubbing her belly.

"Um I thought it was our baby" she said bawling up her mouth like a baby.

"It is babe stop pouting and let's go so you can give my baby some nutrients I know he's hungry." Jasean stresses he wants a boy.

"Whatever let's go before Chynna text me again." She grabs her purse and they head out the door to the elevators. They get off the elevator and everybody is down there waiting.

"Bout time y'all brought y'all ass on here we are hungry. Endy you should have been the first person down here" Chynna spat.

"Girl I'm sorry I didn't want to come out looking like I squeezed in my dress" Endy laughs.

They have a van that's taking everyone to the restaurant but Niema and YaYa are not in place.

"Yo where Ny and YaYa is are they coming?" Endy asks.

"She said they were running behind and will be coming in their own car" Chynna tells her.

"Who cares let's go" Ari said and the guys bust out laughing.
"If that damn child isn't just as ghetto" Endy said shaking her head at Ari.

The whole van just burst out laughing and all just enjoy each other on the ride to the ride.

They get to the restaurant and Endy is still wondering why Niema wouldn't ride with everyone else. . She has texted her several times but got no response.

"Endy you talk to Ny? Where is she at? She told me she was coming" Chynna questions especially since they were about to be seated.

"I don't know I haven't heard from her." Endy's getting frustrated with everyone keep asking her about Niema.

Ari gives Endy this look that let her know Ari too is pissed off.

"What I don't understand is why wouldn't she come with a guy she claims she been dating. She didn't have to fuck him if she didn't want to. Damn! I'm not feeling this YaYa chic at all" Ari says

"Girl you don't even know her like that. How can you say that Ariana? Be nice" Endy shakes her head at her friend. However she knows she meant what she said.

"Yeah, Ari, be nice. You know Endy don't want to upset li'l Niema" Chynna says, trying to be funny.

"Whatever Chynna y'all just don't start tonight" Endy laughs at them.

"What's going on people y'all started without us?" Niema says while being escorted to the table by the waiter. She and YaYa are both wearing short black cocktail dresses with nothing but legs showing which immediately put all the girls in defense mode.

"Girl I almost thought your ass told me a lie. You know I was going to get your ass" Chynna gives her this serious look.

"I told your butt I was coming Chynna. Y'all all met my cousin YaYa from New Orleans right" Niema replies as her and YaYa have a seat.

"No I haven't met her yet. Hi! I'm Ari, Tylon's wife and Endy's best friend. How long you're here for?" Ari gets straight to it.

"Hi Ari I'm YaYa and I will be moving to New York for good. I'm taking a Chief Editor Job there with a high fashion magazine. I got my degree in journalism" YaYa says proudly.

"Well that sounds great girl. You know Endy is a boutique owner and on occasion designs her own clothes. Maybe y'all can hook up on that sometimes" Chynna said trying to soften the mood.

"That sounds great yes Endy we must do that." YaYa throws a smile.

Endy forces a smile in agreement. Niema hasn't mentioned anything to Endy about her cousin moving to New York and she feels some type of way about it. Everyone talking and laughing at the table but Ari notices Endy's somewhat real silent and seem bothered.

"Excuse me, you guys. I have to use the potty" Endy stands as Jasean help her up. He's always been a real gentleman to Endy but since the pregnancy he's been really distant. He wants to show her he is going to do better by her.

"I'm coming with you girl" Niema jumps up looking sexy as ever in her dress.

Endy gives her a dreadful look but don't want to seem like she's being mean so she tells her to come on. The two head to the bathroom and Endy doesn't mutter a word, on the other hand Niema just yapping away. After they use the bathroom, they're at the sinks washing their hands and Niema feels the need to address the elephant in the room.

"E what's up with you? You haven't really said shit to me" Niema blurts out feeling the tension from Endy.

"No I haven't said shit to you because you been M.I.A. not answering my phone calls or even checking in on me. It's like ever since I found out I was pregnant you been acting funny" Endy replied highly upset.

"It's not like that Endy I just been real busy. I wouldn't just ignore you girl you know that I'm ready for my li'l god baby to get here" she said rubbing Endy's belly.

"Well it's like ever since you and Caine broke up you been taking it out on everyone else. Look that was your decision to keep dealing with him after he's constantly disrespected you. So get it together and stop taking the shit out on the rest of us. I haven't been anything but a good friend to you and I would like the same in return" Endy

yelled with her hand on her hip and tears in her

eyes.

"Endyia! I'm sorry boo I didn't know you

felt that way. I have been taking time out for me

it's nothing personal. I was in a bad place and it's

a lot I want to tell you. Things have been going on

that I'm not proud of. I felt alone and depressed. I

really need to get some things off my heart"

Niema grabs Endy hands her voice trembling

holding back tears.

"Ny what's wrong with you? Did

something happen with Caine? What the hell is

going on?" Endy is now.

"What y'all doing we are about to go

gamble. Why do I feel like I walked into a scene

of the Young and the Restless?" Ari said as she

busted in the bathroom. She found both her

friends crying. She startled them both and Niema runs inside one of the stalls.

"Is everything okay y'all?" Ari asks because she see that Endy seem to have been crying.

"Everything is fine we just had a sister moment right then, that's all" she replied. Niema comes out the stall and freshens up her lips gloss as Ari gives her a funny look.

"NIEMA! You sure everything is alright. I know we have our up and downs but I love you always" Ari tell her.

"Yes boo everything is fine I just been having these moments. I'm trying to put things in my life together little by little that's all. I feel like ever since Caine been gone I can't get my shit completely together. I put too much into a sorry

ass fuck boy" Niema said.

"Well you know regardless of what's

going on with you and Caine. We love you and

we're here for you" Ari hugs her.

"Girl I know that. I just wanted y'all to

know I would never distance myself from y'all on

purpose. I don't want y'all to feel like I'm always

being a negative Nancy when I'm around that's

all nothing against y'all. Now come on let's go

enjoy ourselves before these men send out a

search party. I'm telling y'all I'm going to be

okay we all are" Niema assured them.

The group is gambling but Endy is tired

and ready to go to bed. She doesn't want to be a

Debbie downer but the pregnancy is taking a toll

on her. She walks over to where Jasean is playing

poker to let him know she is ready to go. "Bae

I'm tired." Endy whines to Jasean. "Yo let me get a few more hands in and we can go" He said with a look of frustration that framed his face.

"What are a few hands Jay I'm tired and ready to lay down?" she whines again.

"Endy I thought we came out to enjoy ourselves" he snaps.

"Dumb ass I thought we came to spend time together, but excuse me I guess playing poker is more important. So you know what, stay your ass here I'm out" Endy stormed off.

Jasean runs behind her. "E…E…yo, what's up with you?" Jasean grab her arm.

"I said I'm tired! I want to go to the room and spend quality time together something you haven't done with me in over a month" She

shouts.

He pulls her into his chest and hugs her

tight feeling guilty about his actions. He hated to

see her upset especially with her carrying his

baby.

"I'm sorry Ma come on let's go to our

room. Your right this weekend is about us" Jasean

gently kisses her forehead.

About two in the morning Endy gets up to

use the bathroom and notice that Jasean is not in

the bed. She is immediately alarmed to where he

would go especially since it's in the middle of the

night. Endy begins calling all their friends but gets

no answer so now she's really worried. She grabs

a snack and turns on the television but just as she

was about to doze off at about 3a.m. her phone

rings.

"Hello" She answers seeing its Ari calling.

"Hi boo you called." Endy can hardly hear her

because it's some loud reggae music in the

background.

"Where you at? I don't know where Jay is

at? I been calling everybody and no one has been

answering" Endy yelled in the phone.

"Oh Jay good girl we all at this club called

'Cocoa's' but Jasean left like an hour ago did he

not get there yet?" Ari asks.

"He's not here how far the club is from

here" Endy's now alarmed.

"Umm Endy he should have been there he

was drunk as hell give him a few more minutes"

Ari said.

Well I been calling him and he's not answering the phone. I hope he is okay you know people will take advantage of you when they know you drunk" Endy said really worried.

"I'm sure he's good girl maybe he went back to gamble" Ari tried to reassure her everything was okay.

"Girl maybe he is but he can at least answer the damn phone, but I'm about to take my ass back to sleep" Endy said and they wrapped up their conversation.

Right after she hangs up with Ari Endy hears the door open. She sat straight up in the bed and yelled "Where the hell you been at?"

He smirks and shakes his head "Damn E not right now." He said sitting down on the foot of the bed.

"Jay it's after three in the morning in the morning and you have the nerve to say not right now. You better tell me where the hell you been at."

She stands in his face breathing so hard that her nose is flared which lets him know that she's really pissed. Although he's still tipsy and wants to lay down, he knows that won't be happening until he answer her

"You think this shit is funny? Leaving me in a room by myself all night and not answering your phone. I feel like slapping the piss out yo ass" She's yelled and started crying.

"Look E calm down, I was gambling DAMN! We're in Atlantic City right? What the hell I suppose to do while we're here. You being extra as hell man" he dismisses her feelings by walking off and going toward the bathroom.

That only pisses her off more. She rushes his ass from the back and starts swinging on him everywhere screaming, yelling, and cursing. He's trying to hold her arms but she's throwing punches left and right.

"Endy what the hell? Chill out Bae what the hell is wrong with you?" he finally gets a good hold on her pending her down on the bed.

"I'm tired of you Jay! I'm tired of you treating me like shit! I'm tired of you staying out all night like you single. If that's what the hell you want then go Jay. Go be fucking single!" Endy shouts breaking away from his hold.

"Baby I love you I don't want to single why you acting like this?" Jasean's confused.

"Fuck you and damn this trip I'm going home" she started packing her things.

He grabs her pleading for her to stay because he has a special day planned for Valentines. "Baby please don't do this I'm sorry I didn't think it was that big of a deal. I got it Bae I'm here please stop stressing yourself and the baby" he begs.

Endy finally calms down and he gets her to lie down while he massages her body to relax her. After a while she went to sleep and he started tie up some loose ends for his plan.

Chapter 6

Valentine's Day had finally arrived. They had finally started enjoying their trip without any more arguments. Endy is up early because Jasean has planned a full day of pampering for her. She's getting a full spa treatment including a Mani and Pedi, hair do, facial and massage. She is so ecstatic when he wakes her up with breakfast and a beautiful card with the spa reservation in it. She just gives him a huge hug and kiss. Morning breath and all she was so happy with her surprise.

"Baby thanks for all of this I'm so sorry for being so bitchy towards you. I just don't want my family to fall apart and you getting tempted by these whores out here" She said placing her hands on both sides of his face staring him in his eyes.

Their love was so deep and their connection was tight as ever.

"Baby you never have to worry about me being disloyal to you" Jasean assures her. (*Da...Da...da...da...*daaa...there's a knock at the door*).*Endy jumps up to answer the door and it's Niema.

"Girl what's going on? We got to go, why you're not dressed yet aren't" Niema shoots to Endy.

"Bitch don't start I'm coming. I had a long night last night of being nasty with my man" she shot back. She grabs her clothes and runs to the bathroom.

"Well I didn't need to hear that nasty asses. Tell her I will wait for her downstairs. By the way Happy Valentine's Day" Niema said

before walking out the room.

Endy is dressed and down stairs in forty-

five minutes to wait on the driver. "Damn bitch

about time I'm ready to eat" Ari says.

"Girl your big booty can miss a couple of

meals" Chynna said defending her cousin.

"Shut up Chynna I know you're not

talking about nobody big booty" Ari shoots back.

"Y'all bitches come on so me and my

baby can eat" Endy laughs.

"Girl you keep eating like that and you're

going to be big as house" YaYa chimed in.

"You don't worry how big I get my man

likes all this juiciness" Endy snaps back.

"Oh okay I was just kidding sweetie my bad" YaYa throws her hands up.

"First of all I'm not your sweetie so when you talk to me you come correct" Endy pops off.

"Whoa, whoa, Endy chill she was just kidding" Niema intervenes.

A dead silence comes over the group. Endy is pissed by YaYa comments and everybody knows it. Niema is confused on why Endy is being so mean to her cousin.

"Look y'all we supposed to be having a good time" Chynna said grabbing Endy's hand was shaking with fury. .

"Endy I swear I didn't mean any harm I apologize. I was just was trying to make conversation that's all" YaYa pleads with Endy.

"No girl I'm sorry about that I'm tripping because I'm hungry and y'all bitches still standing here" Endy starts laughing and so does the rest of the girls.

"This bitch is definitely bipolar I need this baby to come on "Chynna giggles.

The girls are finally all seated at the Country Kitchen restaurant and everyone seems okay but Niema. She still didn't appreciate how Endy popped off on her cousin. However, she's not gonna ruin the moment because she also knows Endy is hormonal right now.

"Ny why you so quiet" Ari asks.

"Nothing just ready to enjoy this spa treatment" Niema tells her.

"You can say that again" Endy said sarcastically sensing Niema irritated. Niema just gives her an ill look and let it go.

The girls finish up eating breakfast and the driver takes them to the spa. The ride there Niema and YaYa are very quiet. Endy notices it but she doesn't care she because she apologized already.

"Girl my feet so needed some attention" Ari moans.

"You can say that again corn toppers!" Niema jokes on Ari.

"Forget you bitch I know you and Endy not laughing and shit with y'all second long toe ass" Ari strikes back.

The girls continued laughing and cracking on each other having a good time and it started to feel like old times again. Niema wanted to confront Endy about how she spazzed on YaYa, but she's gonna leave well enough alone. She knows her emotions are high right now with the pregnancy. She doesn't want to make the trip ackward. The girls just continue engaging in conversation and enjoying each other's company until it's time for them to go back to the hotel.

After the spa treatments, Niema gets Endy by herself to talk a little in the bathroom. "Hi bestest what's going on with you?" Niema asked her.

"What you mean? I'm enjoying being away from New York and work" Endy responded while putting on her lip gloss.

"You know YaYa does mean well Endy she is also in the fashion industry. Maybe y'all can collab on some work to get E-Class name more out there globally" Niema tried convincing

Endy.

Maybe we can do that but tell me

something. Why I didn't know YaYa was here

New Years? Why didn't I know she was moving

to New York? Why you been so distant the last

couple of months? I'm ready to plan this baby

shower and you're nowhere to be found. Not

answering my calls or texts like that. What have I

done to you Ny?" Endy questions Niema.

"No Endy it's not you. I just been trying to

adjust to no longer being with Caine and getting

use to dating which I must say I have enjoyed"

Niema said with a sneaky grin.

"Gurl umm have you hun?" Endy laughs.

"What girl I got me some and all. Yes it's been great being single and I'm enjoying it" Niema smiles.

"Oh really so who is this new boo?" she asks.

"Umm new boo? No, hun, more like new boooo…ty call" Niema laughs and they slap five.

What's going on cunts? What's so funny up in here?" Chynna asks as she enters to see them laughing. She sees their getting past the bullshit. YaYa comes in behind her.

"Girl Ny been getting it in and didn't tell her sisters" Endy informed Chynna. "What? So who is he chic? Spill the beans Niema Mason" Chynna waits for an answer.

"Oh so y'all don't know him?" YaYa blurts out.

"No they don't YaYa but they will be meeting him soon" Niema replied somewhat annoyed.

Although Endy and Chynna sense that Niema is holding out they really don't understand because they usually share everything.

"Oh so we have secrets now Ny?" Chynna questions her with her hands on her hips.

"Ny why haven't you told them…" YaYa said and was quickly interrupted by Niema "because I'm going to let them meet him when I know where we stand" Niema groans at her cousin who looks confused.

"It's all good as long as your get laid by someone other than Caine" Chynna laughs it off.

"Y'all tricks come on the car is here" Ari shouts in the bathroom for them to come out.

Endy and YaYa still both look a bit confused on how Niema is acting.

"Let's bounce y'all before this car leave us" Niema says walking out the bathroom.

The ride back is quiet Endy is still confused on how Niema was acting all secretive about who she getting it in with. When they reach the hotel, Endy notices Jasean waiting outside the lobby.

"Girl your man must of missed you already damn" Chynna tease.

"Whatever haters that's my baby" Endy has a huge smile on her face.

"Are you alright Ny?" YaYa whispers noticing Niema is really quiet.

"I'm good girl just ready to see how tonight turns out" Niema replied still a little agitated with her

"Well we can't forget we all meeting up at six" Ari mumbles to Niema and YaYa so Endy can't hear.

All they know is Endy is going to be so surprised about what Jasean has planned for the night.

"You know I'm not going to forget that. She is going to be so ecstatic" Niema says.

"Okay he said we need to be in place so y'all please don't be late" Ari grunts rolling her eyes at Niema.

"I'm not bitch damn" Niema groans back.

They both did it so Endy doesn't hear them. As soon as they exit the van Jasean embrace his woman tight and plants a wet one right on her cherry lip gloss lips.

"What's good Bae? You enjoy the spa? Jasean asks.

"Yes Bae, I sure did, it was much needed."

"Well I want you to go upstairs and look at the beautiful dress I got you for tonight" He instructs her. He loves Endy very much and it's no secret.

"I know you're up to something Jasean Newman. I don't know what it is, but I'm sure I'm gonna love it" Endy smiles.

"Okay Jay can you take yo' ass on so she can go and plus I'm nosey I want to see this dress" Ari disrupts the couples happy moment. "

Okay y'all do your girly thing and I will see y'all all tonight" He laughs.

When Endy and her girls get back to the room she sees this beautiful black Polyvore gown which now raise her suspicion. "Gurl this gown is fire hot" Ari shouts.

"Yes it is E, Jay really outdid himself this time. But we are going to go so you can get dress and we will be right back. Time is ticking boo" Chynna adds.

The girls all are walking up the hallway so excited to be part of an awesome event. However Niema is just day dreaming because she's wondering how surprised Endy is going to be when she see Jasean planned something so beautiful.

I wonder how she gon act when she see what he has planned for her because it had to be hard to pull this off and have everyone attend" Ari said to the girls.

"However she feels I know shocked and happy is going to be in there. I'm sure she is going to feel crazy especially with their crazy ass behavior here lately" Chynna says now more anxious than ever.

"Well I'm so happy she has a loving man in her life. I'm so ready to meet this new addition.

I truly love her because she has been a great friend to me always" Niema says all teary eyed.

"Awe boo you know she love you too" Chynna hugs Niema.

Chynna and Ari exchange a look of content to see that she is really happy for her. They have been friends over a decade to let petty mess come between them, especially with Niema being Endy's supposedly best friend. They completely understand her wanting to be distant with all that's going on with Caine, Keosha, and their new baby coming. However, they want her to know they are there and don't shut them out her life completely. "Awe okay group hug damn it" Chynna and Ari breaks in to hug them.

"You too YaYa come get some of this love you're in the family now" Chynna says.

YaYa walks over to the girls and they all squeeze each other tight.

"Next time I'm gonna kick y'all bitches ass" Ari blurts and then came the laughter.

For the first time in a while they were showing love to one another with no arguments. This was Endy's day and they wanted it to be special for her.

The girls are finally gone and Chynna is rushing Endy because everyone is waiting for her downstairs. Endy is wondering what her man has up his sleeve. They finally get downstairs and Chynna directs her away that's not the exit.

"Where are we going, cuz?" "You are about to see girlie" Chynna replied. As they cut the corner down this long hallway, she sees her mom, dad, and grandmother standing at the entrance of this room.

"Hey y'all what's going on? Why are y'all here?" Endy's now confused.

"I asked them to come" Jasean pops up from around the corner.

"What? Why?" Endy asks.

"Because we couldn't do this without them being here" Jasean kneels down.

"Baby what are you doing we are already engaged" Endy said really confused now.

The doors to the room open up and the scenery is beautiful. It's purple lighting and everything in the room look crystalized and seated inside is all their family in friends.

"Jay what the hell is this?" Endy's eyes are now tearing up.

"It's our wedding baby I don't' want to wait another day without you being my wife Endy. I love you with everything in me so if you will baby let's get married now. I don't want our baby to be born out of wedlock. Everything is done just how you wanted it. Except it's in the winter and not summer. So will you marry me tonight baby?" Jasean said still kneeling down.

"Jay, OH MY GOD! I'm so surprised you pulled this off. What about Pastor Barnes?" Endy panics.

"He's here baby" Jasean points to the front of the room.

With her stomach in knots, Endy replies "yes baby of course I will marry you. You're my soul mate Jay" Endy cries.

"Don't mess up your make up baby girl" Tanya tells her daughter kissing her cheek.

"You look beautiful baby girl" Eddie tells his daughter kissing her cheek also. "I'm so emotional right now y'all. But I can't imagine marrying nobody else but you baby" Endy tells him.

"Well let's get to it everyone is waiting" a teary eyed Luella gives her granddaughter a tight hug before being going to be seated.

When the music begins to play for Endy and her dad to walk in she's surprised at what Jasean picked.

"Oh my God" she looks at Eddie. "What?"
he asks "He remembered the song" she says with
tears in her eyes.

Jasean picked "Spend my life with you
with *Eric Benet and Tamia*. Endy's surprised
because she told him that's what she wanted and
he remembered. As she walks down the aisle tears
are just flowing from everyone including Jasean.
He knew after he almost lost her to another dude
he would never want to lose her again. Endy
stomach is doing somersaults as she approached
her future husband. When they finally get to the
alter Eddie steps to Jasean and says "take care of
my baby girl Jay." "I got you pops" Jasean
replies.

"Who gives this woman to be married"
Pastor Barnes asks.

"I do" Eddie replies. He and Jasean shake hands and Eddie sits beside his beautiful wife.

In addition to the couple saying their vows the pastor asked them did they want to say something. Endy was too overwhelmed to speak but Jasean told him yes. As he grabs both of her trembling hands, he looks deep into her eyes and speak…

"Baby I just want you to know from the day we met I fell in love with your heart, mind, body, and spirit. Your loyalty to the people you love is spectacular and I just know you're gonna be a great mother. I wouldn't have chosen a more loving and nurturing person. Your spirit is full of love and patience and I'm forever grateful for God bringing you into my life. I had to learn sometimes it's better to do right then

By the time Jasean finished Endy had tears streaming down her face and the pastor told him to kiss his bride. Everyone just stood up and clapped it was so beautiful and Endy was taken aback by everything. The pastor introduced them as a couple and the family rushed them with hugs and kisses.

"Well you're a married woman now" Chynna smiles as all her girls scurry up to hug her.

"I know I want to thank all of you for being there for me. I love you all so much.

"Aww... girl, we love you too" Ari hugs her.

"Well I just want to say I'm really happy for you Endy. All your dreams are coming true. I can't think of anyone else who's more deserving of true happiness" a tearful Niema said.

"Dang Ny its okay" Endy confused on why she's crying so hard.

"I just want you to know I'm sorry I wasn't there like I should have been but I promise I will be a better friend to you E" She hugs Endy so tight.

Ari gives Chynna a look but they both dismiss it and continue on celebrating the couples union.

Everyone is seated about to eat and Caine stands up to give a toast.

"I just want to say congratulations to my cousin and his beautiful wife. I couldn't think of anyone else who more deserves of this happiness but you two. We had our ups and downs but through all the adversity you two stuck and out. I love y'all and thanks for showing what true love can look like. To one of the cutest couples in the world" Caine holds up his glass.

Everyone cheers except for Niema. Who rolled her eyes at the comments because how the hell he knows what true love looks like when he's dragged her through the mud for years?"

"I need the couple to come to the floor the DJ says playing Luther Vandross song If only for one night. Endy is again surprised at how Jasean remembered so many things from them their past. She laid her head on her husband's chest and just inhaled his scent enjoying every minutes of their dance in the icicle purple ballroom that her baby did so well putting together. She told her family this was all surreal she felt like she was dreaming. While everyone is having a great time and congratulating the newly married couple Ari notice one person who looks very sad.

"Ny what's good Ma? Beautiful wasn't it?" she said wondering why she looks so down.

"Nothing I'm just so happy for them Ari. Like E really deserves this" She puts on a fake smile.

"Look you can't fool me I know you a slight bit jealous come on who wouldn't be" Ari throws salt on Niema wounds.

"Fuck you Ari! You always trying to say some hurtful shit worry about your man" she grunts back.

"No bitch you should've been worried about yours so he wouldn't be over there snuggled with Keosha" Ari strikes back.

"Fuck you. Nobody wants fucking Caine he's a whore!" Niema says loudly now jumping up out her chair.

Chynna and Egypt comes between the two who obviously had too much to drink

"What you gonna do ho? I'm on to your trifling ass" Ari says loudly. Everyone including Niema is confused on what she talking about.

"Whatever Trick I don't have time for this bullshit. I'm not about to mess up my best friend's wedding" Niema throws up a dismissive hand and walk away.

"Ari what is that about?" Chynna asks.

"You will see Chynna that bitch dangerous. All y'all gonna see. She's jealous of Endy" Ari says staggering.

"Okay let me take my baby upstairs" Tylon intervenes. "You get the fuck off me because you know what's going on" Ari mush Tylon.

"Ari what's good babe" Chynna asks again.

"It's noting Chynna I'm taking her upstairs to sleep this off see y'all tomorrow" Tylon hugs everyone so he can get Ari to the room quickly.

Everyone else continued enjoying themselves and Jasean just held his bride really tight and embraced the moment. The guest had gotten back to having a good time and enjoying this beautiful scenery and everything was just laid out so beautifully. Endy was so in awe of how he and her family had everything so perfect she was still in shock over the whole ordeal. That's what let her know that they are destined to be one unit no matter the obstacles they encounter. The music continues to play and it's like their love has touched everyone in the room. Chynna still can't get over how Niema and Ari Carried on. One thing she does know is Tylon can say what he wants, but she know something is going on because Ari don't spit accusations like that. So until she can get to the bottom of it she will leave it alone. Just… for…..now.

The next day everyone prepared to go back home and Niema is extremely quiet. "Ny are you okay you been quiet all morning" Endy asks her.

"I'm good just still a little tired but don't worry about me. You just enjoy your new life" Niema tells her.

"You know I love you Ny. I want the same happiness for you so I can have me some god babies and have play dates. I just want you to give love another try don't let Caine make you miss out on a good man babe" Endy hugs her.

"I'm not Endy I promise. I love you and thanks for always being such a good friend. I just don't think love is for me" Niema tears up.

"He's coming Ny I can feel it God is going to send you a loyal and loving man just be patient sis. Talk to you later okay" Endy tells her and head to the car so they can head back to New York and her Jay packs for the honeymoon to Dominican Republic.

Chapter 7

Summer has arrived and so has Endy's baby shower and she's got a few more weeks before she has her baby girl. She picked this vintage styled restaurant in Brooklyn since all her and Jasean family lives there. She didn't want to make everyone travel to the city if they didn't have to. She's ready to hold her baby; especially, since Caine and Keosha had their baby girl, Cadence, about a month ago. That just got her more excited.

"So how you doing balloon belly?" Chynna teases.

"Shut up bitch I didn't mess with you when you pregnant with Enrique" Endy pouts.

"I know but your huge Endyia that baby has to be nine pounds." Chynna laughs.

Endy shakes her head and walk off to finish getting things together before she goes to get dressed.

"Hi y'all" a familiar voice says and it's none other than their little cousin Karishma with Asia in tow.

"My babies, Rizzy and Asia. Yes, I'm so glad y'all are here. Can y'all get the keepsakes table together for me, please?" Endy asks, giving them both hugs and kisses on the cheek.

"Endyia you know we don't mind helping you" Karishma says.

"As long as your damn cousin don't fuck with me I'm good" Asia adds.

Asia stops it! You and Chynna are blood and y'all argue like y'all not" Endy said.

"Okay cuz just for you but that bitch says one thing to me and I'm airing her ass out" Asia walks toward the back of the venue where the table is sitting that has the keepsake ornaments on it.

"Please just keep them out of each other way Rizzy" Endy pleads with Karishma.

"I'll try girl you know all y'all bitches have terrible tempers like Nana" Karishma jokes with Endy.

"Whew Lord give me the strength" Endy says to herself and continue setting up.

The baby shower started on time and everyone is in attendance. Well almost everyone besides Niema and people are not happy about it. They supposed to be playing games and eating by now but they have been trying to wait on her to arrive.

"Where the hell is your baby's godmother at?" Chynna asks growing impatient.

"I don't know Chynna but we can go ahead and start it. I can't keep waiting bad enough Jasean was almost an hour late doing club bullshit as usual. I'm so sick of them two I don't know what to do" Endy's said also frustrated.

 "I don't know why you even let her be the godmother" Ari grunts.

"Ari you know she always said she wants to be the god mother when me and Jasean has our first baby" Endy reminds them of the countless times Niema has asked her that.

"I know but she keeps being late to shit over and over again like what the hell is she doing?" Ari shouts and everyone look at her.

"Ari calm your ass down. We're not doing this today okay!" Chynna warns her.

"I know she just pisses me off with this bullshit Chynna. Come on even YaYa is here" Ari calms herself down.

"We have to let Endy deal with her. The more we intervene the more she hangs onto her Ari. We got to let her do it on her own." Chynna whispers giving Ari a hug. She knows she's acting out of concern but it's Endy's day and it cannot be ruined.

"Where the hell have you been?" YaYa bum rush Niema who's finally walking in the shower. "I was getting my god daughter gifts together I just ran a little behind" Niema snaps.

"Ny your two hours late and you know Ari has been talking shit too" YaYa gives her a heads up.

"Well Ari is always talking shit what's new" She walks off to go find the others. What's good y'all? Sorry I'm late" Niema says nonchalantly hugging everyone.

"Are you serious right now Ny?" Chynna interrupts her. "What?" She responds.

"Look y'all don't start I'm ready to open these damn gifts and enjoy my baby shower!" Endy yells at them.

"Alright Endy you don't have to yell everything is good" Niema says.

When they all turn around to head toward the gifts, in walks Caine, Keosha and their new baby girl. Niema stomach drops at the sight of them while everyone is more in shock he actually came with the baby. Especially knowing Niema was gonna be in attendance.

"Ny you good!" all the girls say at once.

Despite their constant arguing they all know Niema is very hurt by the turn of events in her relationship. Just like that all her friends sympathized with her and was just interested in her best interest.

"I'm gonna go to the bathroom for a minute" Niema says walking away swiftly.

"Ari go check on her please. I'm gonna go ahead and sit down to open the gifts" Endy tells her. "Okay, I gotchu boo .Go ahead and entertain your guests."

Ari heads to the bathroom and finds Niema in the mirror. "Ny are you okay babe?" Ari let the anger she had toward her go.

"I'm good sis it was bound to happen sooner or later. This is why I keep my distance a lot because I can't take running into him Ariana" Niema eyes tear up.

"I know baby girl but you got to get it together. You can't let them see you sweat" Ari gives her a tight hug.

"I know and I got this boo. I'm good okay let's go finish celebrating Endy's special day" Niema convince her.

They go to the area where everyone is standing around watching her open up one of her many gifts. Niema is on time to assist her bestie. Niema felt Caine trying to get eye contact from her but she continues to ignore him. Her stomach is a knot that she hasn't felt in a long time, her palms was sweaty and her heart felt like it was beating out her chest. Endy's voice sound as if she was talking in slow motion opening her gifts. Niema was feeling as though she was having an outer body experience.

"Niema!" Endy's voice startled her. "Pass me that mint green box, hun," Endy says giving her a strange 'you okay' look. "I'm sorry boo" Niema puts on a fake smile passing her the box.

She is really just ready for this whole thing to be over. After opening so many gifts everyone was getting drinks and conversing around the room.

"Niema" A family voice says coming up behind her as she sits at the bar. "Hello Caine how are you doing?" Niema gives another fake smile.

"Don't do that you can give me a hug" Caine says opening his arms. "Umm I rather not because I hate to have to smack the shit out of your bum ass baby mother" Niema says taking a sip of her patron margarita.

"Okay that's how you gon' carry it Ma" he laughs.

"Look Caine please go ahead because I'm not really in the mood for nonsense.

"There you go" Keosha walks in between them with the baby. "Cadence wants her daddy" Keosha said giving Niema a dirty look.

Keosha removes the blanket from the baby's face. Niema was so in awe with her she looked just like Caine. She began thinking about how she wished it was their baby. How could go and have a baby with another woman.

"What's good y'all? Oh my goodness she's beautiful Caine and Keosha" Chynna says giving Niema a 'what are you doing?' look.

"Yes she is very gorgeous. She looks just like her dad" Niema blurts, giving Keosha a devious look in return.

"Yes, she does" Keosha hands Caine the baby and grabs hold to his arm staring at Niema to throw shade.

"Well let me go tell Endy I'm about to step outside for a minute and grab my camera out the car but it's nice seeing everyone" Niema turns to walk away.

"Maybe one day you will have one of your own, girl" Keosha blurts out. Niema stops immediately and spins around "What the hell did you say?"

"Oh, I was just saying. You know everyone had a baby but you. Maybe you will have one soon" Keosha said with an evil smirk.

"Please don't go there honey because when I do, it won't be to trap no dude to be with me. It will be with the man I'm going to marry" Niema claps back.

"Oh yeah your right that's what we will be doing this September in Vegas. I can't wait" She gives a big grin and sips her drink clapping back even harder.

Niema never felt so stupid, hurt, and embarrassed. "Oh, well, I guess I need to say congraaaaaatulaaashuughhh" Niema jabs Keosha so quick, nobody seen it coming.

"Oh shit! Yo get your girl Chynna!" Caine shouts.

When Keosha hits the floor, Niema jumped on her and got in her ass, for the old and new. I mean she was giving it to her trifling ass.

"Niema let her go" Ari screams pulling Niema along with Chynna.

They're trying their best to get Niema off her but were not successful at all. Everybody is just screaming and finally Jasean and Caine got them apart.

"Niema what the hell is wrong with you?" Endy yells.

"Endy I'm so sorry I didn't…" Niema pause and look around the crowded room. She jump up and ran out the venue.

"Look Caine keep your bitches in check. I'm sick of all this little shit between Keosha and Ny. You knew better than to bring her ass here anyway. You knew Niema would be here" Endy points her finger in his face.

"E, I'm sorry, but that was on ya girl this time around" Caine tries to explain. "Save it Caine everybody just get the fuck on right now" she yells and storms off.

Jasean shoots Caine a pissed off look and swiftly brush past him bumping his shoulder. Keosha stands there, looking stupid, while Chynna and Ari go to find Endy.

"Your best bet is to get this bitch out of here before shit gets real ugly" Luella warns Cain while handing him the baby he threw to her to break up the fight.

He grabs his baby and drags Keosha out of the shower because he knew Luella was not playing with him. Endy's grandmother is well known for carrying a gun and not being scared to use it. She loves her family too death especially her grandchildren she doesn't play about them at all.

"Endy are you okay" Chynna asks her cousin who is crying and very upset. "Hell no I'm not okay. That shit them bitches did is not okay.

Ny gonna have to see me for real. I told her that Caine and Keosha probably were coming and she promised me she would behave" Endy groans.

"Endy now you know her seeing that baby was not a good idea at all knowing how much she wants a baby" Chynna sticks up for Niema.

"Girl she needs to get the fuck over it Caine doesn't want her and she needs to move on" Ari shouts.

"Ari would you shut the hell up sometimes damn the girl is hurt it hasn't even been a year yet they have history you dumb bitch" Chynna snaps.

"Damn you, Chynna, nobody is pacifying Ny. She needs to move on and get her shit together" Ari yells again; this time Tanya walks in.

"Y'all keep it down in here everyone can hear y'all" she tells them. "Sorry auntie" Chynna and Ari both say.

"Baby girl are you okay?" "Mommy I want to kick they ass for ruining my shower" Endy says with her voice trembling. "Well look you got about an hour left all you can do is apologize and let it go" Tanya tells her daughter.

"Yeah cuz let it go and enjoy the rest of your shower. Endy sighs knowing their telling her right but it doesn't dispute the fact she's pissed off.

"Yeah but this shit isn't over like I said Ny gonna have to see me for this bullshit" Endy said standing to get herself together to go apologize to her guests for Ny and Keosha's behavior.

♦♦♦NewSouth™♦♦♦

Niema is feeling very of remorseful about what happen she doesn't know what to do. She's pacing back and forth smoking a blunt trying to figure out how she can make this up to Endy. (Ding dong…the doorbell rings in combination with a knock at her door)

"Who the hell can that be?" she whisper to herself. "Who is it!" she shouts but nobody answers. "This better not be that damn Caine' she storms to the door and snatch it open. "Rocko?"

"I just want to make sure you're alright Ny nothing more" he said.

"I'm good Roc but I think its best you leave I don't want to cause any more trouble. It seems like drama follows me everywhere I go" she starts crying.

He grabs and hugs her tight but realizing their outside he makes his way in and close the door. They walk to the sofa and sit.

"Can I ask you a question?" Rocko asks as he grabbed her hands. "What is it Roc?" she looks up eyes filled with tears.

"Why do you continue to let this man get the best of you and tear you down? Do you even realize how beautiful you are?" He says with the most sincerity and concern.

 "It wasn't that Rocko, I guess, I just…I just couldn't take seeing the baby. Why can't I get over this? Why can't I get over him? I'm so tired of hurting Roc. I'm so tired" Niema sobs loudly.

Rocko continues to console her even though he doesn't like how she speaks about Caine. He's very much in love with her he's just trying to be a friend right now.

"He doesn't deserve your tears baby girl. I hate to see you constantly blame yourself for his behavior. He's a disrespectful asshole and never deserved your heart. I want you to start living and loving yourself Niema because if you don't you're gonna let this dude tear you down" Rocko felt the need to be real with her.

 "I know Rocko I know I really just want to get away from New York for a while. Maybe I need to go down south to see my aunts for a little while. So much has happen over the last few months and I need a getaway" Niema says rubbing her temples.

"Well do it then Ma because you can't keep going this route that you're going. You're either gonna end up in jail or with no friends to lean on. My cousin loves you but she is pissed right about now with your ass" Rocko informs her.

"I know I have to see her before I go anywhere I love her too much to lose her as a friend hell she's loved me more than anyone else in the world. I can't lose her in my life" Niema continue crying.

"Well you better fix it but before you do can I make one request?" Rocko asks.

"What is it?" Niema's concerned of what his request is.

"Can I stay and hold you tonight. We don't have to have sex but I just want to make sure you're alright. I love you so much Ny. I would do anything to make you happy" He grabs her hand which makes her feel so weak and vulnerable. A part of her knows it's wrong to lead Rocko on, but she loves the affection he shows her.

"Rocko um I…" Niema stumbles over her words.

"What is it Ma just spit it out" he tells her.

"Rocko I want to make love to you tonight. I want to feel good tonight" she says surprisingly that it shocks both of them.

"Are you sure?" he asks her confused.

"I never was so sure about anything in my life. So would you? I mean I understand if you're…"

Before she can finish her sentence Rocko grabs and kiss her aggressively. She willingly gave in and started tongue wrestling him right back. They were grabbing each other clothes and taking them off. Finally they're both naked he stops and looks down at her sexy caramel physique. He goes down to suck on her pussy which caught her off guard. He sucks her clit until she has multiple orgasms and Niema was louder than she has been in a while.

 "Ahhh…Ahhh…Roc…Roc" she yells in sweet agony. "I love you baby I promise I got you Ny just give me a chance" he moans slurping up every bit of her juices.

After she cums she lays there stuck. "I told you baby I got you that's all I wanted to do was make you feel good" Rocko kiss her cheek. Before they knew it, they both were fast asleep.

Niema is lying in her bed feeling guilty about her encounter with Rocko last night but she was vulnerable and only wanted to feel loved. (Ding…Ding…doorbell rings).

"ROC! Get up someone at the door" Niema jumps up naked to put on some clothes.

"So what Ny I'm tired of hiding whoever it is so what" he mumbles and turned over to go back to sleep.

"Roc, Roc! We got to get up it's almost nine o'clock I told Aunt Sally I would go to church with her this morning damn" she says putting on some plush Victoria Secret pajama pants with the tank to match. She runs to look out the window of the front room and see that it's Caine.

 "Shit" she grunts. "Who is it Ny?" Rocko asks putting on his clothes.

"Its Caine ass" She says holding and shaking her head. "So what you still fucking this dude?" Rocko snap pissed off.

"No I'm not fucking him Rocko I don't know why the fuck he's here! But I do know it's not going to look right if he see me and you here like we just woke up" She tries to reason.

"I don't give a fuck what he see he don't give a fuck about you Ny. He's only here because he feels guilty about yesterday I'm telling you and your ass gonna fall for it again" he snatch his shirt and walk toward the front door.

 She runs behind him "wait where you going? Hold up Rocko please don't leave!" She begs. His love for her won't let him continue walking so he just kissed her and said "get rid of him Niema or I will."

 "Okay Bae; please just go sit on the couch. I got this okay" she says getting herself together to open the door. However when she opens it he's not alone, Endy's right beside him

"Hello Ms. why aren't you answering your phone?" Endy asks with her arms folded.

"I was getting ready for church and…"

"What's good cuzzo?" Rocko pops up before she can finish. Endy frowns up her face looking back and forth between the two. In fact you can see Caine whole facial expression change.

"Okay, okay, okay what the fuck is going on?" Endy gives a little sarcastic laugh with one hand on her hip and the other on her big belly.

"It's not what you think E, Rocko came by to check on me that's all" Niema knew they didn't believe her but she was going to try and convince them anyway.

"This is not a good look at all B" Caine adds. "Dude, don't worry about what's a good look or anything concerning me, with your wack-ass" Niema screams on him.

"Are you fucking serious Ny? This shit is beyond trifling" Caine bucks back. "Please Caine fuck you get out your feelings and stop worrying about what I got going on" Niema yells jumping and Caine's face.

Rocko quickly jumps in between them which shock Niema. "B who the fuck you supposed to be!" Caine blows up at Rocko.

"I don't think you want to find out!" Rocko yells standing face to face to Caine which makes Endy jump in between.

 "Y'all please don't do this. Ny what the fuck you done got started? You got too much shit going on!" Endy cries screaming she blamed Niema for the commotion.

"What the fuck you mean? I didn't start shit. Y'all came to my crib with this bullshit Endy. Why everything always fall on me? I can have who the fuck I want at my house. I pay the bills at this motherfucker!" Niema's upset too.

"You better back the fuck up and take your lil ass on somewhere" Caine warns Rocko. "Make me move motherfucker if you feeling gully" Rocko boasts up closer in Caine's face. You can see the fury building up in Caine's eyes.

Meanwhile Endy is trying to pull her cousin away, and as she tries to diffuse the situation Caine throws the first punch. It goes down after that and Niema pulls Endy out the way so she's not caught in between. Both men are swinging and tearing Niema's house the hell up. Specifically her screen door glass is shattered and her curio is knocked down.

"Y'all stop it please Caine! Rocko!"

The women are screaming but they continue going at it. I mean punches are going back and forth with so much force between the two that's until Aunt Sally arrives and commence to hitting them with a broom stick which ends up breaking. They finally break apart with Aunt Sally

screaming and curing

"WHAT THE HELL IS WRONG WITH Y'ALL? It's

the Lord's day for God's sake!" Aunt Sally yells at the

top of her lungs. Rocko stands there with a bloody nose

and mouth and Caine has a blood shot eye. "

OMG!!" Endy yells. "What Endy" Niema panics. "My

water just broke" she yells again.

Niema looks down at her wood grain floors and it's

confirmed Endy's water has broken. Niema immediately

calls Jasean to meet them at New York Methodist

Hospital. Despite the altercation that just happened

everyone got it together and rushed to the hospital with

Endy.

"I see this is gonna be a long day" Endy says rubbing her

stomach as they ride down belt parkway to get to the

hospital.

When they arrive at the hospital mostly everyone that needs to be there is there besides Jasean. "Where the hell is Jasean at? They said Endy is already 8 centimeters" Tanya asks Caine and Niema.

"Ma I'm trying to figure out the same thing. I haven't heard back from him yet?" Niema says pissed off. They all have been calling him for the last hour and a half and still they haven't gotten a response.

"Hi girl what's going on with Endy?" YaYa pops up out of nowhere. Niema greets her with a hug

"Hi YaYa she's good we are trying to get in touch with Jay right now. He hasn't answered the phone or anyone texts"

"Wow has anybody spoken to him today?" YaYa asks. "No girl and she's already 8 centimeters. I know she will be devastated if he misses the birth of the baby.

"Yeah I bet" YaYa adds.

"Yo! Where my wife at?" Jasean bum rushes the waiting area a few minutes later. "Boy where have you been?" his aunt Marilyn (Caine's mother) asks.

"I was working on some last minute stuff for the club. Where is she?" he brush his aunt off.

"She's in room 24B hurry your mother and Tanya are already back there" she tells him. He kiss her, tells everyone else hello, and rush to the back where his wife is about to give birth to his first born and he's too excited.

"Ahhhhhoohhhahhhooohhh" Endy yells as Jasean enters the delivery room where his mother and mother in law are already dressed in scrubs. His eyes got big as fifty cent pieces because he couldn't understand the pain that his wife was enduring but he knew he wanted to be there for her.

"Jay...jay…JAY!!!" she tried to call Jasean in between contractions. "Breath baby girl breath" Tanya and Evelyn (Jasean's mom) tells her. Jasean is frozen because he didn't know having a baby was gonna be this intense. Anyhow he jumps in ready to see his seed and cut the cord.

The rest of the family is anxiously waiting for the princess to arrive. Endy's been in the back now about two hour. It is a lot of tension floating around and a lot of questions unanswered as to why Rocko lip is swollen and Caine eye is blood shot. Ari already knows it has something to do with Niema and she's pissed about it.

"Ny you good babe you been really quiet" Chynna questions Niema's mood she seems a little standoffish. "Yeah girl I'm good just nervous for Endy she was screaming really bad when I went back there" Niema throws on a smile. Rocko keeps trying to get eye contact but she is constantly avoiding him.

"She's here everybody" Jasean comes shouting in the waiting area. Everyone jumps up to congratulate and hug him.

"Our baby is here girl. We gonna spoil her up something too" Chynna says hugging Niema who is smiling although she's really overwhelmed by the whole ordeal.

"How much did she weigh" Eddie asks being that him and Luella had a bet.

"She's a beautiful healthy eight pounds and nine ounces" Jasean says proudly.

"We should have known by the way her tail was eating" Luella says making everyone laugh.

"Well after she gets cleaned up four people at a time can see her but y'all can visit the nursery now. Let me go give my wife a big kiss and let her know how much I love her for giving me the best gift ever" He smiles and head back to the room.

Everyone goes to see the baby but Niema and Chynna notice that she is missing and no one knows where she went.

"Yo! You see Ny?" Chynna asks everyone. "No I thought she was back there with Endy" Tanya says preparing to go home since they been there most of the day.

"No she's not and Endy is asking for her. I don't see YaYa either" Ari adds.

"Well why would she leave without seeing the baby?" Evelyn asks. "I already told y'all the bitch is jealous" Ari says. "She with Ms. Marilyn outside smoking a cigarette" YaYa interrupts Ari remarks. "Well Endy's looking for her to see the baby since she is the godmother" Ari snarls.

"You know what you be having a lot to say about my cousin" YaYa growls back. "And what you gonna do you about it bitch" Ari starts toward her. "Bitch I'm not scared of your ass" YaYa starts right back towards her.

However Caine meets them mid-way and he grabs YaYa and Chynna grabs Ari. "Who is this YaYa?" Luella questions. "She's Ny cousin Nana" Chynna replies.

"Well y'all keep a close eye on her I don't trust her far as I can see her" Luella gives them a concerned look. "I feel the same Nana" Ari slaps Luella five. "Girl get your crazy ass on. I don't know what I'm gonna do with you child" Luella laughs at Ari.

"You know I don't play about Endy and Chynna they're my babies" Ari snarls again. "Look let's get back here and see this baby again" Evelyn says.

While they are all in the room someone enters "I'm here" Niema spoke loudly with Caine's mom Marilyn alongside whom she's still very close too.

"I'm sorry you guys it's been a long morning" Niema explains hugging everyone. "Okay y'all ready let's name this baby" Niema excitedly says. "Okay y'all ready her name is Patience Loyalty Newman!" Endy yells out. "Aww that is so beautiful, cousin" Chynna says.

Waaawaaa" Patience screams out.

"I guess she likes her name. "I'm the happiest man in the world right now" Jasean kisses Endy. "Awe..." the whole room says making the two of them blush.

Chapter 8

After spending some time with Endy, Niema realize she still has the situation with Caine and Rocko lingering. She knows once Endy gets out the hospital she's gonna have some explaining to do but these days she just really don't care. She feels that she don't have to explain shit to no one especially who she's screwing being that everyone holds secrets when they feel like it. (Ding…ding)Niema phone rings and it's YaYa

"What's going on cousin?" Niema says answering the phone. "Ny we got to talk its important" YaYa says in a distressed tone.

"What wrong YaYa? Why you sound like you're in trouble?" Niema asks her concerned. "Nothing like that I just really need to talk to you and show off my new truck so can I come over or not?" YaYa says in an agitated tone.

"Okay bitch come on I'm home now" Niema yell back at her.

"Okay bitch I'm on my way then" YaYa quickly hangs up and rush over to Niema's house fast as she could. While driving she calls a number "What's good? Look, I'm heading over to Ny's house now. I think we need to tell her what's going on? I mean everything. You can't keep avoiding my phone calls" she yells.

♦♦♦NewSouth™♦♦♦

"Can I see Patience please?" Endy looks up and it's her cousins Rocko and J. J.

"Hi y'all here she is" Endy has this wide grin across her face.

"Wow E she's gorgeous but why she has Chinese hair" J. J. jokes because the baby has real straight hair and chinky eyes like her dad.

"Shut up jerk don't be messing with my princess"
Endy says kissing her forehead. "Nah for real cuz she's
pretty as hell. I can't wait to have me another one" Rocko
says as he reach to hold her.

"Another one! What the hell you mean? Shit you
and Taiya can't even stop arguing long enough to have
another damn baby" Endy laughs slapping five with J. J.

"Who the hell said it will be with Taiya?" Rocko
responds all nonchalant which stuns them both. "So….
who the hell you gonna have another baby with then?"
Endy asks.

"Don't worry about it but it won't be with her"
Rocko laughs it off. "Okay don't be pulling any surprises
on us Rodney Hinton" Endy warns him. "I got you cuz"
he laughs again.

"Well when you get to go home?" JJ asks. "I go home today and I'm so ready these damn nurses been getting on my last damn nerve" Endy chuckles.

"Fam...Lee, what's good wit cha?" Jasean walks in loud. "Jay shut up I just got Patience to sleep" Endy holds her finger to her lips.

"Sorry Ma, are y'all about ready to go? They already checked the car seat. I got you a push gift downstairs" He says giving his wife a kiss. "What kind of present Jay?" Endy's now suspicious of what it could be.

"Don't worry you about to see soon. But what y'all been up too." he brush her off. Endy just shakes her head and go into the bathroom to put on her sundress her mother brought her that matches the baby coming home outfit.

"Nothing too much you know how it goes" Rocko says giving him a pound. "Nah I heard you been on some corny ass bullshit" Jasean says to Rocko letting him know

he heard about the situation.

"Yo that was your fam B, not me. He came at me

so what was I supposed to do" Rocko says. "I feel you on

that son but y'all some faggots for that bullshit" Jasean

reply right before Endy comes out the bathroom.

"Okay is mum gonchu leaving us already huh?" A

West Indian nurse jokes as she sees Endy getting her

things together. "Yes I am because y'all have not been

letting me get no damn sleep" Endy laughs. "Oh, chu not

gon get no sleep. Baby keep you up" The nurse replies.

"You ready E" Rocko asks grabbing her bags.

"Yes I'm ready the nurse has to wheel me and Patience

downstairs" Endy reminds him. "Okay we will meet y'all

down stairs" Jasean tells them.

They get downstairs and Endy starts looking for

her BMW in the lineup of cars in front of the hospital.

"Where the hell is Jay at?" She says. "He's right there" Rocko said shock because Jasean hops out silver BMW X5.

"What the hell Jay? Who truck is this?" Endy says just as shock. "Surprise Ma It's my present to you because you gave me the best present in the world" Jasean smiles giving Endy a kiss. "Oh my God Jay when did you do this? Oh my God it's so pretty Jay" She's crying tears of joy. "It's yours and Patience you deserve this and so much more" Jasean kiss her again and helps her get into her new truck. "I don't know what to say baby you're the best husband any woman can ask for" Endy has tears just falling.

"Yo B this shit nice as hell. You did that for real my dude that's love man. You make us good dudes look bad" Rocko says with much approval because he knows Endy's a good woman and deserve nothing but the best. "Well y'all go home and get settled we'll be seeing y'all soon” J.J. kisses Endy and daps Jasean, and him and

Rocko head out.

Endy’s been home for a few weeks now and she

hasn’t seen or heard from Niema but twice and both times

she said she would be by but never shows up.

“Ny this Endy what’s good you haven’t been by

to see your god child since I been home why would you

fly to Vegas when you knew I was coming home? I

thought you was my bitch call me. (da, da,da, da, da a

knock at the door). Endy hangs up the phone and go to

answer the door.

“Hi Pooh I heard you needed some helping hands

since Jay is back at work” Chynna comes in with bags

along with Ari and Egypt behind her also carrying bags

with all the kids in tow.

"What is all this stuff?" Endy questions because they came in with hell of bags.

"This is our girls' night in stuff and the rest of the gang is on the way. We thought we would surprise you" Chynna tells her giving her a great big hug. She knew she could use the company especially with Jasean putting in so many hours at the club. "Awe... thanks, you guys. I sure could use the company. Patience wants to sleep all day and be up all night. Girl I don't see how you bitches do it" Endy grabs her head.

"Uh huh I told your ass it's a lot when their new born Enrique is 17 months old and still tries that getting up shit" Chynna agree with Endy's frustration.

"I love my baby don't get me wrong but I'll be so glad when she gets her days and nights together" Endy chuckles.

"Well can you go get my pudding for me please?" Egypt asks Endy anxious to see her baby cousin. Endy heads to the room to get Patience so they all can enjoy their time with her.

"Where the hell is Ny at anyway?" Ari asks because she's been M.I.A.

"Girl I heard about Rocko and Caine getting into it at her house. What the hell was Rocko doing at her house anyway?" Egypt asks.

"I don't know but they claim it was innocent and nothing happened" Chynna says skeptical because she knows it's more to the story.

"If she's fucking Rocko she's on some real thot shit for real" Ari snarls shaking her head.

"Well I don't know what happened but I'm going to take their word for it if they say it is innocent then it is what it is" Endy says wanting to end the conversation. "Well let's put on some music and play cards or something" Ari jumps up to turn on the stereo.

The doorbell rings. "I got it y'all" Egypt race to open the door. "What's going on y'all we want to party too?" Karishma yells holding up a bottle of wine with Asia behind her. "Bout time you bitches got here I thought y'all weren't coming" Chynna says giving her cousins a hug.

"Umm Where's Ny at?" Asia smirks. "I don't know. Why?" Chynna asks.

"It's mighty funny that she and Rocko both are out of town at the same time. Plus Taiya called Lynasia saying she thinks Rocko and Ny is messing around and if she finds out she's gonna beat her ass" Asia says shaking her head.

"Who's getting their ass beat?" Endy asks Asia as her and Ari comes from the kitchen with some glasses and snacks. "Your damn friend that's who" Chynna says.

"Who? What Friend?" She asks confused. "Niema that's who how about Rocko is out of town too. Something just doesn't seem right to me." Chynna says.

"Well I'm not gonna jump to any conclusions let's just wait until Ny comes back and we will have our normal round table like we always do when something comes up okay" Endy tries to get off the subject.

"Okay but if that bitch fucking Rocko I'm gonna whip her ass" Ari groans. "And why would you do that?" Endy gives her a suspicious look.

"Because it's not right Endyia and she keeps doing little stupid shit. I think when she left Caine she left a part of her brain. The good part" Ari burst out laughing.

"Bitch you stupid let's play some spades" Chynna laughs at Ari comment. The girls played spades, talked and listen to their music all night to make Endy feel good.

The next morning Endy gets up and text Ny because all the rumors and stuff being said is getting to her. She would hope her bestie isn't lying to her but she can't help but wonder with all the accusations everyone is making.

Ny I don't know what's going on with you and Rodney but I need you to come and have a real conversation with me because it's starting to be too many coincidences.

She sends her the text hoping she responds soon. "What you doing up so early? I didn't hear Patience cry" Chynna asks her cousin who is just sitting up alone.

"Oh I just put her back down and couldn't go back to sleep. I'm okay though" Endy says in a down mood looking down at her phone. "You don't sound good what's up?" Chynna asks because Endy just looked stressed the whole time they been there.

"Nothing I just need a break from the baby from time to time. Jay is hardly here and when he is it's late at night or not until the next morning. I just feel like he may need to get another type of job" Endy says as her voice cracks.

"Oh my goodness Endy Why didn't you say something?" Chynna hugs her cousin who she strongly believes is going through postpartum depression. "I told you Endy this shit is hard man" Chynna express to her cousin because she too has been in Endy shoes.

"I don't know if it's me in my feelings or me being overwhelmed with Patience, but Jay is still not home or answering his phone. He knows I hate when he doesn't answer the phone for me. Anything could happen" a frustrated Endy shouts.

"I know baby but he has to make that money. Do you want me to talk to him? You know I will" Chynna asks.

"Nah I'm gonna talk to him. I just want him to know that he has to be more responsible now not answering his phone is not okay with me. I will be letting his ass know that too" Endy says pacing the floor.

"I thought I heard y'all up" Asia comes in the living room to join her cousins. Endy shoots Chynna a don't say anything look.

"What y'all? Did I just walk into something?" Asia asks because of the look on her cousins' face. "Endy is just a little overwhelmed with the new baby that's all" Chynna tells her. "CHYNNA!" Endy yells.

"What? She needs to know so we can all pull together to help you. STOP TRYING TO BE SUPERWOMAN!" Chynna shouts back.

"Why you do that all the time Endy?" Asia shakes her head. "WHAT ASIA?"

"Why do you feel like you have to try to prove a point to everyone? If you needed help with Patience why you didn't say something? Come on now Rizzy, Egypt, and I don't have any kids we don't mind Endy" Asia stands up to give her cousin a hug.

As they are about to get the day started the door opens. "Well hello there did you forget where you live at?" Endy says with her hands on her hips. The girls quickly scurry in the kitchen to let them talk.

"What you talking about now E?" Jasean plays it cool. "You know what the hell I'm talking about why haven't you been answering your phone?" She shoots him a heated look. "Look I just feel asleep at the club that's all baby damn" He grabs her by the waist and kiss her.

"Nah I told you anything can happen with me and the baby you need to be on alert at all times Jay" She push him away. "Damn Endy I'm trying to make money so we can be straight until you go back to work" He snaps.

"Who the hell you think you yelling at you're the one who didn't answer the damn phone" She snaps right back.

"Look Baby I'm not trying to argue I need to take a shower and take you out to eat this evening. Do you think someone can keep the baby?" he grabs her hand pulling her close to him.

"Don't try to butter me up punk" she smirks but still furious with him. "I'm not Bae it's been a while and I want to feel my warm puddle of goodness" he says squeezing her butt. "Stop it before someone walk in here. I'm serious Jay when I call, you need to be answering the phone man" Endy mush his head.

"Okay babe dang" he gives her a kiss. "The baby crying y'all want me to get her" Egypt comes to ask them.

"Nah I'm on daddy duty y'all go ahead and I will get my baby girl. Daddy misses her anyway" Jasean boast and head to the nursery.

"Girl I know he does some crazy shit sometimes but at least he provides because half these men today don't know what that word means" Egypt tells her cousin. "I know girl he's a good man. I'm just spoiled that's all and still getting use to this new part of my life being a new mommy that's all. Hopefully I am done with this emotional part soon" Endy laughs.

"Okay y'all mushy bitches can we please eat" Ari interrupt their sentimental time. "Girl you will mess up a wet dream" Endy throws a pillow at her.

"Girl I'm hungry y'all have to come on now" Ari rubs her stomach. "Okay girl we coming now" Endy said and they all go into the kitchen to eat the breakfast Egypt and Ari prepared for everyone.

"Good Morning boo how you feeling this morning" YaYa says to Niema. "I'm good about to get ready to meet up with Endy she sent me a text this morning about wanting to have a conversation about me and Rocko" Niema shakes her head.

"Girl don't worry about what they think if you love Rocko fuck it girl y'all figure it out not everybody else" YaYa gets fed up. "I know that YaYa but it doesn't help that he is still with his daughter's mother. No matter how I look at it; I'm going to still be looked at as the side chic" Niema throws her arms up frustrated.

"You know what! Fuck it! Stand up for yourself for once Niema. Damn do what makes you happy forget what everybody is going to think" YaYa is now furious because she can't stand when Niema tries to be so pleasing to people who talk shit about her. She wants her to just do her for once and stop worrying about what other people will have to say. "YaYa I know what you're saying but I have to make sure he handles shit on his end too. I can't just jump out there and expect him to leave his family because my shit is messed up" Niema get frustrated with her cousin.

"Okay it's your life and your grown I just want to see you happy Niema" YaYa calms down because she don't want to argue with her. "Look I'm just gonna come clean with her I made my bed so I got to lie in it" Niema shrugs as she finish rolling her blunt.

It's a beautiful summer August day out as Endy is seated at the girls' favorite seafood restaurant in City Island waiting for Niema to show up so they can chop it up. She is trying to remain calm but she has a bad feeling Niema is going to tell her something she doesn't want to hear. Niema is on her way there butterflies all in her stomach but she knows she needs to come clean with her friend so they can get pass the tension. Endy see Niema as she walk toward the table. She stands to give her a hug.

"What's going on girl? Ms. M.I.A" Endy says sarcastically. "I know E I just been trying to get it all together. I didn't want to continue burdening you with my problems. I do have to be honest with you E" Niema takes a deep breath.

"Just tell me Ny are you and Rocko messing around first of all?"

"Yes Endy we are and have been since around Christmas time" Niema puts her head down. "Ny! What the fuck? Why didn't you just come and talk to me? Why did I have to hear it through the grapevine? Come on you know better you can tell me anything whether good or bad. This doesn't just affect you Niema" Endy rolls her eyes.

"I know that E, but you were pregnant and things were going good for you I just didn't want to drag you down with me. My life was going in a downward spiral and still is." Niema sighs grabbing her head.

"I know Ny but we're supposed to always be there for each other. Shit I haven't really heard from you like that since my pregnancy announcement New Years and now I see why" she shouts making Niema cry.

"So what is the plan now? What are you and Rodney planning to do about this situation because you know Taiya is about to flip the fuck out. The family is going to be very disappointed in y'all Ny. Plus everyone

is already insinuating anyway so y'all not slick" Endy

informs her.

"WHAT! I know bestest this is the worst thing I

could have ever done. I don't want to break up his family

I love Rachelle. I'm going to tell him we need to chill

because I know nothing good is gonna come out of this. I

was just acting on my own hurt trying to hurt Taiya and

Caine. When I should have been left Caine ass alone" she

begins to cry which make Endy feel bad.

"Well something gots to give and he knows I'm

coming for his head with this bullshit here. Y'all two

know y'all something causing all this damn drama Ny"

Endy's still angry. "I'm sorry for shutting you out but you

don't know how hard it has been for me these last few

months. I'm sorry Endy I love you and I would never try

to hurt you intentionally" Niema squeals.

"It's okay bestest we are going to get through this. Even though I don't agree with what y'all did, I still have your back at the end of the day. Now where the hell do we start at because Nana about to get in y'all ass about this one" Endy laughs still teary eyed.

"I know but I made my bed now I must lie in it" Niema says relieved. "Give me a hug girl I know you need it" Endy says giving Niema a tight hug. They both start crying because Niema knows she hurt her friend and Endy know her friend is hurting.

"I'm so sorry I wasn't there for you more Endy. You have been nothing but a great friend to me all these years. Even when people wanted you to leave me alone" Niema tears flow heavily.

"Well we gonna work this out but right now let's just hold tight because the storm is about to come big time but I'm with you Ma okay" Endy reassures her friend. As they are walking to their cars, Niema notice Endy walking to the BMW Truck.

"Uh oh Girl is this you?" Niema shouts hugging Endy. "Yes girl Jay got it for me as a push gift girl" Endy holds up shaking the keys. "Girl this is nice but why YaYa got the same truck girl that's crazy" Niema says nonchalantly.

"She does?" Endy frowns up her face. "Yeah girl she just let me see it that's crazy as hell" Niema says. "Yeah that is crazy well I got to go get Patience from mommy but I will hit you up later" Endy says as she gets in her truck. "Okay I'll talk to you later and thanks for being my friend Endyia. I will forever be grateful for you" Niema says before walking off.

As Niema head to her car, her cell phone rings and its Rocko. "Hello?" "What's good Ma how you're feeling today?"

"I'm good just left from talking to Endy. I came clean to her about us" Niema just blurts it out. "What you mean you came clean it wasn't any of her business" He shouts in the phone.

"First of all who the hell you yelling at and second what are you trying to hid if you claiming to love me so damn much" Niema yell back. "I'm just saying Ny you should have told me before saying anything to her" he shouts again.

"I don't have to tell you nothing first of all. We're adults and we made a gown up decision to have sex so if you felt like you needed to hide then you should have told me that part ass hole. I'm not jeopardizing my relationship with Endy for no one not even you Rocko" She snaps.

"I'm sorry Bae yeah your right. I just know this is about to be some shit but we got to face it because what's done is done. So with that said I got something to tell you Ny" Rocko nervously says.

"What now Rocko spit it out?" "Okay, Okay Ny whew" He sighs. "WHAT!" she yells.

"Okay Niema I hate to tell you this but Taiya is pregnant" Rocko just spits it out. "WHAT THE HELL YOU MEAN SHE'S PREGNANT?" Niema yells in the phone.

"Ny please I'm gonna fix this let me explain please" Rocko tries reasoning.

"NO FUCK YOU RODNEY DON"T HIT ME EVER AGAIN" she's now crying.

"Ny I'm sorry baby please" Rocko says but its silent. "Hello. HELLO!" he yells in the phone. "Damn she hung up.

Chapter 9

It's been a few weeks since Niema and Rocko seen or evens spoke to each other. Niema has been trying to keep herself busy hanging out more with Endy and Patience. They have been talking more and went on a couple more lunch dates. Niema is missing Rocko's company and becoming depressed again. She knows she has to tell Endy she's pregnant but she hasn't even decided if she's gonna have it yet.

"So girl what's going with you today? You all quiet and shit so I know something is up" Endy asks Niema.

"Girl I have so much going on right now it's not even funny" Niema stated with a stressful look on her face.

"What's going on now Ny? You know I'm gonna find out so just tell me" Endy tells her.

"I have something to show and tell you but I don't want you to be upset with me" Niema which alarms Endy even more.

"Ny we are good babe. What is it? Please just spit it out" Endy reassures her. Niema digs in her purse and pulled out a pregnancy test.

"Ny oh my God you're pregnant?" Endy screams excitedly.

"Endy this is not good. It's not good at all" Niema cries.

"Why? You said you're ready to be a mommy right?" Endy's confused.

"Yes but in the right way not being pregnant by someone who I'm not with and who is already with someone else" She whines. Endy gets up and give her a hug letting her know she will be there every step of the way.

"Girl you're going to be good Rodney and you mind as well let everyone know what's going on now. This is something y'all will not be able to hide forever" Endy remind her.

"I know Endy, but you must not know everything that's going on right now" Niema says to her.

"What do you mean Ny? What don't I know?" Endy questions

"Endy, Taiya's pregnant too and I haven't told Rocko about me for that reason. I know this is going to be too much and it's becoming a real life nightmare. Like what the hell have I gotten myself into" she yells loudly making the baby jump.

"It's going to be okay Niema we are going to get through this together. One thing I know is Rocko loves you he always has furthermore he's going to be a great father to this baby" Endy tries convincing her but Niema just doesn't feel confident just yet. Especially since he doesn't even know she's pregnant yet.

"I hung up on him when he told me about Taiya because I already had a feeling I was pregnant. It's been almost two months since I had a period" Niema shakes her head in disbelief.

"Damn y'all were screwing up something huh" Endy laughs trying to soften the mood.

"It's not funny E you know Nana and the rest of the family are going to flip out. I'm going to be looked at as a home wrecker and whore. This is just too much right now Endy" Niema panics.

"Ny you have to calm down! The first step is to have a conversation with Rocko then go from there. Don't make any sudden decisions please. At the end of the day, nobody has to take care of that child but you and him. Please consider having it" Endy begs her. The look on Endy's face let Niema know she was right. She had to at least let Rocko know she's pregnant it was only right. She knew at the end of the day he loves her to death and besides he's told her many of times he would leave but Niema told him no.

"Okay Endy I'm about to text him and tell him we need to talk. Gurl I know this is not going to turn out good. I have to do it though" Niema sighs.

"It's going to be alright boo I got you if nobody else does" Endy hugs and comfort her friend. "I'm gonna be a god mommy. Yay Payday we gonna have baby" she burst out loud.

"Bitch your crazy" Niema starts laughing and go ahead and text Rocko.

♦♦♦NewSouth™♦♦♦

As Rocko lay in his lavished condo in Midtown his phone vibrates and he looks and sees it's a message from Niema that reads:

"Yo Roc we need to talk ASAP it's an emergency. Just hit me up when you get time."

"Lord what can be wrong now? I'm not in the mood for any more bad news. I'm ready to see my baby" Rocko grabs his head mumbling to himself.

Taiya walks into their French antique furnished living room. One thing for sure is Rocko has great taste and he tried to pass that on to Taiya, but she just won't leave her hood ways behind. Rocko is not bad on the eyes at all with his olive skins and big locs of curls on his head.

"What's wrong one of your ho's done pissed you off?" Taiya giggles.

"I'm not in the mood for your bullshit Tai" Rocko grunts.

"I'm just messing with you dang why you acting so fucked up Rocko" Taiya snaps.

(Da, da, da, da, da…a knock at the door). "Who is it?" Rocko yells at the door. "Rocko, it's J.J, yo open the door, B" JJ yells through the door. Rocko opens the door and J.J. can tell he's upset about something.

"What's good B?" J.J. asks him giving him dap and taking a seat on the sofa.

"Well I'm about to go lay down I'm tired see y'all punks later" Taiya said as she went to the bedroom.

Rocko just gives her a disgusted look and sit across from J.J. who peeped it out.

"Yo cuzzo what's the deal with you and Taiya? And better yet what's the deal with you and Ny? The streets are talking, my nig you better be coming up with a solution quick" J.J. says, smirking.

"Man I got myself in some shit. Me and Ny have been messing around for like nine months B, and now Taiya ass is pregnant," Rocko whispers to J.J.

"What?" He shouts so loud that Taiya can hear him.

"Yo shut up I don't want her ass trying to be nosey. This shit got me stressed because I want to be with Ny. I don't know how to tell Taiya this shit man" Rocko groans.

"Damn Man you're going to have to make a decision. You and Ny how the hell did that shit happen" J.J. said trying to take everything in his cousin is telling him.

"Cuz you know I been wanting Ny for years well after the Christmas party last year shit finally went down. I promise you man it was everything I expected it to be" Rocko smiles as if he's reminiscing.

"Roc, you got to make a decision, yo, and fast; because this shit is about to get ugly real fast. You know Caine is coming for your head. But you my FAM so if shit gets ugly so be it. He should have treated her right while he had the chance. I just still can't belee this shit" J.J. said shocked.

"Yeah man I just hate how everything is going down and now Endy knows. I know she's about to let me have it. My only concern is to make sure my baby comes here healthy and I talk to Niema ASAP!" Rocko stresses.

"I know man well you know I'm here if you need to chop it up at any time of the day man. You are like my brother Roc but I need you to get this shit handled man" J.J. stands up to leave.

"Oh now you want to run off" Rocko laughs.

"Yo B, with all you just laid on me I need a damn drink. I'm about to meet Lynasia at the bar in Brooklyn." J.J. dapped him up.

"Okay man I will hit you up later" Rocko walks him to the door and reality sets in. "Damn I got to get to Ny before she gives up man" he picks up his phone to text her back *"Yo we need to talk."*

"So we work all night now? Endy snarls as Jay walk in the bedroom at six in the morning.

"Look E please don't start I got to work we got bills" he spat back.

"Jay I know your ass not snapping on me and you're the one in the wrong. I'm the one up with Patience when you're not here motherfucker so don't yell at me" Endy jumps out the bed.

"ENDY CHILL DAMN WHY YOU TRIPPING? You know the club don't close until 4 sometimes 5 in the morning. I am doing this for us babe I have the fall bash coming up along with the Halloween party it's a lot. Caine all knocked off his fucking game because of what Ny and Rocko got going on. It's just been stressful damn I want my home to be a place a peace" Jasean rants.

"Okay Jay all I'm saying is you can call me sometimes I be worried that's all" Endy felt bad after listening to him.

"Look baby I understand that but please ease up I'm just working to build something for us that's all. I want us to be in our new house by next year. We can't keep staying in this tight ass Condo" Jasean walk over and grab her hand.

"I be missing you Jay like damn it's been two weeks since we had sex and it's been sparingly since I had the baby. I'm starting to feel like you're losing interest that scares me" Endy sadly state.

"I would never lose interest in your E you're my soul mate I will forever love you. I made you my wife because no other woman has ever done it for me. My heart will always be with you babe" Jasean reassures her. The touch of her man hands rubbing up and down her arms and the sensual kiss he plants on her forehead calmed her right down. Then he kisses her lips slowly

grabbing her by the waist and picking her up to carry her

to the bed. He laid her down slowly and lowered his head

down to the place he missed so much.

"Uhhhhhh" Endy let out a loud moan and the rest

well you know…

After a few of hours of making love to her

husband, taking a nap, a hot shower and feeding her

beautiful baby girl Endy's in the kitchen making Jasean a

good old lunch of chicken and waffles she's been dying

to use her waffle maker since they had the girls night a

couple of months ago.

"Hi bae that smells good and I need it since you

took all my energy this morning" Jasean said as he

walked in the kitchen with just his basketball shorts and

ankle socks. His body glistening made Endy want to take

him down again.

"I know you're probably hungry. I got to get to the store and get Patience to my mom and Aunt Lisa. She puts her arms around his neck giving him a kiss.

"Damn baby you not gonna eat?" Jasean asks as Endy's rushing through the house.

"Babe I have to go check on my shop. I will get off early enough to see you before you leave" she grabs Patience and brings her so Jasean can give her a kiss.

"What your mom got going on today?" he asks her as she slaps a wet one on his lips. "I don't know probably shopping knowing my mother. You know she probably want to show her off" She says putting her in her car seat.

"Tell her don't be letting motherfuckers put they lips on my princess" he spat.

"Boy please she doesn't even want us kissing her. I love you hit you when I get the store" Endy says as she leaves out the house.

"Dang I love you too" Jasean mumbles finishing off his delicious lunch his baby made for him.

(Ding….dong…the doorbell rings). "Who is it?" Jasean yells walking to the door. "Its ya cousin open the door!" J.J. shouts through the door. Jasean opens the door and let him in.

"Come on in Bruh, in here eating and shit what brings you to Brooklyn?" Jasean asks him as he goes back to the kitchen.

"Nothing much man I was Downtown doing some shopping and thought I would stop by to see y'all. Where cuz at?" J.J. asks sitting down on the sofa.

"She went to the store and the baby with Ma Tanya" he says with a bottle of Patron in one hand and two glasses in the other.

"Okay well I want to smoke this L so let's hit the terrace" J.J. stands up to go on the terrace that overlooks most of Brooklyn and Queens where they usually chill at.

"I know you so what's on your mind?" Jasean asks knowing something is bothering J.J.

"Well man shit is about to hit the fan and we all fam so we got to get a handle on this shit" J.J. begins.

"What the deally, yo?" Jasean frowns. "Well it's about all this shit with Caine, Rocko, and Ny ass. Yo know I spoke to my cuz and they are fucking" J.J. spits out.

"You fucking with me B come on nah man this shit can't be real" Jasean jumps up. He knows nothing good is gonna come out this situation. He can't be mad at Niema for moving on but he is upset that Rocko broke the bro code even though he's always been in love with Niema. He knows Caine is going flip the hell out.

"Yeah man and that's not all" J.J. informs him.

"Please don't tell me it gets worse" Jasean shakes his head no.

"Yeah B it does. Roc is planning on leaving Taiya to be with Ny. And to top shit off Taiya pregnant" J.J. grunts.

"What! This shit is getting crazy what the hell is really going on with everybody?" Jasean is pissed now. Once Caine know this shit is really official it's gonna be some blows thrown. Caine and Rocko are both cocky as hell and neither will back down but can the family join forces to diffuse this situation.

"Jay we got to put a stop to this shit at the end of the day Rocko fucked up big time. Although Caine had a baby with Keosha, Ny and Roc should have never pulled no shit like this. But we can't let this shit divide the family. Endy will be devastated and so will Ny. Despite everything I know she loves everyone involved" J.J. says looking over and noticing Jasean staring off into space.

"Yo B you hear me?" J.J. yelled seeing Jasean not paying him any mind.

"Man I hear you but this shit is bad it's no way around it. Look we gonna have to have a real men sit down on some grown men shit because shit is about to get ugly J I feel it" Jasean groans.

"I know man we gonna do that but first I want to talk to Ny because I want to know what the hell she was thinking" Jasean adds.

"Well let's put this shit in motion and I mean with the quickness" J.J stands up slapping five with Jasean.

"Alright I'm gonna get at you" Jasean stands to walk J.J. to the door.

"Alright man love" J.J. said and walks off.

"Yeah man Love" Jasean responds back as he close the door and lock it behind him. He notices his phone flashing it's Caine that left a text message:

"Jay I need you to hit me up ASAP I got some shit to tell you"

"Dam he got to be talking about this shit with Ny and Rocko" Jasean picks up his phone to call him. (Phone rings).

"Jay, damn, I been hitting you up for the last hour. What's good, my man?" Caine yells loudly in the phone.

"I was chopping it up with J.J. what's good" Jasean asks.

"What he talking about? I'm about to touch his bitch-ass cousin, for real, yo. He crossed me in the worse way" Caine tells Jasean.

"Man y'all need to stop this bullshit man. The family can't be beefing over any bullshit" Jasean pleads with him.

"Look! Tell your snake ass cousin in law that was bullshit. I didn't do nothing but look out for that pussy" Caine growls.

"I know that man but y'all all had a part in it. I'm not about to let y'all put division in the fam for real Caine" Jasean growls back.

"Man I know you not switching teams on me I'm your family. I don't give a fuck if you and Endy married or not that man needs to be dealt with end of story" Caine says

with all seriousness and Jasean know it.

 "Look man meet me at the club tonight you know I got

you man but we have to figure this shit out I don't need

you doing no stupid shit for real" Jasean pleads with him.

"Jay I will meet you at the club but I'm telling you that's

not gonna change shit. I'm putting hands on that

motherfucker on sight Jay" He says hanging up the

phone.

"CAINE!" Jasean yells in the phone but he already hung

up. He flops down on sofa with his face in his hands

shaking his head. "This dude done lost it I have to get to

him before his ass see Rocko" Jasean mumbles.

◆◆◆NewSouth™◆◆◆

Endy have texted Rocko to meet her at E Class so she can talk to him about this whole ordeal because she has a bad feeling shit about to get out of hand.

"How is my beautiful cousin doing?" Karishma asks laying out the newest fall fashions they have of jeggings and sweater crop tops both with E Class signatures.

"She's good she with Mommy and Aunt Lisa. When Rocko get here I'm going to my office to speak with him so make sure if you need me let me know" Endy informs her.

"I'm good cuz! I got this handle your business" Karishma says all sassy.

"Girl you're a mess" Endy laughs. The store door bell chimes and in walks Rocko. "What's going on cuz?" Rocko speaks. "What's going my tall brown sugar?" Karishma teases Rocko.

"What's going on beautiful?" he gives her a tight hug and kiss on the cheek. Now Karishma is the baby of the family. She's a beautiful pecan tan with green eyes and curly black hair. She has a mixture of black and Panamanian so all her cousins just loved her to death and was very overprotective of her. Rocko walks and give Endy a hug as well and by the way she hugs him back he knows she upset about him and Niema.

"Well we about to go to my office if you need me holla" Endy says heading to the back of the store.

She sits at her desk and before she can speak her phone rings she look and see its Niema. Any other time she would answer but because everything that's going on she know she's gonna have to call her back.

"Roc what's good with you bruh?" Endy says giving him a very disappointed look. "Look Endy I know you talk to Ny but please let me explain?" He says throwing his hands up like you would for the cops.

"I don't know how you gonna explain this bullshit. What the hell were y'all thinking Rocko? Like did y'all even think about the rest of us that will now be in the middle of this bullshit? This is so fucking unfair to everyone involved" Endy shakes her head.

"Look Endy I know it's a fucked up situation but I love Ny and I want to be with her. She's always had my heart you know this" he's filled with emotion.

"Rocko how the hell y'all think this is gonna fly with the family especially Nana? You know she is gonna flip on y'all asses Mommy and them too. Like what the hell were y'all thinking? DAMNIT" Endy yells jumping up pacing back and forth.

"Endy all I can say is I love her man. I'm in love with her she could be Ms. Hinton for real like that's how serious I am about this shit" He says. Endy stops in her tracks and look in his eyes. She knew then that he was serious and this shit is worse than she thought.

"Rocko you are for real! I can see it in your eyes and hear it in your voice. Damn it why y'all have to do this to me. You know I'm a sucker for love" Endy calms down.

"Well what about Taiya? You know Ny told me she's pregnant right."

"That's what I need to figure out you know I'm going to look out for my babies but I'm going to need them to be with me. I can't trust that bitch with my kids' man" Rocko says sounding stress.

"Well you mind as well know everything Roc because your troubles are only just beginning" Endy holds her head overwhelmed.

"What E spit it out?" "Roc you may need to talk to Ny and I mean now" she tells him. "No come on E spit it out I won't say nothing come on you're my family" he begs.

"Whew Lord why y'all doing this to me but you do have a right to know" Endy fights with herself.

"Right to know what" Rocko is getting nervous.

"Fuck it! Niema is pregnant too Rocko and she's scared to tell you because she is thinking about getting rid of it since Taiya's pregnant" Endy finally spits it out. Rocko is stunned.

"Endy are you serious? That must have been what she texted me about. I'm happy as hell nah I'm about to go talk to her she's having that baby fuck that" He rush Endy with a bear hug.

"Damn so you're not upset?" Endy asks.

"HELL NO! Did you just hear what I said I want Niema I'm so in love with her Endy for real" he express to Endy.

"Well you better go talk to her because she is a nervous wreck. She was going home to rest she haven't been sleeping well. However in the meantime y'all better find a way to tell the family about this bullshit because this is about to be some shit. I'm still upset with y'all but the baby has nothing to do with y'all poor decision making" Endy says mushing his head.

"I know this situation is messy but I will fix it babe we don't need the families clashing" he said hugging Endy again.

◆◆◆NewSouth™◆◆◆

As Beyoncé's" *Dance For You"* plays through Niema's laptop speaker as she lay on her sofa in a cashmere pink robe crying her eyes out. Her phone rings and she see it's Rocko and push ignore. Then a knock comes to the door. The knock startles Niema but she pause the music and race to see who it is. When she peeps out the window she sees its Rocko at the door.

"Ny open the door I know you're here we need to talk"

he yells through the door.

"Rocko just go away we done made a big enough mess"

she begs him.

"Baby please let me in we got to talk" he pleads with her.

She finally opens the door and he sees she's been crying.

"Baby girl come here" he grabs her and plants a strong

passionate kiss on her lips.

 "Rocko what are you doing" she looks at him strangely.

 "Endy told me baby and I'm happy as hell" he tells her.

She turns to walk in the house and he follows her.

"Ny I got you and the baby you know that. I love you so

much I got y'all I promise you that" Rocko says grabbing

her hand to sit beside him.

"Rocko did you forget Taiya is pregnant too how you gonna do that. I'm gonna have to get an abortion" she cries.

"I be damn if your killing my baby Ny we gonna be alright please don't do this. I got my kids you know that" Rocko begs.

"Roc I don't want to have a baby by someone I'm not with" Niema says.

"Well you don't have to because I'm about to finally just do what I should of done before" He states standing up.

"What do you mean Rocko?"

"I'm leaving her she can have the condo I will cop me a crib uptown so I can be closer to my job. "Rocko I don't know about this baby" Niema's unsure of the whole situation.

"Ma I got this we gonna be good. Shit you just don't know how happy I am right now. I wanted to be with you since we first made love Christmas last year Ny. I love you so much and I promise I got you" he leans in and kiss her again this time longer.

"Can you stay with me tonight?" she asks him.

 "Here?" he's shocked. "Yes here crazy everybody knows now it's nothing to hide. Well everybody but Taiya" Niema says.

 "Forget that let me enjoy knowing your carrying my seed" he says.

He then pulls her up and opens her robe exposing her naked body. "Damn you're so beautiful" he says bending down to kiss her stomach. He's too excited to have his dream woman pregnant by him.

"I want to make love to you without rushing it. I want

you to know just how much I love you" he says grabbing

her by the waist and starts to kiss her soft lips again.

"Ooh" she moans. After that he knew she was ready. So

he picks her up and she wraps her legs around his waist.

He gently lays her on the floor and before he knew it she

grabs his tool and took all of him in her mouth which

made him yell out unexpectedly

"Whoa Damn Ny" He stutters.

 "You like that baby lay back and let me do what I do"

she says pushing him back on the carpet and continued to

pleasure her man like never before.

"Damn, Ny! Shit, you must of missed me like I…I…ahhh

shit…Damn, Ny. You got a motherfucker speechless" he

moans. After sucking him off for another few minutes,

right before he cums, she gets up and put his wet, stiff

dick and place it in her soak and wet kitty.

"Ahhh!!!" she yells. The connection was deeper than ever before and they both felt it. Niema bounces up and down on him and Rocko can feel her kitty getting wetter. It wasn't long before Niema can feel Rocko's dick hitting her spot which made her kitty get tighter and wetter. Rocko was in heaven because sex with Niema was a whole other level then he's had in his lifetime.

"Damn girl this shit feel so good."

"It feel good baby" she responds back. He then grabs her waist so he can go deeper inside her walls and when he does they both feel themselves about cum. She then slows down and grinds slowly back and forth until they both couldn't take it no more.

"Ugh baby I'm about to cum...I'm about to cum...Shit!" Niema squeals out loud.

"Me too baby…damn Ny…I love you so fucking much…ugh…ugh…damn I'm cumming" Rocko groans letting off all inside Niema.

"Ahhh…yeah…yeah…yeah" and she came right along with him.

They both collapsed and how they laid is how they slept. Not worrying about what the future holds because at the end of the day it is what it is and they will have to deal with it.

Chapter 10

Taiya wakes up another morning to Rocko not coming home all night which wasn't anything new. She didn't care because she was doing her own thing. She's been contemplating leaving and just putting him on child support, but she knew if she did that she wouldn't be able to live the lavish lifestyle she was use to. Although she always cheated on Rocko and he took her back, she's just not use to him totally ignoring her. To not even call to check on her made her suspicious especially with him knowing that she's pregnant. (Ring…ring) Taiya cell phone rings scaring her.

"Hello" "Girl I'm so done with fucking Caine. This bastard is locked up" Keosha shouts in the phone.

"What? What happened, Keosha?" Taiya asks confused.

"This motherfucker had a gun in the Mercedes girl stupid as hell. Not to mention his ass was drunk and then I'm hearing he's trying to fight Rocko over Ny. Tai I'm so sick of this shit man. If he wants her then he can go the fuck on and leave me alone!" Keosha starts crying.

"Calm down Keosha! Where is Cadence?" Taiya asked.

She's with Ms. Marilyn so I can go get him out. I should leave his stupid ass in there." Keosha is hurt and Taiya could tell.

"That bitch again I don't know what dudes see in her I'm sick of her ass" Taiya groans.

"I can't keep blaming her Caine knows better I just feel like he is still not over her. Ugh well I am going to have to decide what I'm going to do because I'm not gonna keep battling this bitch over him" Keosha complained.

"Well girl Rocko hasn't been home all night and I know something is up. You know how he is on my ass usually and now he hardly even talks to me. I'm not stupid he has a bitch somewhere" Taiya get pissed all over.

"Well girl let me go get this ass hole. I'll hit you up later" Keosha tells said to her before hanging up.

"Okay boo go do that just hit me up later" Taiya responded and hung up the phone.

It's ten in the morning and Rocko still isn't home.

"Mommy, can I have some waafulls" Rachelle said, standing by the kitchen, holding a baby doll.

"Yes baby come on let's go eat some breakfast" Taiya picked up her baby girl who is the spitting image of Rocko same almond skin color and curly hair.

"Where's daddy?" Rachelle rubs the sleep out her beautiful brown eyes.

"I don't know where daddy at but he better be home soon" Taiya kissed Rachelle's rosy little cheeks and sat her to the table in the kitchen.

As Taiya watch her baby girl eat her eyes water because she doesn't understand why Rocko is acting so distant. She knows she has her faults in their relationship but doesn't want to lose him.

"DA…DEE!" Rachelle screams excited as Rocko walked in the kitchen. Taiya was so engulfed with her thoughts she didn't even hear him enter the house.

"Hi baby girl daddy missed you" Rocko picked her up and kissed Rachelle on the nose.

"I missed you daddy where was you at?" Rachelle asked still holding her baby doll.

"Daddy was out making money for you so I can buy you that tablet you asked for" he told her.

"Yay Mommy daddy getting me a tabbit" Rachelle squeals in her kiddie voice.

"I heard him, ma ma. Why don't you go to your room and turn on your TV shows?" Taiya told her, so she could talk to Rocko.

"Okay mommy" Rocko puts her down so she can go in her room. He knows he's in for it but he doesn't care because he had something he wanted to say himself. When Rachelle is clear out of sight Taiya immediately goes in.

"So Rodney what's the deal with you? What's going on with us because I don't want to be surprised so give it to me straight" She said with her arms folded across her chest that was heaving in and out. He saw she was upset and understood but with all the cheating she's done on him he felt justified in what he's done.

"First of all you're right it is something going on and it's time we get it out in the open no since to hide it no more" he starts off.

Before he can finish Taiya spits out "I know you're not gonna tell me this about another bitch because if so you and that bitch going down. I'ma fuck both of y'all up I promise you that" She shouts.

"Taiya, calm down and don't start acting like you care for me now. I already know you were running around with them dudes in Harlem with Keosha, so stop it" He spat back at her.

"Are you fucking kidding me? You're going to try to do this shit now after I'm pregnant" her voice started to quiver.

"Look don't pull that crying shit you been fucking over me a long time and despite motherfuckers telling me to leave you alone I stuck it out for my daughter. To keep it 100 with you I'm in love with someone else. I just think our time together has expired a long time ago" he explained best he could.

"Look dude you won't leave me stuck with two babies while you go carry on with some random ass bitch I tell you that. I built this family and held you down. All the money I made on the pole went to your ass so don't think you just gon'' leave me high and fucking dry. I will put your ass on child support" she yelled.

"Do what you got to do Taiya I'm not about to argue with your stupid ass. I will be there for my babies but me and you are done" he groans walking away.

"Fuck you Rocko get your shit and get the fuck out!" She yelled again this time throwing a big serving spoon that just missed his head.

"Are you crazy? Fuck this! I'm leaving." He grabs his jacket and head out the door, but Taiya is not giving up without a fight.

"Ahhggg" she leaps at him swinging.

He grabs her arms to restrain her by pinning her on the sofa as he does this he hears "Daddy no don't hurt mommy daddy" Rachelle yelled.

Rocko looks at his little girl crying but can't release Taiya because she's still hysterical crying, swinging and kicking him.

"TAIYA CHILL THE FUCK OUT DAMN YOU SEE RAE CRYING!" He screams in her face.

She looks in his eyes and spits dead in his face. Before he could react, Keosha rushed in the wide open door to the tussling duo.

"Y'all stop it, Tai…Rocko… y'all stop it! Rachelle is crying." Keosha screamed and Rocko jumped up, grabbed his jacket, picked up Rachelle and ran out the house.

"Don't let him take my baby Keosha! Don't let him take my baby he's trying to leave us for some bitch!" Taiya cries still hysterical.

"Taiya, you got to calm down, please" Keosha kneels down on the floor to hug her friend.

"You're gonna be alright, Tai. Baby, please calm down" Keosha pleads with her.

After a few minutes, she had calmed down. She jumps up and shouts "fuck it I got him. I got that motherfucker he will pay for me and these kids I promise he will."

A bewildered Keosha jumps on the phone to call Lynasia. "Yo some shit isn't right about all this! Taiya and Rocko just got into a big fight and he took Rachelle. She said he just told her he's leaving her for another chic" Keosha said on the phone.

"What oh my God I knew this shit was going to happen. Look I am on my way it's something she should know but I have to tell her face to face Ki Ki" Lynasia explained

"What is it? Tell me what's going on?" Keosha begged but Lynasia didn't budge.

"Okay well please hurry up because this bitch has gon''' crazy" Keosha said before hanging up.

"I can't belee this bitch tried to come for me" J. J. spat, pacing back and forth.

"Why would Caine try to come for you behind Rocko's bullshit" Chynna asked her cousin who is pissed.

"Rocko was supposed to meet us there. Me and Jasean was planning a sit down with them behind this Ny shit" J.J. replied

"Babe I be back I got go to the drug store. You need anything?" Lynasia asked J.J. She was ready to go because the fake and phony she didn't feel like dealing with.

"Nah I'm good Bae I'll be here" J.J. kissed her on the cheek.

"See y'all later" Lynasia said to Chynna and Reeko.

"Alright check y'all later "Reeko said although Chynna just stand there giving her a dirty look. Reeko just shake his head at his girl.

After they knew she was out of sight, they grill J.J. for more information. "So are you telling me that Rocko and Ny really are messing around?" Chynna asked with the most furious look in her eyes.

"Messing around hell Niema is pregnant and Taiya is pregnant too" J.J. blurts out.

"What the hell?" Reeko said stunned.

"PREGNANT! This bitch is pregnant by Rocko. Oh my goodness this shit can't be real" Chynna jumps up. The door opens and it's Rocko with Rachelle in his arms.

"I'm so glad you are here. Negro somebody better tell me what the hell is going on and I mean quick" Chynna groans at him.

"Yo, I just got into it with Taiya her ass acting crazy. I had to get my baby out of there" Rocko snaps sitting Rachelle down.

"I would be acting crazy too if I knew you had another chic pregnant especially someone so close to the family" Chynna snaps back.

"Hey shit happens! Me and Ny love each other and I don't give a damn what nobody got to say" Rocko told them.

"Roc you told me you were gonna meet me at the club and you never showed then Caine tried to come for me and threaten me with burners and shit" J.J. roared walking in Rocko face.

"Man I didn't know that shit was gonna go down. I went to see Ny and she told me some shit" Rocko explained unaware of what was going on.

"We know what she was telling you that her trifling ass was fucking pregnant and it must have gotten to Caine because now he is tripping" Reeko informed him.

"So what, this man came at you because of me? Yo man I got this that punk motherfucker not nobody but a womanizer" Rocko said frustrated with everything that's going on.

"Look somebody got to act like they got some sense this shit has gotten way out of hand. For all we know Niema probably told that man so she can throw it in his face" Chynna adds.

"Ny isn't on that bullshit I'm telling you we good she loves me and I love her. Motherfuckers just gonna have to accept it. She didn't even want to have the baby I told her to have it. Taiya know she can't spit shit to me all the dudes she done ran through while she was with me" Rocko said.

"Are you fucking kidding me Roc? Stupid ass don't you see you're a rebound? She wants Caine; she's using you because she's hurt Rocko. Use your fucking brain my dude" Chynna pleads with her cousin.

"Yo Chynna we blood and all but I ain't trying to hear shit you're talking about because I know Ny love me. We gonna be together and have our baby" Rocko says confident.

"I don't know what the fuck you were thinking but y'all better come up with a solution because this shit is gonna get uglier before it gets pretty" Chynna grab her purse, kissed Rachelle and head out the door.

"Y'all know how y'all cousin is she just loves her family and want peace that's all" Reeko said dapping J.J and Rocko and also giving Rachelle a kiss.

"We will get up man I'm just gonna chill here for a minute" Rocko tells Reeko.

"Alright Holla" J.J. said closing the door behind him.

Once he left J.J. sat in the recliner looked at his and cousin and said "We got to get to the bottom of this shit or it's about to get real. The sat in silence the next few minutes

"I'ma get us a drink so I can tell you what happen last night" J.J. gets up.

"Aight I'm gonna put Rachelle in the room while she taking a nap." Rocko responds taking Rachelle to lil J.J. room.

J.J. pours both of them a glass of Henny and shakes his head "What the hell he done got us into." he mumbled.

"Hello is anybody home?" Lynasia shouts as she enters Taiya house.

"Girl, I'm so glad you are here to talk to this bitch. She's going crazy," Keosha shouts. "What is she doing?" Lynasia asked.

She sees the house trashed and Keosha with a worried look on her face. Next thing they know Taiya comes walking in the living room waving a gun in her hand.

"Taiya what the hell are you doing?" Lynasia yelled frantically.

"That's right I'm gonna kill this motherfucker!" Taiya yelled back waving the gun in the air.

"Tai please chill out I don't want you doing nothing you will regret!" Lynasia shouts.

FUCK THAT SHIT NAY THIS JERK THINK HE'S GONNA JUST LEAVE ME WITH TWO KIDS AND MOVE ON WITH SOME TRICK? HELL NO!" Taiya screamed still waving the gun.

"This shit so not worth it Taiya like fuck him don't give up your freedom and your children because of him. I know your upset but I'm not going to let you destroy yourself behind this boo." Lynasia scream back at her.

Taiya is shocked by Lynasia's firmness but she knows at the end of the day she's right.

"Nay I know I messed up in the past but Rocko knows I love him I just was too stupid to see he was a good dude. I wanted the hood bullshit but the luxury lifestyle he provided me. I wanted my cake and eat it too but I'm sorry I get it now" Taiya burst out in tears dropping the gun to the floor.

The girls hurried to her side to comfort her. Keosha is so hurt to see her friend in such a vulnerable state. It made her look at her life and all she has gone through to be with Caine.

"Taiya, I know this shit hurts like hell right now, but you got to pull yourself together," Keosha says, pulling Taiya's hair back that's all over her head.

"I'm still surprised he's doing this now after he knows I'm pregnant again" Taiya sobs louder.

The girls cuddle her to calm her down. "We are here for you Taiya and that baby is gonna get so much love. I just need you to calm down and take it one day at a time. Rocko probably was talking out of anger" Keosha told her.

"But he's the one who stayed out all night I supposed to check his ass on that" Taiya tells them.

"Stayed out all night doing what?" Lynasia questioned.

"That's what I wanted to know but now I know it's another bitch involved I want to know who it is" Taiya groans.

"Knowing who she is will not solve anything Tai if he wants to leave it's nothing you can do. We can't keep holding on to these men who don't want to be held down" Keosha said.

"Don't compare my relationship to your bullshit you have with Caine. Your shit was built on lies from the beginning. Rocko ain't ever done the shit to me like Caine has done to you" Taiya yelled.

"Bitch please don't come for me. No he didn't but you sure fucked off on him plenty of times" Keosha shoots back.

"Stop this bullshit; y'all are saying shit y'all don't mean!" Lynasia screams at them.

"No she wants to try to call me out let's get it all out because I been biting my tongue long enough" Keosha jumped up.

"Let it out then. What the hell are you are biting your tongue about? It's nothing you can say to make me feel bad at all. My life with Rocko is nowhere near as messed up as yours with Caine. He is still out here chasing after his ex like what the hell is it gonna take for you to see the fact that you were his second choice if Niema wouldn't have left him alone" Taiya barks back.

"Keosha, no don't go there" Lynasia begs, as she sees the look of defeat creep up on Keosha's face.

"Bitch let me give you some facts your man and my man got into it because of the same bitch when Endy had the baby. And from what I hear he's still fucking Ny so you wanted to talk facts here you go. The only reason I didn't say anything, is because I didn't want to hurt your feelings," Keosha yelled.

"Are you fucking serious? He's fucking Ny and y'all bitches didn't tell me?" Taiya screams at them both.

"Taiya I was coming over to talk to you about all this bullshit I just found out. Caine and J.J. got into last night at the club because of the fight" Lynasia explains.

"Oh my God he's been sleeping with this chic since Endy had the baby and y'all just now telling me. Get the hell out of my house! GET THE HELL OUT BOTH OF Y'ALL!" she screams enraged.

"Gladly, bitch! You always try to call somebody out on their shit, but the tables always turn" Keosha grabs her coat.

"Bitch fuck you just take your ass on out my crib before it be a situation" Taiya warn her this time walking towards her.

"Y'all chill we all need to be pulling together during this time not pulling apart" Lynasia jumps in between them. Keosha walked out the door, slamming it behind her.

"I know she didn't just slam my door" Taiya growls pacing the floor pissed to the max. She don't know who she's mad at the most but one thing she does know is that Niema is gonna have to see her real soon.

"You know I'm gonna find that bitch I promise you she will be seeing me real soon" Taiya sat shaking her left leg up and down.

"Lord I can see this whole shit going the wrong way" Lynasia mumbled.

◆◆◆NewSouth™◆◆◆

"This shit is becoming a fucking nightmare man. We have to make this shit right my family and your family can't be beefing with each other" Endy said to Jasean.

"I know this E but what the hell can I do? These are grown ass men!" Jasean responds

. "Endy the only people who can fix this whole bullshit is Niema and Rocko. They brought all this drama between everybody whether you want to face it or not. Ny knew better than this bullshit right here man" Chynna adds.

"Look I understand their wrong really I do but Caine getting physical with everybody isn't helping shit.

302

J.J. had nothing to do with the decisions Rocko's made"
Endy snaps back.

"What do we do now because somebody better talk to Caine? He is nowhere near letting this shit go right now. They were together too long he loved Ny despite everything Endy" Chynna stated.

"Well we know we can't let this shit continue on like this because somebody is gonna do something they are gonna regret. We all supposed to be like family at the end of the day" Reeko says.

They all hear the front door open and in walk Ari and Tylon. "What's good everybody we're finally here" Tylon announce as he and Ari carry in some bags.

Damn y'all act like y'all seen a ghost what's the deal!" Ari said as she notices everyone just sitting quieter than usual.

"Girl it's a bunch of shit we got to catch you up on" Chynna told her.

"Well let me get a drink because this sounds like some real drama type of bullshit" Ari says going to Endy's kitchen.

"Yes let me get one too" Chynna gots up to follow her. After everyone gets situated back in the living room, someone knocks on the door.

"Lawd, I'm not gonna ever find out what's going on. I know it has something to do with this Niema and Rocko shit" Ari blurts out.

"Girl that's not even half of the story girl… it's so much more" Chynna comments.

Endy opens up the door and who's standing there? "Ny you must of knew we was about to talk some shit about you" Ari exclaims.

"Bitch fuck you I came here to see Endy not none of y'all asses" Niema said as she put her right hand on her hip while holding her keys and purse in her left. She gives Ari a *don't fuck with me* look.

"Bitch Fuck you! Who the hell you think you talking to? You're the one around here being a li'l trick and you have the nerve to say fuck me" Ari shot.

"Girl I'm not up for none of y'all shit today I need to talk to Endy so if you mind I will get at you later. Know your facts before you come for me trick" Niema shot back.

"Bitch I will slap you tasteless" Ari jumped up walking towards Niema.

"I wish you would put hands on me" Niema shouts as she saw Ari charging towards her. Reeko quickly grabs Ari and Endy drags Niema towards the bedroom.

"Y'all better chill out in my crib my daughter in the back" Jasean scream at both of them.

"Besides Ny you need to chill your pregnant it's not good for the baby" Endy told her before thinking about it. The room falls silent as everyone has a '*did I just hear that right' look* on their face.

"You trick! And you had the nerve to get pregnant" Ari groans. Endy knows she messed up now just by how pitiful Niema look at her.

"Look yes I'm pregnant and it's by Rocko's I'm sorry if I caused a bunch of bull shit. I didn't want any of this shit to happen" Niema pleaded with the group.

"Bitch is you fucking serious? You got dudes that were like brothers ready to pop each other over your trick ass. Then you have the nerve to say you didn't want this shit to happen" Jasean bucks at Niema.

"Jay chill out don't call her out her name she's going through enough damn it" Endy shouts.

"Dead ass this some bullshit we got to diffuse this situation ASAP because it's not gonna just go away" Chynna intervenes.

"You had the nerve to be talking shit about Keosha and her crew…and you were just like them" Ari said with her arms folded, shaking her head.

"BITCH FUCK YOU!" Niema yells trying to go towards Ari but Endy warns her she's in her house.

"Let her go I will drag her li'l ass in here! " Ari told Endy.

"Y'all stop it, you're not going to jail for fighting this girl while she is pregnant" Tylon's warns his wife.

"I'm so sick of everybody trying to check me on some shit when nobody is perfect" Niema says.

Chynna phone starts ringing "Lord what mommy want? Hello!" She shouts in the phone.

"WHAT? I'm gonna kill that bitch! Ughhhh!"Chynna shouts again hanging up the phone.

"What happen, Chy?" Endy asks kind of scared of the answer.

"That bitch fucking shot my cousin" Chynna screams which leaves everyone else confused. Endy doesn't know what cousin but she jumps on the phone to call her mother but before she can finish dialing Chynna scream out "Taiya shot Rocko and he's on the way to the hospital. Reeko come on now" She grabs her purse and run out the door. Everyone has officially started to panic and Endy's still in shock about the whole thing.

"Oh my God please no this cannot be happening" Niema's started crying and although Endy tries to comfort and calm her down, Jasean is in pure disgust about the whole situation.

"Look Ny we have to calm down and make sure he's okay first before we panic" Endy told her.

"E, come let's go we need to see what's going on" Jasean interrupted her with Patience already in the car seat. Endy grabs Niema to get up "You just ride with us" Endy advised her. Jasean is not pleased but he goes along with it to avoid an argument. They are settled in the car and Endy forgot her phone.

"Oh shit let me grab my phone" She jumped out the car and ran back in the house.

"Look we need to talk because I don't need Endy to get hurt because of some bullshit" Jasean groans. Niema just shakes her head yes and Endy jumps back in the car. Niema's only thought is if Rocko going to be okay.

Chapter 11

Everyone has arrived at Jamaica Hospital where Rocko is in ICU and the family is in the waiting area to hear about his condition. Everything has become a mess but everyone manage to pull together during this tragic time. Well, almost everyone besides Lynasia, Keosha and Caine. Caine's not answering anyone calls and Keosha's at 113th precinct on Baisley Blvd in Queens trying to post Taiya's bail but no one knows

"What is taking them so long to let us know something" Luella cries.

She is totally upset by the whole ordeal. Niema too has been rushed to the ER for passing out twice. Her Aunt Sally and Cousin YaYa are there with her. Emotions are raging at this point and all Endy knows is that she has to stay strong through this terrible storm.

"Nana I'm telling you that bitch gonna die y'all better not ever let me see this bitch. She shot him in his back, shoulder, and arm" Endy's all worked up.

"Endy you got to chill out we got stay strong for nana and them. The nurse said he is in surgery but he should be okay. Have faith cousin" Chynna tells her.

"Look at Nana Endy! All this bullshit happened because of your fucking friend and our stupid ass cousin selfishness" Chynna snaps.

"Chynna, let's take a walk," her dad, Marlo, tells her.

"Daddy I don't feel like walking I want to beat the shit out of Taiya and Niema right now. If we aren't walking to see them then leave me alone" Chynna shouts at her dad.

"Chy what the hell is wrong with you? We are supposed to be pulling together right now and you pulling this bullshit. It's a time and a place for everything" Lisa now shouting at her.

"Well everybody needs to know that all this shit is behind Rocko and Niema ass sneaking around. Taiya found out and shot Rodney. Now we at the hospital because of Endy's hoe ass friend" Chynna yells again crying.

"Chynna stop it don't do that it's wrong but you should never try to take somebody life behind cheating hell she could of took her ass on and left his ass alone" Tanya growls at Chynna.

"I'm sorry y'all I'm just pissed the hell off how can she think it's okay to sleep with Rocko and get pregnant and there was not gonna be any repercussions behind it" Chynna said and bust out crying which made the rest of the family start sobbing too.

Endy's now stuck in the middle of being there for her cousin and being there for her best friend. He cousin got shot three times all behind bad decisions.

"So Ny really thought it was okay to sleep with Rodney knowing that it would cause problems with the family? I can't believe y'all withheld this type of information from the family" Luella said shaking her head in disgust.

"I know Nana, I know it's not right what she did but she's carrying your great grandchild right now either way. So the best thing for us to do is figure this out as a fucking family" Endy snaps.

"I'm sorry that Niema has caused this entire ruckus with y'all" a voice says and when they look its Aunt Sally.

"Awe Sally Niema didn't make this mess by herself Rocko knew better too. They were selfishly thinking and not considering how everyone else was gonna feel. Our main concern is to make sure both of them are alright and the baby arrives here healthy and safe" Tanya walks over

and grabs Aunt Sally's hand.

"Thanks you all! I love y'all like family and I would hate

for a stupid decision these kids made tear us apart" tears

stream Aunt Sally face as she spoke.

"Never that Sally, you have nothing to do with what

Niema and Rocko has done. They are adults at the end of

the day" Lisa adds.

 "I thank y'all. I thank y'all all because if I lose my only

support system in New York I don't know what I would

do. I tried my best to keep her on the right path. Caine

ruined my baby. He knocked her down until she just

made a mess of her life" Aunt Sally sobs.

"It's okay Auntie, we are all in this together so don't beat

yourself up about it okay" Endy said and gave her a tight

hug.

"Endy your right, how is Niema doing Aunt Sally?" Chynna asks now feeling bad for her behavior with her.

"She's doing okay she is really worried about Rocko but the baby is doing just fine. She didn't even tell me and we never keep secrets" She replied.

 "Well all we can do is continue praying and ask God for order in this situation because this is a big mess to clean up. Rocko and Niema have a whole lot of repenting to do in this situation. I don't see it getting any better no time soon" Luella painfully stated.

"I just want everyone to calm down and come together right now please until we know what's going on with Rodney. We have plenty of time to place blame, but the main concern is Rocko, Niema, Taiya, and the babies" Endy explains.

"What you mean babies?" Aunt Sally asked confused which let everyone know that she didn't know Taiya was also pregnant.

"Yeah Aunt Sally, Taiya is pregnant also so that's why we said this mess is going to get worse before it gets better" Endy explained.

"Oh my goodness does Ny know this?" Aunt Sally wails.

"Yeah she knows and was just waiting for the right time to tell everyone. It was already bad enough that she was sleeping with Rocko, but to be pregnant and his baby mother pregnant too was a bit overwhelming I guess" Endy said.

"I can't imagine what is going through Niema's head right now this has got to be the worse feeling in the world" Tanya sympathized.

"Well we gonna sit here and continue praying for our family's strength because we are gonna need it" Luella adds. They all joined hands and prayed.

◆◆◆NewSouth™◆◆◆

"Ny you got to eat something! At least drink some water" YaYa tells her cousin.

"I just want to see Rocko or at least know how he's doing!" Niema weeps.

"I know babe but they are not going to release you until you get your blood pressure under control" YaYa counters back. Niema is so upset at this point and they want her to stay calm for the sake of the baby.

"Okay but tell Endy or Aunt Sally to come here so I can at least know if he's stable or not. I'm going crazy just sitting here not knowing what is going on" Niema cries. The door opens and it's Caine walking in with flowers.

317

"What the hell do you want CJ don't come stressing me out" Niema shouts.

"Ny Please calm down! You have to for the baby" YaYa begs her.

"So you are really fucking pregnant by this dude Ny? You mean to tell me you stooped that low to get back at me. That's some real ho shit Ny" Caine spat.

"CAINE FUCK YOU WITH YOUR BITCH ASS! I know you're not talking about stooping low when you have been fucking that stripper bitch on me for two to years. Then to add insult to injury, you got the bitch pregnant, had a baby and you say I stooped low Caine" Niema screams.

"Caine please just leave she don't need this shit right now like damn haven't you done enough" YaYa intercedes.

"Look bitch you shut your ho ass up" He snaps.

"HO ASS! Are your fucking kidding me? Bitch you better step before you get dealt with" YaYa says stepping to Caine.

However before anything physical transpire the security and nurses enter the room. "Sir you're going to have to leave" the little Hispanic nurse says.

"Fuck this shit bitch I hope you and that baby die" Caine yelled before swinging open the room door and leaving out.

"That bitch ass dude had the nerve to come here talking noise Ny. Are you fucking serious this motherfucker needs to be dealt with immediately" YaYa shouts still very upset.

"Yo chill that dude don't want no smoke because if he do we will give it to him. He's right what the hell was I thinking" Niema started crying. "Mam we need you to calm down," the nurse says.

The door opens and Endy enters the room. She walks in startled by the commotion that goings on. Two nurses are trying to restrain Niema and a security guard has YaYa by the arm.

"Ny what's going on baby? YaYa what happen to her?" Endy asks grabbing Niema trying to calm her down.

"That bitch ass cousin in law of yours came in here talking noise" YaYa shouts.

"Who Caine? What the hell was he doing here?" Endy's upset now.

"I'm tired E why don't everyone just leave me alone. I know I fucked, I know, I know and God is making me pay big time but all I want is for my baby to make it here healthy" Niema cried as Endy have her cradled in her arms. YaYa gives them a look and says

"Ny I told you let's just go to N.O. and leave this bullshit here" YaYa blurts out.

"No she's not fucking leaving and taking my cousin to New Orleans you must be tripping. Ny I know shit not looking too good right now but you got this" Endy rolls her eyes at YaYa.

"Girl bye it's her decision if she knows what's best for her she would get her shit and leave all y'all bipolar ass motherfuckers alone" YaYa bucks back.

"Bitch who the fuck you calling bipolar your five minutes in the circle ass. You don't know shit about us ho so you better mind your mouth" Endy now stands up.

"Y'ALL PLEASE DON'T START THIS BULLSHIT NOW!" Niema yells as she sees the argument getting heated.

"No tell this bitch don't start I'm just saying these motherfuckers act real funny style" YaYa observes.

"Bitch you don't even know me like that so you need to fall all the way back!" Endy yelled back.

"Endy please sit down you don't want it" YaYa advise her.

"Don't want what bitch? You better take your country ass down south with that bullshit. Like bitch really, jump because you barking like you have mad issues with me so let's get to it bitch" Endy groans taking off her heels.

In the heat of the moment Aunt Sally, Tanya, and Lisa enters the room just in time to diffuse the situation.

"Yo, yo, yo... what the hell are y'all doing?" Aunt Sally shouts grabbing YaYa arm.

"Endy stop this now! You know better than this bullshit in this hospital" her mother grabs her.

"Mommy talk to this bitch she came for me talking shit calling us bipolar and shit, who the fuck she think she is?" Endy spat.

"Who the fuck are you bitch? A backstabbing ass friend with a man who you think is better than everybody else. That dude is no better than Caine" YaYa yells as Aunt Sally pulls her out the door.

"Fuck you bitch why you worried about my man? We happy bitch so don't worry about what we have going on" Endy yells infuriated.

"Endy stop it come on we have enough going on with the family right now" her aunt Lisa told her. Niema is crying her heart out so regretful of her actions right now.

"Endy look at your friend we have to find a resolution to this mess" Tanya informed her as they both watch Niema sobbing.

"I just want this all to be over auntie. I didn't want anybody to get hurt. Look at this mess I caused Lord I just want it to stop. I just want everything to be over" Niema continued to cry harder.

"Ny I'm sorry babe but your cousin took it there. I'm going to take a walk because I hate to be the cause of you going into pre –term labor" Endy said giving Niema a kiss on the cheek.

"I understand bestest just come back and check on me please" Niema throws her shivering arm around Endy.

"Please calm down Ma I need my god baby to be safe and healthy" Endy says a little worried.

"I am but please let me know how Rocko doing" Niema cries.

"We will baby girl just stay calm and let God take care of the rest" Tanya affirms giving her a kiss on the forehead.

"I love you Ny I will be back soon but promise me you will calm down " Endy tells her.

"I will I promise just please let me know that he's okay" she begs.

"I will" Endy eyes tear up. They head out the room and they see YaYa and Aunt Sally sitting in the waiting area having a heated argument.

"See you Aunt Sally we are to head back downstairs to check on Rocko" Endy says putting on a fake smile.

"Okay baby we're praying he's okay" Aunt Sally replied. Endy and her mom head to the elevators just in time. "Girl your ass is plain out trouble" Tanya chuckles as the elevator doors close.

♦♦♦NewSouth™♦♦♦

"I'm still shocked that you shot your baby daddy," Keosha says to Taiya as they leave the precinct and walk to Lynasia pearly white Cadillac truck in the front with her in the driver seat waiting for them to come out.

"I didn't mean to, it just happened, he said shit I didn't want to hear at that point and I just snapped Keosha" Taiya said still shook up from the mess that happened the day before.

"Well you know them Hinton's are ready to rock your ass right about now" Lynasia warned her.

"Fuck all them motherfuckers especially them punk ass cousins of his. Let them come for me I'm gonna let them bitches have it" Taiya said.

"Bitch we not about to let you fight or get all crazy with that baby. You need to lay low and chill out right now Tai! Please just let this shit play out" Lynasia begs her.

"Look I'm not running like no scared bitch out here I didn't do shit. He came taunting me and throwing that baby up in my face" Taiya starts to cry.

"BABY! What baby?" Keosha asks.

"Girl yes Niema is pregnant by Rocko" Lynasia informs her.

"Are you fucking kidding me right now?" Keosha let out a giggle.

"THIS SHIT IS NOT FUNNY BITCH!!!" Taiya yell.

"Girl, calm your ass down. I know it's not funny, I'm just saying. How these bitches been so quick to talk shit about us but Ny out here being a sideline ho?" Keosha explained.

"Look dead all that I'm going to need you to lay low and chill out while I see what's going on. We put our family on the line for this bullshit so like I said chill out" Lynasia groans at her.

"Okay I hear you bitch I just want to know if he's okay at least" Taiya pleads.

"TAIYA!!! I know you're crazy-ass don't think you're going to the hospital" Keosha scrunched up her face.

"No I know I can't go up there I just want to know if he's okay at least" her eyes tear up.

"I know you do but right now we have to get you calm and then we can worry about the rest later. I'm sure everything is going to be just fine babe" Lynasia reassured her.

"I don't know what I would do without y'all" Taiya begins to sob.

Keosha grabs her hand from the back seat and they ride the rest of the way to Taiya's house wondering what is in store for them.

♦♦♦NewSouth™♦♦♦

"What's going on cuzzo?" Chynna said to Endy who's sitting in their Nana's living room.

"Girl I'm still disturbed by all this mess man this shit is too much Chy" tears stream down Endy's face as she tries to whisper not wake up Luella.

"I know E but we got to stay strong you see how upset nana was especially since she helped Uncle Rodney raise him. That bitch gonna get hers in due time just watch. Right now we have to be there for the family. Rocko made it through the surgeries so we have to be thankful" Chynna said and give her hug.

"I am but I'm ready to put that bitch six feet under but I know she's carrying my blood inside her. If it wasn't for that I would go to that bitch ass on sight" Endy grunts. (Ding dong…the doorbell rings).

"I got it you just sit here and relax" Chynna jumps up. She opens the door and its Egypt, Asia, and Karishma.

"Girl you are not gonna believe this bullshit"
Egypt walks in pissed and loud which startles Luella.

"What's going on?" Luella jumps up.

"Oh sorry Nana I didn't mean to wake you but
I'm so pissed right now" Egypt said with tears forming.

"What happen Egypt spill it" Chynna demands.

"Okay here it goes! Taiya is out on bail. I heard
that Lynasia put the money up to get her out" Egypt told
her family who are all in a state of shock.

"I'm so pissed they let this trick out of jail and my
cousin is laying in the hospital fighting for his life" Asia
said furious.

"Egypt how you know this baby" Luella ask her
granddaughter.

"Nana my homeboy seen her leaving a couple of weeks ago with Lynasia and Keosha's ho ass" Egypt explained.

"Aye stop all that cursing I know you girls are upset but we have to handle this situation rationally okay. Do y'all hear me" Luella grills letting the girls know she means business.

"Okay Nana your right but how can they release her without Rocko being cleared of his condition. It just seems really messed up" Chynna adds.

"Look y'all I know it's hard but look what God has done. Rocko got through his surgeries and he's stable so we have to be thankful for that" Luella explains to them.

"I just want my cousin home. I miss his jokes, his laugh, his presence man just everything about Rocko I miss. This some bullshit Nana how this bitch is out walking the streets" Endy cried and her cousins comfort her. Everyone knows they are close.

As they all try to comfort Endy the doorbell rings.

"I'll get it" Karishma says walking to the door. When she opens it, who was standing there? Caine and Jasean. "I know y'all don't want to see me but we've all known each other too long for this bullshit" Caine said to Chynna who is standing behind Karishma as she opens the door.

"Yo, if you coming here for some bullshit CJ leave now because I'm not up for it today" Chynna snaps. She just didn't understand why Jasean would bring him there knowing the family is going through hell right now.

"Babe we come in peace we just wanted to make sure y' all are okay and to get an update on Rocko's condition" Jasean said.

"At the end of the day we family no matter what the situation is" Caine adds.

"Who is that at the door?" Endy shouts.

"It's me babe" Jasean replied looking at Chynna for approval to come in the house. "Y'all come in I just don't want Caine ass to be on no bullshit" Chynna forewarn them giving Jasean a hug. They walk in the living room, everyone frowns and get quiet when they see Caine with Jasean.

"CJ what the hell is he doing here?" Endy jumped up.

"Y'all calm down Jay and CJ come in y'all are still family and we have to find a way to get through all this bullshit together. No matter how messed up the situation is we have to find peace within the families" Luella told them.

"Babe it's not like that C.J. came in peace he understands the realness of this shit. We want to make sure everyone is good for real come on" Jasean pleads with his wife. Endy shoots Jasean a mean look.

"Endy I know your upset we all are but this not the time to be arguing. I had time to think about the whole shit and we got come together right now" Caine said.

"Yeah we need to come together cousin" Karishma agrees.

"Your right Rizzy" Endy says and gives her husband a hug.

"We all know this situation is unfortunate but we have to think about the ones who are involved which is Rocko, Niema, and even Taiya crazy ass" Luella said.

"Your right Nana we need to just be there for Rocko, Niema, and even Taiya because at the end of the day this is going to be a lot to process for them all" Chynna adds.

"Taiya she the one that started all this mess my cousin is lying in a hospital bed because of that bitch!" Endy shouts.

"I know your angry but we have to be honest Taiya was acting on emotions she loves Rocko and pregnant with his child. Only to find out that Niema has been sleeping with him and even worse she's pregnant too. It's not right but I have to be real babies we can't say what we would have done in this exact situation" Luella explained.

The girls all look at each other knowing their grandmother was right but they just couldn't forgive her just yet.

"Nana I get what you're saying but I'm just not on the road of forgiveness yet" Endy states.

"I want my wife to be okay. I love you E, I hate to see you so torn up like this" Jasean sat beside her with his arms around her shoulders hugging her.

"Aye all we can do right now is continuing praying that everything turns out for the best with Rocko and for them babies" Egypt interjects.

(Ring...ring...The house phone rings). "Hell-Low!" Asia answers all ghetto.

"I'm sorry I came at you like that Caine we are family. I just want all this shit to go away and my cousin to come out the hospital okay" Endy tells him.

"I know E I love y'all we've know each other over a decade so I will not let this break up the family. I will just have to stand tall, eat this shit and find forgiveness in this. I'm trying to be a different man for my daughter sake" Caine explains to Endy.

"When?" Asia yells which makes everyone in the house quiet.

"What happen now?" Luella asks concern.

"Yo they said Taiya and YaYa got to fighting at the hospital and YaYa got arrested. Uncle Rodney and Aunt Tanya are on their way up there" Asia informed them.

"What! I know the fuck they didn't do that shit" Endy shouts.

"That's J.J. on the phone now with Nana" Asia replied.

"Okay let me call Ny and see what's going on" Endy said pulling out her cell phone.

Everybody has a worried look on their face because they're trying to figure out why Niema or Taiya was at the hospital. Niema was put on bed rest after her pre-term labor scare and Taiya supposed to lay low and away from Rocko.

"Oh no I'm on my way up there now" Endy yelled in the phone.

"Endy what happen?" Jasean asked.

"Mommy said NY was visiting Rocko and Taiya came up there with Keosha. She said they passed words and Taiya charged Ny and YaYa jumped on her ass. Her and Taiya were fighting in the damn hospital room" Endy said putting her pink and black Adidas sneakers on that matched her pink and black Adidas sweat suit.

"I'm going with you Endy" Chynna said putting on her coat.

"Well we will stay here with Nana y'all just keep us posted" Asia hugs her cousins as they walk out the door with Caine and Jasean right behind them.

◆◆◆**NewSouth™**◆◆◆

"The nerve of that bitch trying to put her hands on me" Niema screams.

"Baby you got to calm down I know you're upset and emotional but you have to chill out" Tanya told Niema.

"Well Taiya is gone and YaYa had to go to the precinct just for a cooling off period and Sally is on the way to the precinct now. This whole situation is just getting more and more out of hand" Lisa said sitting down next to Niema and Tanya in the hospital waiting room.

340

"I just want Rocko to be okay and we sort this out for the children auntie. I swear if I can take this all back I will but I can't what's done is done." Niema bury her face on Tanya's shoulder and sob loudly.

"Now this bitch wants to cry after all she has done" Taiya yelled as she is being taken on a gurney to the ER to be checked out.

"HO FUCK YOU! If you know what's good for you bitch you would stop talking to me" Niema yelled trying to jump up to the point where Tanya and Lisa had to hold her down.

"Ny stop it now! Don't go there with her she's upset and your upset. Rocko is still lying in this hospital you have to calm down for the sake of the baby" Lisa told her. Niema continues to cry because deep down inside she knows this is all her fault and she can't do anything to fix it. What has been done it's no coming back from and she just wants to find peace in this fucked up situation.

"Look babe Rocko open his eyes and reacted that's good sign even if it was due to the drama that happened in his room. His lungs are working better and he's responding so let's just continue praying for a speedy recovery and leave the drama on the back burner baby girl" Tanya told Niema while holding her and rubbing her head as she cried a river on her shoulder.

"MA! What happen?" Endy shouts as she storms in the waiting room.

"Endy everything is good your cousin is responding well and crazy as it is, it was all due to the fighting in the room. He woke up trying to talk but his vitals went high so now they are just trying to keep him stable" Tanya tells her daughter.

"Okay Mommy I'm sorry I will calm down I just want my cousin to be okay and Ny I need you to try to relax for this baby" Endy kneels down in front of her grabbing hold of her shivering hand.

"I know Endy but it's just too much coming back-to-back. I don't even know if I want to keep this baby" Niema cried.

"Ny stop now we not about to go there that's all you been talking about is having a baby even before I had Patience. Now we are all gonna get through this one way or another" Endy assured her.

"Hinton Family" a black nurse shouts.

"We're Hinton family" Lisa ran up to her.

"Mr. Hinton is doing well and you all are able to see him now" She said.

"When can we go" Endy asks.

"I came to bring you all back" the nurse said and the family follows her. They get in the room and Rocko is wide awake. They are stunned and happy all in one.

Chapter 12

The holidays are right around the corner and Rocko is able to be home right in time to be with the family. He still has quite a bit of physical therapy to do but he has progressed tremendously considering the bullet just missed his spine.

"I'm so excited that see my cousin comes home today" Endy said to Ari who is going with her to the hospital to pick Rocko up.

"Girl I know you are ready to see him. All this was going on and you didn't say anything to any of us" Ari argued giving her a look.

"I know I should have said something but it was like everything happened so fast. Plus I just was trying to be a loyal friend. I couldn't have imagined that it would of gone this far" Endy explained.

"Girl this shit went beyond far, motherfuckers went to jail, got shot, two babies on the way I mean this shit is a real lifetime movie man" Ari laughed.

Endy just gives her a look and laughs too. "Girl I have to laugh to keep from crying and cursing. I'm just glad he and Caine made peace but he is not feeling Ny at all right now" Endy informed her.

"Hell can you blame her girl. They were together since we all were in Junior High School. It just seems crazy him and Ny hooking up after all these years" Ari says.

"I know but we have two beautiful babies coming into this world and mad as I am at Taiya I'm gonna have to find peace with this situation for my cousin" Endy said reluctantly.

"Well girl let's go because I am ready to see him you know I couldn't do that hospital shit with him man"

Ari clarified since she didn't go see him at the hospital like that.

"Girl please I'm just excited for everything to get to some type of normalcy for a change because my Nana is going through it and you know Rocko and J.J. is her babies' girl. So yeah let's get it I know everyone is going to be happy to see him it's been over two months" Endy stated grabbing her beige Givenchy purse that has the pea coat and knee boots to match. Jasean gets his baby all the flyest clothes before they even hit the store racks. They take Ari Escalade since it's bigger and the doctor wants Rocko to use the wheelchair a little bit longer.

"Girl I don't know how I can thank you enough for taking off work and doing this for me" Endy expressed.

"Girl it's no biggie that's what friends are for. I know you've been through so much. I just wanted to take some of this baggage off of you" Ari replied.

"I really hope that Roc, Taiya, and Ny can come to some type of agreement because this is not going to be pretty. The whole situation is messed up. He has to take his first baby mother to court for shooting him and then deal with the betrayal he's done against his homie. I just wish them all peace in the end" Endy shakes her head.

"I know boo but you can't keep worrying yourself about Caine, Ny, Rocko, and Taiya it's taking a toll on you and your marriage. What is going on with you and Jasean y'all seem a little distant" Ari questioned wondering why Jasean hasn't been real supportive of Endy at her time of need.

"Girl I don't want to jump to conclusions but I found a hotel key card in my truck and when I asked him about it he said it was Caine's. But Ari my intuition tells me that it's more too it but like I always say what's done in the dark will come to the light" she stated brushing it off. However Ari knows her friend and she know it's more to this hotel key card mess but she will let it go just for now. Ari is the one in the group that will confront and get to the bottom of any situation no matter how messy it is.

They took the elevator to the hospital trauma section and when they reach their destination and exit the elevator who's standing there?

"How y'all doing ladies?" It's Taiya who spoke with Keosha beside her.

"What the hell are y'all doing here? Y'all better not have been anywhere near my damn cousin" Endy barked heading straight toward her ass but Ari pulled her back.

"I don't know what y'all bitches thought y'all had going on but I'm gonna tell y'all this much, y'all ass better fall back before you get pushed back. I swear I'm not trying to catch a charge today" Ari adds.

"Look nobody scared of y'all first of all, we just came to make sure my baby was okay and to check Rocko was okay damn!" Taiya barked back.

"Bitch you and your homie better get missing real quick before y'all end up missing!" Endy shouts mad as fire because security has intervened.

"Dis es sad ya know, chu people cunt get elongfo tee sake of the mon" the tall, black, Jamaican, security officer said. He was the one who had to stop YaYa and Taiya from fighting the last time.

"Like what are y'all doing around here? She shouldn't even be allowed around my cousin at this point man. This hospital will be sued if she was anywhere near my damn, my damn, cousin I tell y'all that much" Endy started stuttering pissed off because she want to beat the hell out of Taiya right now but she knows she can't.

"Mumm we sorrdeechee jus cum here and no been in thee rumm yet but me is sordee for dat" the security guy replied in his Jamaican accent.

"Look Endy chill we need to let them do their job and get Rocko so we can get our ass home. We will handle them chic's accordingly" Ari told her. "Yeah your right" Endy agrees. Meanwhile, the security is escorting Taiya and Keosha back to the lobby to leave the hospital premises.

♦♦♦NewSouth™♦♦♦

"Niema I wish you just cut these Hinton people off like they are all for themselves" YaYa yaps at her cousin.

"Girl Endy has been the most helpful to me than anyone else" Niema spat back.

"What the hell that supposed to mean?" YaYa asked insulted.

"Girl you know I didn't mean it like that. I'm just saying it's like you don't want me being friends with Endy. We've known each other since we were kids. She's the only person who has ever stuck by me even when others thought she shouldn't have" Niema explained.

"No I just feel like you give her too much credit as a friend where is your praise as a friend to her. It's always made like you're a bad friend. I'm so sick of them damn people." YaYa gripes.

"Well YaYa either you live with it or take your ass back to N.O. I'm sick of you trying to get me to feel like Endy is being a bad friend when she's not. I did get jealous of her pregnancy and marriage. They had a right to say what they were saying. I wasn't there for her like a friend should" Niema admits but YaYa doesn't want to hear it.

"Girl you are so blind all that shit was to make you mad and jealous. Jay ain't any better than no other nigga" YaYa blurts out and Niema gives her a suspicious look.

"YaYa that's the second time you done said that bullshit. Is there something you need to say?" Niema questioned.

"No girl I'm just saying no man is perfect, all men cheat. Didn't you say he cheated in the past?" YaYa asked.

"Yes YaYa but so what he's changed and he did it because she wasn't taking his shit" Niema responded

"Whatever Ny I believe the old saying once a cheater always a cheater point blank. He is no better than nobody else" YaYa remarks rolling her eyes.

*I don't know what I ever do without you from the beginning till the end you've always been here right beside me so I call you my best friend, through the good times and the bad one whether I lose or if I win, I know one thing that never changes and that you as my best friend…*come blaring through Niema's phone.

"Oh shoot that's Endy hand me my phone off the table please" Niema asked YaYa. She brings it to her rolling her eyes with an attitude but Niema pays her no mind.

"What's up girl how is Rocko doing?" Niema answers smiling for ear to ear.

"Girl What!" Niema jumps up and shout. She now has YaYa attention she comes from the kitchen drinking a glass of soda.

"Endy calm down babe please I will meet you I'm on my way" Niema said before hanging up the phone.

She is already dressed in cute plush black sweeter she got from Macy's with some blue skinny jeans and her black leather knee boots she got from Aldo's. She grabbed her black leather coat and her big black Gucci purse to match.

"Ny what happened? Where you going? Do you need me to go with you?" YaYa interrogates Niema as she watches her rush to Endy's side.

"No you stay here, you and Endy not vibing right now. I'm not up for no bullshit today. She suggest to her as she rushed out the door and to her car.

Niema can't believe that Keosha and Taiya slashed Ari tires and scratched her car after they were escorted from the hospital knowing damn well they was picking up Rocko. She just continues driving in disbelief. She called Endy back once she's alone.

"Yo, why would they do that knowing y'all went to pick Rocko up from the hospital?" Niema asked.

"Girl these bitches must be nuts if they thought there were gonna get away with it" Endy laughs.

"Bitch ain't anything funny about none of this shit going on. I'm gonna whip Taiya's ass so she can match her bestie ass whipping" Niema snapped.

"I'm out, yo see when you get here we don't have time to be messing those petty-ass birds we better than that" Endy criticized Taiya and Keosha. "Your right, okay be there in a few" Niema" agreed.

When Niema arrive at Luella's house she's hesitant to go in because this will be everyone first time seeing her and Rocko in the same place at the same time since everything has erupted.

"Lord please be with me as I go in here" Niema mouthed a quick prayer to herself. She gets out the car unbeknownst of what will be said and how the family will react to her. She rings the doorbell once she reaches

the door and the main person she did not want to face
first answers.

"Oh hi it's you Ny" Chynna spoke leaving the
door open and walks away.

"Hello to you too Chynna" Niema shook her head
entering the house and closing the door behind her.

"Everybody it's Niema" Chynna said as they both
enter the living-room.

"Niema baby girl, how are you holding up?"
Luella jumped up to give her a hug and so does the rest of
the family.

"I'm okay how are y'all doing?"

"I'm doing okay happy my boy is home and doing
great God is good" Luella replied raising both her hands
up in the air.

"I know that's right Nana that he is. He's always on time too" Niema tried to make small talk.

"Well go see your man" Tanya laughs.

Niema shook her head at the comment and asked "Where is everybody at?" Niema notice that no one else was in the living room.

"Oh their all in the den baby and don't think we stop loving you but you know this here is a damn mess" Luella remarks. Everyone else just laughs and gives Niema hugs. She walks to the den feeling crushed but she knew it was coming. When she enters the den you can cut through the tension that filled the room.

"Hi boo how you doing?" Endy's the first to get up and give her a hug.

"Aye Ma how you been?" J.J spoke also giving her a hug. Tylon goes to hug her but Ari push him back down on the chair.

"Hi to all of you too" she spoke noticing that Chynna and Reeko barely spoke.

"We all know you're here to see Rocko so go ahead and see him" Ari snarled.

"Girl look don't start I came to see everyone but yes I did want to see him too. We are about to have a baby together" Niema snarls right back.

"And you have the fucking nerve to think this shit is cute. Like do you really understand the enormity of this situation? People got hurt because of y'all hidden secrets Niema. I mean motherfuckers could have died and you come in here like everything okay. I just think it's real fucked up" Ari yaps still a bit pissed.

"Come on y'all this shit gots to stop ASAP! Y'all are getting on my damn nerves" Endy interrupted them.

"Your right Endy I'm sorry about that it's not the time or the place. How are you doing? Did y'all find out who messed with Ari's whip?" Niema asked caring less that Ari car was scratched and tires flattened.

"Girl not yet they're looking over the security cameras of the parking lot to see if they caught anything. Their some real punks" Endy rants pacing the floor.

"Hopefully they can see who did it because that's some real cowardly shit" Niema agreed.

"Look at the pot calling the kettle black" Chynna mumbled.

"Chynna you got an issue with me? FINE! But you're not gonna keep throwing shade at me. I already know this shit is a messed but I really need y'all support at this time man please I'm begging y'all. It's nothing else I can do to change this situation I have prayed and asked God for forgiveness that's all I can do right now. So you can hate me but you will not continue to taunt me about this shit Niema barks.

"I keep telling y'all let the petty mess go we have bigger fish to fry. Ny you go on ahead to see Roc. Chynna please chill Nana don't need their bullshit today" Endy warned her cousin.

"Your right look I'm about to go and see who knocked on the door. I don't have time for you or your messy ass bestie" Chynna rolled her eyes and exit the den.

"Whew girl give me another drink because this drama driving me crazy" Ari laughed and so does Endy.

"Bitch it's not funny this is one downward spiral right here" Endy sighs.

"Hi babe" Niema announce as she entered Rocko's old room. Rocko looks up and see it's Ny and his face lit up with a big grin.

"Yo, come over here" he told her sitting up in the bed. She rushed over and gave him the biggest kiss.

"Baby I missed you so much Roc. So much has gone on with everyone I feel terrible man. Maybe I don't need to go through with this pregnancy" Niema tears up.

"Babe everything is gonna be okay we can't turn back now. Everyone will just have to adjust just give them time" Rocko gave her reassurance.

He been gone a couple of months but he's full aware of what the two of them are going to have to face. He no longer wants to be with Taiya but he doesn't want Niema to aboard the baby. He was thinking once Taiya knew what was going on that eventually she would be the one who wanted an abortion. Well that didn't happen and truthfully he doesn't want to get rid of none of his babies but he doesn't want anything to come between him and Niema.

"Rocko I know we planned on being together eventually but I feel like the baby is making the relationship be more rushed. We haven't even started living together yet. It's just too much happening too fast for me" Niema admits.

"So what you saying Ny because I can't let you get rid of my baby."

"Roc I just think we can try again sometime down the line when we've been together longer" Niema explains.

"HELLNO NY I'M NOT TRYING TO HEAR THAT BULLSHIT!"

"Okay Rocko chill stop yelling like you crazy in Nana house. I just want to make this whole situation easier. You were messing with both of us and you told me y'all stop. How will I know that you won't do this shit again?" Niema is now skeptical.

"Ny come on I know I messed up baby but I love you. I promise I will never hurt you like that. It happen a couple of times if that" he pleads with her.

"Rocko I just don't know it's too much stress" Niema said as she sat down on the bed beside him.

"Baby I got us I promise you the last thing I will be is a deadbeat dad" Rocko gently takes her hand in his. She knew at that moment that he meant it by the look in his eyes.

"I'm just coming to get my daughter I can't believe this bullshit" they hear a familiar voice yell.

"I know that's not who I think it is" Niema frowns.

"Yeah that's Taiya ass go see what's going on Ma" Rocko told her. Niema jumps up shoots out the room and fly down stairs to see what all the commotion about but when she gets to the living room Taiya and Endy is nose to nose.

"Endy she's not worth it she knows what she is doing" Chynna said pulling her back.

"I know y'all don't have this bitch around my baby" Taiya rants turning her attention to Niema.

"Taiya this is my house and Niema is always welcome. What y'all have going on keep that mess out my house" Luella said them.

"Nana fuck this ho she better step because I will slap that face because her face not pregnant" Chynna yelled while Tanya pulled her toward the back of the house. Everyone is cursing and shouting at the same time.

"You have the nerve to bring your ass here after what you done. Mommy call the cops she not even supposed to be here around any of us" Tanya shouts.

"Look Taiya go on home don't make things worse on yourself. At least do it for the baby if you're not thinking about yourself" Luella begged her.

"I'm not going anywhere why is it that she can be here and I can't" Taiya pointed to Niema.

"Bitch because you shot him and have the nerve to bring your ass here" Niema bucks back.

"Ho fuck you that shit you did was what started all this shit in the first place" Taiya started crying.

"Taiya go home and just leave us alone. We love the kids and their always welcomed but as for you are concerned I'm done sweetheart now please just go"

Luella explained to a sobbing Taiya.

"LOOK I'M NOT GOING NO WHERE UNTIL I

SEE ROCKO!" she screams and Niema charges right

towards her, and they intertwine together letting out acts

of tension both of these women been holding was let out

on each other.

"Get them" Lisa yelled at Chynna. They done tore

the living room up even busted one of Luella's antique

lamps she got from one her friends from Guyana. Finally

Reeko and Tylon were able to split them apart. Rocko

has now come into the mix of the commotion.

"You're really trying to play me with this nothing

ass bitch Rodney" Taiya squealed as Reeko and Big

Rodney walk her out the door.

"WHAT THE HELL! Why y'all just sit here and

let them fight" Rocko screams.

"Boy who the hell you yelling at you the one brought all this drama to the family. Don't sit here and act like this mess is our fault this is all you're doing. You and these grown ass women so don't come talking about what the hell to us" Luella jumped up and point her finger in Rocko face very stern.

"I'm sorry Ma I didn't mean any disrespect to you or the fam" he softened up real quick. Luella is known to light you up with her .38 revolver if she feels disrespected. She walks off to the kitchen still mumbling to herself livid at her grandson.

"Boy you know better than that" Endy slapped his head.

"I know E where's Ny" He panicked

"She's in the bathroom with Mommy Rocko. She's okay I just need you to calm down for real man" Endy told him.

"Okay I'm going to go talk to this girl and let her know exactly how I feel" Rocko walked toward the door but Lisa jumps in front of him.

"No Roc don't do this let her ass go the police are on the way and they will make sure she gets off Mommy property. Just let it go and focus on getting your strength back because your children are going to need you. Look at Rachelle she's scared to death. When he turns around and saw Rachelle she was holding her baby doll looking so pitiful.

"Where is mommy? Daadee, are you okay" Rachelle sadly murmurs.

"Yes baby daddy is okay come here" she ran and jumped in his arms and he squeezed his baby girl so tight.

"I'ma tell y'all this, the cops better take care of this bitch because if not I will" Rocko said. He takes

Rachelle upstairs to calm her down and the family stands there speechless.

"I will go and try to calm him down y'all stay here and keep shit calm down here please" Luella asked as she go to talk to Rocko.

"Endy this mess is a fucking nightmare all this for what? We shouldn't have to go through this bullshit" Chynna complained.

"Chynna I know, you're right, we shouldn't but babe we are family. We have to fight through this storm and pull together to push through the mess. Everything is going to be alright it's just so much happening at one time. You don't think I'm mad? I'm fucking pissed but beating motherfuckers' asses is not going to solve the problem. We're going to have to let this shit play out because anything we do will just make matters worse" Endy explained. Endy tried to get her to understand that retaliating is not in the best interest of the family right now.

"Something has got to give because we can't keep letting this shit with them affect Nana like it has been. If shit keeps going this way then I'm going to handle these ho's myself" Chynna gripes. Endy phone rings and she see it's the hospital number.

"Hello?" Endy quickly picked up.

"Is this Ariana Lewis?" a male voice asked.

"No who is this?" Endy's asks confused.

"It's Ronald, the security guard y'all spoke to earlier about her tires being slashed. I wanted to see if she can come down here and see if she can identify the person on the video footage we have" he informed Endy.

"Yes hold on Sir, let me run to get her" Endy heads to the kitchen where Ari is sitting with Luella at the table. "Ari this is the security guard at the hospital he said you can come down there and see if you can identify the person in the video" Endy rushed in handing her the phone.

"Hello?" Ari jumped on the phone.

"Yes I will be right down there with my husband" Ari yelled excitedly handing Endy the phone back.

"You want me to go with you?" Endy asked.

"No Endy you stay here and chill with the family I'll hit you after I'm done" Ari gives them a kiss and rush out.

"Endy no matter what's on that video let the cops handle it you hear me" Luella told her granddaughter as she entered back in the living room.

"Nana I will chill for now but we can't keep letting Taiya come at the family she's going way too far" Endy groaned.

"I know baby but I also know you and Chynna tempers are just like mine. Please just let the Cops handle it" Luella begged Endy.

"Nana I promise to hold my temper. I don't want you anymore upset than you are now" Endy gave her nana a hug. "God has a plan for this entire situation baby girl" Luella kissed her granddaughter on the forehead.

Chapter 13

"Ny why don't we cook Thanksgiving dinner at Aunt Sally's house" YaYa suggests.

"We can do that, but we got to do it early because you know I'm going Nana's house around six" Niema reminds her as she grab her coat and keys to head to her doctor's appointment. She and Rocko are going to see what the sex of the baby.

"Why can't you just spend at least one holiday with your family? You're always around them like we don't exist" YaYa snaps.

"YaYa I don't know what's going on with you lately but you know I always spend time with y'all and with them. Regardless of what you and Endy have going on I love both of y'all. I'm not choosing sides so just chill the fuck out its stupid anyway!" Niema spits back.

"Okay damn do what you want, but Aunt Sally
needs us and she's worried about you Ny" YaYa stated.

"I know that, but I can't stop living my life
because of my mistakes. I'm a grown ass woman who
knew better and knew what I was doing. I just want to
make sure my baby gets here healthy that's it" Niema
throws her arms around YaYa shoulders empathizing
with her feelings.

"Ny you're a good person I just want your friends
to recognize it too that's all" YaYa gave her a hug.

"I'm good cuzzo trust and believe my eyes are
open but just know Endy has been a very good friend to
me even when I wasn't to her" Niema says defending
their friendship.

"Okay whatever you say just know I'm going to
be on it because you're my cousin and I love you" YaYa
bush it off.

"Okay well let me get going girl Rocko is going to meet me there he is so excited. You would think this is his first child" Niema laughs.

"Well I'm just happy he is sticking by your girl thank God for men like him" YaYa told her.

"I know right. Well I will hit you later and keep you posted okay. I'm so excited to see what we're having" Niema smiles rushing out the door.

When Niema gets to the doctor's office Rocko is nowhere in sight but Endy is there waiting for her with Patience. "Hi bestest how you and my baby doing today?" Endy eagerly greets her.

"Hi boo" Niema gives her a hug.

"Don't panic Roc is on his way" Endy says not wanting Niema to get upset. "Okay but where is he? Is everything okay?" She questions.

"Everything is fine him and Nana are on the way now let's just relax" Endy pulls her to sit down.

"I hope I'm not late" Rocko said which prompted Niema to jump up and smile. "Baby I thought you were gonna miss it" she said wrapping her arms around his neck.

"Not for nothing in this world I told you I'm recording this for my little man" Rocko smiled proudly.

"Whatever Rodney we are about to see" Endy counters back.

"NIEMA MASON" The Nurse shouts.

"Uh oh you guys here we go I'm so freaking nervous man" Niema exclaimed.

"Don't be, this is a blessing baby girl. Come on Ny you got this" Endy convinced her. Niema gets up with Rocko right behind and followed the nurse to the back.

"Hello I'm Yesinia (Ya-Sin-Ya) let's see what Mommy and Daddy should be expecting" the cute little Puerto Rican nurse says.

"I am very nervous and excited all in one "Niema grins ear to ear.

"Don't be everything is going to be just fine" Yesinia assures her. They finally reach the room and she gets them settled in the ultrasound room.

"So is this you two first baby?"

"Yes for me but not for him" Niema answered.

"Yeah I have a four-year-old daughter so I want a boy" Rocko grins ear to ear. "What about you Ms. Mason?" the nurse asked.

"Either is fine with me as long the baby is healthy" She smiles at Rocko.

"Okay well Dr. Blake will be in shortly and congratulations on the baby" Yesinia leaves closing the door behind her.

"This is really happening" Niema shook her head.

"Well I want you to know that I love you and will always be here for y'all no matter what the future holds" he grab her hand so passionately. This is exactly what made Niema fall for him because he was so in tune with her needs and she always yearned for that with Caine.

"I know baby the way you have protected me through all this drama with Taiya, Caine, your family and mines has proven to me that you will never let harm come our way and for that I love you" Niema palms his face and lays a passionate kiss on his lips that made Rocko melt all over. He has always loved her and to have her in his life is a dream come true for him. He is just praying this he will not have to regret his decision to break up his family and be with her. He knows he should have been left Taiya who treated him like a piece of shit but he never wanted to do it this way.

"Oh I see how we got here now!" Dr. Blake joke as she entered the room to them kissing.

"Hi Dr. Blake" Niema chuckled.

"Hello Niema we are finally here" Dr. Blake gave her a hug.

"I know right but I can't lie I am very nervous but I'm ready to see how the baby is doing since I didn't have any pre-natal care in my first trimester" Niema confessed.

"Yes I know and why is that?" Dr. Blake expresses concern.

"Well I didn't know if I was going to go through with the pregnancy of not.

"WHAT? Your mother will roll over in her grave if she heard you talking this nonsense" Dr. Blake grilled her.

"I know but it's a crazy situation" Niema replies.

"I see excuse my rudeness and whom may I have the pleasure of meeting" Dr. Blake extends her hand to Rocko.

"Hello I'm Rodney Hinton" he shook her hand.

"This is Endyia's cousin and my new boyfriend Dr. Blake.

"Oh wow then you're like family to me. I have most of the women in your family as my patients" she laughs.

"Yes so I hear" Rocko also laughs.

"Okay so are y'all ready for this" Dr. Blake asks.

"Yes we are" Rocko eagerly replied.

"Okay let's do it, lay back my dear and you go stand right beside her so you can see the screen" she instructed them. She applied the cold gel on Niema stomach and puts this little gadget to her stomach which lets them hear the baby's heartbeat.

"Oh my God that's my baby heartbeat!" Niema shouts excitedly.

"Yes hun that is it, now let's get the screen on" Dr. Blake turn on the screen and shows them the baby. She scrolls through showing the head, ribs, legs, and there it was "We are having a boy" she says.

"YES! I knew it" Rocko shouts kissing Niema.

"Oh my God I'm having a boy" Niema starts to drop tears of joy.

"Okay now let me get your vitamins and iron, and we will be ready to go. Again congratulations you two" Dr. Blake walked out the room.

Rocko just embraces Niema again and kisses her continuously until there was a knock at the door.

"Come in" they both yelled.

"Hi you guys here is the prescription, vitamins and ultrasound pictures" Yesinia hands everything to Niema.

"We are having a boy" Rocko blurts out.

"Oh wow congratulations I know you two are going to spoil him up something serious.

"Yes we are" Niema said with the biggest grin.

"I wonder how it's going back there" Endy says to Luella.

"Everything is going to be fine" Luella told her.

"I just know Ny been under a lot of stress and I know if something is wrong with the baby she will just blame herself" Endy says.

"Everything is just fine you watch. God didn't let us come this far our family has been hit we need some good news right now" Luella adds.

"Aye y'all" Rocko said coming from the back holding Niema's hand.

"What we having?" Luella anxiously asks.

"We're having a boy!" Niema shouts in the waiting room and everyone claps at their happy news.

"Oh my God I can't wait to see him and we have lots of shopping to do" Endy is overly excited.

"Yes we do I need some more boys in this family I'm so tired of y'all split tails" Luella hugs Niema.

"Thanks Nana you know I love and respect you to the utmost" Niema tells her knowing the situation has caused so much turmoil in the family.

"I know Ny and we all make mistakes I just want you all to come to a peaceful agreement" Luella says.

"I know Mama and we will. I am going to do all I can to take care of all three of my children I promise you that" Rocko promised her.

"I know baby I know" Luella hugs her grandson. They all walk out to leave so they can share with the rest of the family.

Endy pulls up to Luella's house to see Ari outside pacing back and forth on her cell phone. "What's wrong with Ariana she looks mad" Luella asked.

"I don't know but she texted me and said she will meet me here" Endy replied. They get out the car and Ari runs over to Endy.

"Girl I am really trying to figure out who would have done that to my car and the only conclusion I can come up with is Tylon is messing with some trick" Ari spits.

"Ari babe let's not get ahead of ourselves" Endy tried calming her down.

"Endy what other reason will there be? It wasn't Taiya or Keosha, so who else would want to fuck with my car" Ari cried.

"Ari I doubt Tylon is cheating maybe them bitches got someone else to do it. Have you ever considered that?" Endy told her.

"Endy if I find out that they had anything to do with my tires being slashed I am going to beat the breaks off both of them tricks I'm not playing" Ari groans.

"I know you are girl calm your ass down we got good news today. Ny and Rocko are having a little boy" Endy smiled.

"Endy I want to be happy but this whole situation still has me a little shocked. How do they expect this whole thing to work as far as Caine and Taiya? I just feel like it's not going to get any better no time soon" Ari express concern.

"Well as far as Caine he's still in his feelings but he and Rocko have squashed their beef he's just no fucking with Ny right now which is understandable. He expressed his hurt and Jasean is not happy either" Endy adds.

"Well what do you expect we were all close and it's like now everyone is falling apart. Events are being broken because certain motherfuckers don't want to be around each other Endy this situation is a mess and I won't sugar coat or pacify their behavior" Ari told her.

"Well I respect your opinion but I love my family and I will support them right or wrong. I know y'all feel like Niema is not a real friend to me and maybe she's not but I know she loves me. She may has a fucked up way of showing it but I know at the end of the day when it's time to ride she has my back. She's been through a lot Ari and I would think you would be the one person who understands that being that you are without your mom also. Just try to find it in your heart to forgive her and be there Ari please do it for me" Endy beg her.

"Ugh you and this damn Niema Mason are driving me nuts. I will try to be better to her for you but I can't make any promises of what may come out my

mouth sometimes" Ari laughed.

"Girl comes on so we can get this menu together

for Nana and have a great Thanksgiving okay" Endy

wrap her arm around hers and pulls her towards the

house.

"I can't stand you Endyia Hinton" they both laugh

and go upstairs to join Luella in the house.

♦♦♦NewSouth™♦♦♦

Niema is moving and shaking around Aunt Sally's

house listing to Aretha Franklin's '*Jump to it*' dancing

around and finally feeling like everything is going to be

okay.

"You sure is in a good mood' Aunt Sally states as

she stands in the door way of her kitchen watching her

niece she raised since her sister passed away, dance

around like she's full of joy. She is so happy to see her in good spirits despite everything that's going on.

"Aunt Sally I just feel good! Where YaYa at? She damn near curse me out for saying I was going to Nana's house and then she don't even bother to come help with Thanksgiving dinner" Niema said.

"I know where is that child at she should have been here two hours ago" Aunt Sally adds.

"Well I'm about to call her because she wanted us to have an intimate Thanksgiving dinner and she is not even here" Niema picks up her cell phone to call her but when she does it goes straight to voicemail. .

"Her phone is either dead or she has it turned off because she is not answering" Niema shrugs.

"Well she better get here quick I don't know who she think she is but we will not do all the work and she just come and eat" Aunt Sally said cutting up onions and peppers for potato salad. "*Jump, Jump, Jump To It*" Niema said singing along with Aretha. (Ding, dong...The doorbell rang). Niema runs to the door and when she opens its Rocko standing there.

"Yo what's up why you haven't been answering my calls" he asked.

"Baby I just need some time to soak all this in I just don't want to make matters worse for you. I know all this is a bit much for everyone" Niema explained.

"Babe look I'm with you all the way. Please don't shut me out not now after I found out your carrying my son I want to be there every step of the way I love you Ny" Rocko begs grabbing her hand.

"Come in crazy" Niema laughs and pull him inside the house.

"Hi Rocko! How are you doing?" Aunt Sally gives him a hug.

"I'm blessed Aunt Sally" Rocko gives that sexy but sly smile that all the women love.

"I see my little nephew is gonna be one handsome something" Aunt Sally smiled and goes on back to the kitchen. (Ding, dong…The doorbell rings again).

"I got it babe go on to the kitchen I'm coming" Niema said going to open the door. When she opens the door she see a disheveled YaYa standing there holding her purse.

"Where the hell have you been?" Niema groans. "Look I'm not up for your shit today" YaYa counters back brushing past Niema.

"Girl what is your problem now?" Niema became irritated.

"Who is in the kitchen?" YaYa hears laughter.

"Rocko and Aunt Sally."

"I should of known you couldn't make this about us them Hinton's gonna be in the mix somehow" YaYa rants as she removed her coat and scarf.

"Look he is my baby father like damn I suppose to just cut them off because you feel like I need to YaYa it doesn't work that way" Niema yelled.

"Girl please those people got you wrapped around their finger they say jump and you do it. Like Damn Ny get some balls about yourself I know my auntie is turning over in her grave."

"DON'T YOU EVER MENTION MY MOTHER AGAIN?"

"What the hell is going on in here?" Aunt Sally rushed to the living room to see what the commotion is about.

"Ask your niece she's the one all sentimental and shit" YaYa smirks.

"Like I said don't mention my mother no more that will get your ass kicked" Niema spat back.

"Y'all please don't do this it's Thanksgiving we supposed to be showing love to each other right now" Aunt Sally pleads with the women.

"Your right Auntie I'm just gonna go upstairs and freshen up" YaYa says.

"Yeah take your punk ass upstairs and get that alcohol off your breath because you're feeling yourself and letting that liquid courage buy you medicine that you're not ready to take" Niema warns her.

"Whatever Niema we're not young no more"
YaYa hops up the steps.

"Bitch what" Niema tried to charge at her but
Rocko quickly grabs her.

"Ma chill you can't be stressing the baby."

"I'm so sick of her damn mouth she always has
something to say. I really think this ho is jealous of my
relationship with y'all it's sickening" Niema shouts so
YaYa can hear her.

"Baby please do what Rocko says because your
emotions are all over the place right now" Aunt Sally told
a seemingly upset Niema.

"Auntie your right I will not let her mess up my
day" Niema exhaled and apologize to them for her
actions.

"Now let's go back in the kitchen and finish cooking so we can eat sometime today" Aunt Sally laughed.

"Yeah because y'all know I'm eating for two" Rocko said and they look at him crazy.

"Well I wish you could carry him too so you can feel all these crazy symptoms" Niema said.

"For you I will that's just how much I love your mean ass." He pulls her close to him and gives her a kiss.

"This is really going to take some getting used to for me" Aunt Sally chuckled.

"What auntie?" Niema had a big grin on her face.

"Y'all that's what I just want y'all to be happy and raise that boy right."

"I promise I'm gonna make sure my prince has the world Aunt Sally that's a fact. You will never have to worry about that I promise" Rocko said with all sincerity.

"I know you will baby I just want y'all to settle this mess with Taiya and get on one accord. This whole situation has gotten way out of hand" Aunt Sally tells him.

"Yeah I know and I am but I'm so pissed with her right now because she took things way too far. All I want is to get my daughter fully and keep her in a safe environment Taiya is too unstable at this point. I may be part to blame but she had been doing me way longer than I have her" Rocko said.

"I understand sweetheart but if it was so bad you should have been left her alone" She respond.

"Your right but you got to trust me auntie I won't hurt Ny and I'm all in when it comes to her and this baby" He said and she has no choice but to take his word.

"Auntie what do you need me to do" YaYa came in the kitchen a little more refreshed.

"Look you and Ny better let this mess go. I don't know what's been going on but y'all have to pull together at this time. Y'all are blood for Christ sake" Aunt Sally shouts putting her hands on her hips.

"Auntie it's not me she has some pinned up anger towards Endy and I don't know why. My friends and who I deal with should not be of her concern but she continues to judge my situation and talk shit" Niema said.

"You're the one around here acting like you and your friends shit don't stink y'all aren't nothing but a bunch of disloyal bitches who are always talking about and judging other people" YaYa shoots.

"YaYa are you serious right now? Disloyal? Girl bye I see what this is I didn't want to say it but I think I'm completely right. You are jealous of me and Endy's relationship and that's so sad because you're my blood relative like come on now" Niema shot back.

"Please nobody jealous of you if anything your jealous of your friend's life and trying so hard to duplicate it with somebody else baby father. Bitch bye!"

"Bitch I'm gonna show you who the bitch is" Niema said walking towards her. For the fear that she would harm the baby, Rocko jumps in front of the two.

"What your pregnant ass gonna do?" YaYa groans which makes Niema even more pissed.

"Ny let's just go baby this is not worth it."

"You're not worth it!" YaYa yelled at Rocko.

"Look I'm talking to my girl I don't have shit to say to you" Rocko replied pulling a vexed Niema out the kitchen and toward the front door. It is hard as hell for him because he is trying his best not to hurt her or the baby.

"Fuck you bitch I hate you ever came here you been nothing but trouble since you be here" Niema screams as Rocko finally get her out the door.

"Fuck you Ny take her over there with her adopted family she don't give a damn about me or Aunt Sally."

"Would you shut your mouth Ni'Yana what has gotten into you too. I thought y'all were closer than this come on" Aunt Sally grab her head.

Eventually Rocko get Niema to the car and they pull off. A disappointed Aunt Sally just closes the door and goes back to the kitchen to finish cooking without uttering one word to YaYa. That itself made YaYa feel bad, and she grabs her stuff and leaves too. She goes to her car and sit in hope that her aunt comes out behind her but she doesn't. "I know she heard me leave. I bet if it was Ny she would have flew out here to make her stay. I'm so tired of feeling unwanted" YaYa whisper to herself as a tear falls from her right eye and No Air by Chris Brown and Jordan Sparks play on the radio. She cranks up the car and drive off crying her heart out.

♦♦♦NewSouth™♦♦♦

"Mommy can you get the door" Endy shout from the kitchen.

"I got it Auntie" Karishma runs to the door. Luella and the girls are putting the food out so they can start eating soon.

"I'm so hungry and this food looks so good especially that Mac and cheese Endy" Chynna smiles.

"Thanks cousin your potato salad look tasty too"
Endy replied.

"Y'all tell everybody to come on" Tanya told
them.

"Okay Ma I will get them" Endy goes to round
everybody up. When she reaches the living room she lets
them all know.

"Where's Jay at" she asked Reeko and J.J.

"Hell if I know! Is it time to eat yet Ma?" J.J.
asked.

"Yeah Nana said come on we about to say grace"
Endy replies going to the back toward the bathroom.

"Jay!" She yelled trying to see where he's at. He
comes out the bathroom in a rush.

"Yo what's good?"

"What's good?" Endy frowns.

"Yeah you yelling and shit" he snaps.

"Yeah I was telling your black ass to come on so we can eat" she look down at his right hand as he ends a call.

"Who were you talking to?" she questioned.

"Look it was business babe come on it's Thanksgiving. We have big things popping out here man."

"So you have to take business calls in the bathroom now?"

"Yo I'm not about to fuck up my day with this stupid shit" he said and walked away. She stands there in silence confused and unsure of why he has become so touchy when questioned about certain things.

"Endy come on!" She hears her mother call out. She pulls herself together and goes to join the rest of the family for dinner.

"Everything okay" Lisa asked her niece who seem a little agitated.

"I'm good auntie just a little hungry she grabs Patience and put her in her seat next to her. (Ding…dong...The doorbell rings).

"Lord who will come right when we about to eat" Luella jumps up.

"Oh that's probably Roc and Ny" J.J. said.

"No they supposed to come by later tonight" Endy objects.

"Nah he called and said something about Ny and YaYa almost got to scrapping at Aunt Sally crib so they were on the way here" J.J. explained.

"Why the hell didn't you say something J.J.?" Luella asked.

"I'm sorry Nana I thought they would have been here by now" he answered going to get the door.

"Why his crazy tail didn't say anything sooner?" Chynna said.

"I don't know but that damn YaYa been trouble ever since she been here" Endy shakes her head.

"Hi family sorry we late I was trying to get here as soon as I could" Rocko states coming in the dining room.

"It's okay Rocko y'all just get to the table so we can say grace and eat" Luella told them grabbing her two daughters' hands.

"Ny are you okay?" Endy asked. Niema just looks around the room and quickly runs off to the front room.

"Good let her go. She got all this mess started and then want somebody to feel sorry for her ass" Jasean groan.

"Yo you better watch it she carrying my baby and already been through some bullshit. I know you don't like it but you will respect it" Rocko defends his woman.

"Dude you won't ever get no respect from me. Y'all some file motherfuckers."

"Jasean and Rocko don't start this mess today we trying to have a nice family dinner" Chynna scream on them both.

"Man I'm not even hungry no more I'm about to be out" Jasean jumped up.

"I know your ass not about to leave your wife and daughter on Thanksgiving Day" Tanya buds in.

"Mommy I got this" Endy tells her.

"Okay baby your right that's your husband."

"So you're that disgusted with Ny that you will leave your family on one of the most important holidays just to prove a point" Endy asked with her hands on her hips.

"I'm leaving because I'm not about to sit here and argue over the person who is the root of the problem" Jasean walks to the living room. Endy follow him and grabs him by the arm.

"Are you freaking kidding me right now?"

"E I'm not about to put up a front for your friend so I'm good on Thanksgiving dinner y'all enjoy. I will see you later" Jasean quickly kiss her but she moved.

"Hell no, don't put your lips on me like this shit supposed to be okay. You been acting real funny lately and I want to know why" Endy asked him.

"Endy I'm good babe I'm just tired and I don't want to argue with you or none of your family. Let me just go" Jasean pleads.

"Go on then Jay take your ass on" Endy yelled and walk away.

"E come on don't be like that" Jasean yell to her but his words fall on death ears because she quickly disappear back in the kitchen with her family. When he gets outside to his car he has a smirk on his face. Niema see everything from the corner where she walks to get away from the drama.

"Yeah Jay I got your number just wait" Niema mumbles to herself.

Chapter 14

"Hi sweetie what the hell is going on" Ari walk up and hug Endy who she is meeting up with for the Black Friday sales Downtown, Brooklyn.

"Girl Thanksgiving was a disaster and I may be on the verge of getting a divorce honey" Endy replied.

"What? Endy what happened?" Ari asked as they to walk down a crowded Fulton Street to shop.

"Girl first of all Jay got to the house all hung-over and shit. Then Ny and Rocko ended up coming because she and YaYa almost got to fighting at Aunt Sally's. Not to mention Rocko and Jay got into it because Jay started to throw jabs at Ny and of course you know Rocko wasn't having it. Lastly Jasean ended up leaving and so did Ny and Rocko so dinner was a mess. Girl I just took Patience and went to Nana's room and cried. I don't know what the hell is going with Jay but he better put his big boy pants on and get it together because I'm not about to tolerate no bullshit. I know he has been working his ass off at the club but that was his decision to run it so he will not take his frustrations out on me" Endy responded as her voice trembled because she really just wants to just cry.

"E I know shit seems hard right now but maybe what you and Jasean need is a vacation. I mean both of y'all been working so hard that y'all are bound to get aggravated with one another. Now about Ny and YaYa what the hell went on with them two?" Ari questioned.

"Ari I don't know, we never got any details on that because everything happened so fast yesterday" Endy explains.

"Wow that was crazy but you know all this that has transpired is really going to take some getting used to for everyone involved. I really don't think that Rocko or Ny are thinking about how their decisions affect everyone else. I understand it's too late now but I really hate how all this has gone down. I love them both dearly but this is a hot ghetto mess girl" Ari laughed trying to cheer Endy up.

It works they are laughing and shopping until she had completely forgot that she was so upset a couple of hours ago.

"Let's get something to eat" Ari insisted.

"Your ass always thinking about some food and the smallest one out the bunch" Endy chuckled.

"So what I need to eat y'all bitches got booty for days and I got a bump" Ari laughs too.

The two of them decide to go to Ki Sushi on Flatbush between Prospect place and St. Marks Avenue. As they get seated and prepare to order their food who comes in the restaurant? None other than YaYa ass herself and you know she has to let them see her.

"Girl this bitch just walked in the restaurant" Endy whispers to Ari.

"Who?" Ari scrunched up her face.

"YaYa ass just walked in and she spotted us" Endy told her as YaYa makes her way over to them.

"Hi ladies how y'all doing" She gives a fake smile.

"We're good how you are doing" Endy sarcastically reply.

"Girl bye you know you don't like us it's no need to be faking" Ari says all cocky and brash.

"Ooookay... well, I wasn't trying to impose on y'all. I just wanted to speak - that's all - but let me go. I'm not trying to get in a squabble today." YaYa flings her Brazilian virgin hair she wears so well.

"SQUABBLE! Bitch it's not gonna be no squabble it's gonna be a beat down if you keep running your mouth" Ari jumps up.

"Ari chill it's not that serious boo. I was just speaking and you had to go and get all hood and shit" YaYa bucks back.

"Stop it y'all we're in a damn restaurant for goodness sake we can handle this bullshit another" Endy yells jumping between the two.

"Yeah bitch I'll see your ass again" Ari warns her but YaYa giggles, fling her hair again, and walked away.

"I don't like the bitch either but she's not even worth the air we breathe Endy laughs as they sit back in their seats. The girls continue talking and enjoying each other company until Endy phone vibrates from a text. She picks it up and look its Niema:

"Please tell me y'all didn't try to jump YaYa? She has already called me"

"Is Ny serious?" Endy is shock when she read it. "What she say?" "She just texted me saying she knows we didn't try to jump YaYa" Endy frowns. Ari just waves a dismissive hand to it.

"I'm about to text her back because why would she just not call me and she knows her cousin is crazy. Endy texted her back:

"First of all, she came in the restaurant being fake and why didn't you just call me to get the real story. Your cousin is on some bullshit and I don't have time."

Niema looks at her message and feel like Endy is being funny because she is around Ari and now she is pissed.

"No First of all if something was going on why wouldn't you call me? You call me any other time you always acting real funny style when you're around Ari and I'm sick of both of y'all bullshit"

"Yeah this bitch in her feelings and I don't have time for it. I have enough going on with my own family" Endy brush it off and put down her phone. Instead of replying and they get to arguing Endy figured she will let her cool down.

"What she say E?" Ari asked again.

"Nothing Ari let's just leave it alone her hormones are raging that's all."

"Okay I'm gonna chill out for you Endy but she come at me with some bullshit then I'm gonna give her some real naked truths about herself" Ari told her.

"Alright deal! Let's enjoy the rest of our day we can't let nonsense ruin it" Endy said digging into her shrimp and chicken Hibachi dish.

♦♦♦NewSouth™♦♦♦

"This bitch didn't answer me" Niema grunts putting her phone down on her coffee table. She gets up to get her something to eat because she has been feeling real nauseous all day. Soon as she gets in the kitchen it's a knock on her door.

"Lord as soon as I go to get me something to eat somebody wants to knock on the door." Niema stops in her tracks and turn around to go answer the door. "WHO IS IT? She yelled as she approaches the door.

"Marilyn!" Caine mother yells back.

Niema stands in her tracks stunned that Caine's mother is at her door. "Umm hold on!" Niema yelled again straighten up the living room contemplating on letting her in or not.

"Niema I just want to talk that's it I don't want to start no nonsense I just want to talk to you" Marilyn said. Niema walks slowly towards the door and open it. "Hi Ma Marilyn I was just about to grab a bite to eat" Niema shows guilt all over her face. Marilyn looks flawless as usual in her diamonds and fur. Her eyes focused straight to her stomach. She sees the little bump and reality hits that everything that's been said is true.

"How are you doing baby girl?" Marilyn breaks the silence and gives Niema a hug.

"I'm good and you come on in" Niema said not trying to show the irritation she is feeling at the moment.

"Thanks I just wanted to come by and check on you to just make sure everything was alright" Marilyn exclaims walking toward the sofa.

"I'm doing okay beside the obvious" Niema responds knowing that Marilyn came to see if she was pregnant.

"I just want to get an understanding of what is going on" Marilyn sat crossing her legs.

"Well me and Caine broke up because he got another chic pregnant. I was a dark place and I made a mistake that hurt a lot of people" Niema explained.

"Why would you do something like this? Two wrongs don't make anything right honey" Marilyn told her.

"First I don't mean any disrespect Ma. Marilyn but I didn't do anything but fall in love with a man who has been like family to me. Yes it was wrong to break up his family but as far as CJ I have no sympathy for his ass at all. I do feel terrible about all the drama it has caused everyone else" Niema firmly states.

"Baby I want you to be happy. I hate you and CJ had to end things but I do understand. I feel like you deserve a man who is going to love and respect you. I never thought he would turn out like his father but he has. So now I have to see the reenactment of what I went through in the women my son dates and believe me it hurts me to my soul that he is so hurtful and disrespectful" Marilyn voice cracks as tears fill her eyes.

"Ma please don't cry. You know I loved CJ very much but I had to let go or I was going to have a nervous breakdown. I was depressed and losing myself. So see I had to do this for me Ma" Niema voice cracks because she really loved Marilyn and didn't want to hurt her either.

"I know baby I am happy for you on the new love and baby like I said I just wish everything went a different way. Too many people got hurt and it all was all so unnecessary and could have been avoided if you and Rodney handled things a better way but it is what it is. All we can do now is pray that everyone finds peace in the situation. As far as that Taiya is concerned she dragged that boy and hoed around Brooklyn for years so she should have known eventually he was going to get tired. I love you Ny. I just want you to know that as much as I know Caine is hurt he brought on his own misery" Marilyn expressed and Niema shakes her head in agreement.

The doorbell rings in the midst of this emotional conversation. "I be right back" Niema scurry off to open the door.

"Who is it?"

"It's your man" Rocko replied back. Marilyn hears him also and immediately grabs her purse to leave.

"Hi babe" Niema gave Rocko a big hug.

"I'm just here talking to Ma Marilyn" she nervously said knowing he was about to become uncomfortable with the idea of her being there. He instantly knew this had something to do with

Caine.

"Hi Auntie! How you doing these days?"
Rocko spoke putting on a front.

"I'm doing okay considering. How are
you coming along your looking much better I see"
Marilyn puts on a fake smile.

"Yeah I'm back to myself these days.
Feeling much stronger than I had been" he replied
grabbing Niema's hand.

The room falls silent and Marilyn says
"well let me go I just wanted to check on you Ny
and make sure you're holding up okay."

"Yes and thanks for coming and talking to
me" Niema gives her a hug.

"Anytime baby girl well I got moves to make but y'all take care and keep me posted on the baby shower" Marilyn said walking toward the door.

"Okay we will do that be safe out there and we'll see you soon" Rocko responds ready for her to go so he can ask Niema what went down.

Niema locks the door and come back to the living room with a big smile. "Hi baby I'm so happy to see you right now" she cuddle beside her man.

"Everything okay ma?" he asked.

"Yeah I'm good I got a call from my cousin saying Endy and Ari tried to fight her at Ki Sushi a little while ago. I text Endy and she came at me real sideways and all I was trying to do is see what was going on. Every time me and her get on a good path Ari comes around and all hell

breaks loose" Niema expressed.

"Well I doubt if they tried to jump her.

Y'all women beef over the craziest shit" Rocko

laughed.

"No Endy just acts funny when she is

around Ari and I can't stand that shit. Me and

Ariana could never get along because she has

always been so jealous of me and Endy's

friendship."

"Look Ny I am not trying to get in y'all

little catty shit man what was up with Auntie

being here? What she wanted?" Rocko questioned

getting straight to the point. "Well you know we

talked about the whole situation. I just told her

how I felt about everything. I let her know that my

only concern is my baby getting here health. I am

trying to be stress free as possible" Niema replied.

"What about us?"

"What you mean what about us we're good? Why would you ask me that?" Niema answers agitated at his question.

"I'm just saying you keep saying all your worried about is the baby like our relationship don't matter" he stated.

"It's not that, you know I love you Roc come on now" Niema said not understanding why he is feeling some type of way.

"I just don't want motherfuckers to come filling your head with nonsense. I want all this stuff to just blow over. I got court with Taiya and still have to explain to my baby that she may be away for a while" Rocko shakes his head.

"Awe baby come here" Niema cuddle next to him as he laid his head on her shoulder.

"Ny I don't know what I'm going to do man. I just want to be happy and raise my baby girl to be the best woman she can be that's it" Rocko gripes.

"Roc you're going to do it I believe in you babe" Niema said giving him the faith he needs.

"That's why I love you Ma. You're always so optimistic that's why I know I need you on my team this is meant. I know it doesn't seem like everything is going to be good but I promise you and the baby will have nothing to worry about" Rocko kissed her.

"I know baby I know."

"So have you talked to Rocko at all since Thanksgiving and why the hell are you smoking cigarettes? You know that's not good for the baby" Keosha says.

"I know that bitch but I'm stressed to the max. I haven't talk to his ass or seen my daughter. Christmas is in a few days and I want to see her" Taiya freaks out.

"Okay damn I'm just trying to help. I will just shut my mouth and be here for moral support" Keosha snaps back.

"I'm sorry Keosha I don't mean to take this shit out on you but I just want to see my baby. I am so ready for all this shit to be over" Taiya settle down.

"I know Hun, but you got to chill this ranting and raving will only make matters worse. Just get through these last days and let God handle the rest" Keosha gives her sound advice.

"I just want to see her face at least these phone calls are wack as hell man" Taiya is frustrated when a knock comes to the door.

"Can you get that please?" Taiya plop down on the sofa. Keosha goes to answer the door being that Taiya is staying at the house and Rocko hasn't been home like that since the incident only to get his things.

"It's Lynasia, girl," Keosha announced, as they both walked back in the living room.

"Hi Pooh! How are my babies doing?" Lynasia rushed over to give Taiya a hug.

"I'm good girl just ready to see Rae that's all" Taiya shook her head.

"Well y'all bitches ready for some juice?" Lynasia asked with a devilish grin.

"What you mean bitch? What happened now?" Keosha asked

"If it's bad news girl I don't even wanna to hear it" Taiya says.

"It's juicy girl your gonna want to hear this shit honey" Lynasia jumped up dancing crazy.

"Okay, crack head, tell us what it is" Keosha is now anxious to hear.

"Okay y'all guess who was about to get jumped?" Taiya and Keosha give each other a crazy look.

"Who bitch?' Taiya demanded.

"Gurl...YaYa ass!" Lynasia spat.

"What? When? By Who?" Keosha asked.

"Gurl by Endy and Ari. They bumped into each other at Ki Sushi downtown. J.J. said Endy claims she came up being all fake and Ari put her in her place" Lynasia informs them.

"What? Those bitches always trying to be extra I'm so sick of them trying to act like they run Brooklyn or some shit" Taiya snarls.

"Girl that's not it I got more. That same day my ass ran into YaYa on Fulton Street while I was shopping. Girl she said Endy and Ari gonna have to see her and that they are some coward bitches. Then she said Endy gonna get what's coming to her because everyone that claims they love her really don't. Which I feel she is talking about Niema" Lynasia adds.

"Girl Ny always been a disloyal envious bitch over what Endy got. Endy dumb ass just don't see it" Taiya said.

"Girl it won't be long before all those bitches get what's coming for them they always thought they were better than us since we were younger. Rocko want that trash box he can have it I just want to make sure my babies straight and that's it" Taiya said disgusted.

"Yeah you're so right Tai and I admire your strength through all this. I know I haven't been here with you like I should but believe me my loyalty and love is still the same for you boo" Lynasia comforts her friend.

"I know that Nay I will never question your loyalty ever" Taiya gives them a smile.

"There it goes I been wanting to see that beautiful smile forever. Taiya is a beautiful caramel colored girl with real curly hair and a small waist and big ole booty. She has a past and ran around on Rocko for years and obviously he got tired of being played and got her back and she is regretting it like hell. She is smiling on the outside but feeling dead on the inside because she knew at one point he loved her and she had him where she wanted. She should have known sooner or later it would all come to an end.

"I know I did Roc fucked up I can admit that but why out of all women in Brooklyn he had to pick Niema's ass. And not just are they together but she is having his son I just feel so betrayed and hurt" Taiya sadly stated.

"I know baby and despite what you did this isn't right. He had a choice to leave or stay, and he chose to stay, so don't beat yourself up" Keosha told her.

"I just wish I would have appreciated him when I had him. I don't want to have to raise two kids alone and I definitely don't want them being raised around Ny if I go to prison. It's just so much I'm facing because I let my emotions get the best of me. I don't want to go to prison and have my baby in there. My mind is all over the place. I just don't know what I am going to do" Taiya's tears fell.

"We got you Tai and the babies I hope you know that" Lynasia assured her giving her a tight hug. She hate to see her friend in so much pain but it's one thing about them Hiltons' they stick together right, wrong, or indifferent. She just really want her to be prepared for what was to come of all this.

"So when do you all have court? "Keosha asks, sitting on the opposite side of her on the sofa with Lynasia.

"Girl two weeks after New Year's my lawyer asked them to give me time to spend with my family before they start the trial" Taiya replied.

"Damn Tai I just wish I was there to help you through this because them Hinton's are not going to let up. You know how much Nana loves her grandchildren especially Rocko baby I need you to get prepared for a fight because them Hinton's are going to hit hard." Lynasia explained trying to prepare her.

"So what about what she went through? And what about hurt that they caused her? I mean, it's like you're taking sides" Keosha bucks at Lynasia.

"Girl ain't anybody taking sides! I'm just keeping it real because this some serious shit. Come on she shot the man in his back, shoulder and arm. They ain't gonna just let that shit fly Keosha. I just want her to be prepared" Lynasia bucks back.

"Come on y'all I don't need us to fall apart right now. I'm gonna really need y'all to have my back and stick together. I don't have anybody so y'all please stop this bullshit" Taiya begs them.

"I'm sorry Tai I just know how ugly this mess is going to get but never question my loyalty to you girl. We go way back and I will always have your back" Lynasia gives her a hug while cutting her eye at Keosha.

"I know that and your right I have to be prepared but right now my only focus is seeing my daughter and spending time with her before this court shit even starts" Taiya tears up again.

"I know Tai hopefully he comes around before then but if he doesn't just know Rachelle knows you love her" Lynasia said trying to give her friend hope. Nothing is working she just continues to cry off and on. At the end of the day her friends are there to console her and at this time that is all she needs to hold her together.

◆◆◆NewSouth™◆◆◆

"What's going on girlie?" Endy says as she greets Chynna at door.

"I was in the neighborhood shopping so we stopped by to see y'all. Where's Patience at?" Chynna walks in Endy's house with Enrique in her arms anxious to see her baby cousin.

"She is in the room go get her it's about time for her to get up and eat anyway" Endy told her knowing she needs to get up anyway.

"Hi my handsome boy auntie misses her baby" Endy said kissing all over Enrique cheeks.

"Girl she is so beautiful and chunky man. You make me want to try again for my little girl" Chynna melts over how big and beautiful Patience has gotten.

"Girl you don't want no girl they take all your beauty from you Endy laughs. "Girl I'm here to put you up to speed first of all, when is the last time you spoke to anyone?" Chynna asked.

"I spoke to Ny about a couple of weeks ago and I talk to Roc yesterday. Why?" Endy questioned.

"Well let me say that YaYa has been going around saying you and Ari tried to jump her. Then Taiya called upsetting Nana saying that she wants to see Rae and Rocko won't let her. Then she went on to say what kind of people are we to support him with keeping Rae from her. Yeah you're looking the same way I was looking when mommy and Uncle Roc told me this bullshit" Chynna stated.

"First of all, we are not supporting shit that was the court's decision because of her mental state. Second nobody tried to jump YaYa she going around spreading that bullshit to look innocent. What happen was she come up being fake as usual knowing she doesn't like us and you know Ariana she called her ass out on it. They were about to fight and that I had nothing to do with. She just knew Ari was about to bring it to that ass that's all. You know I'm not into no punk ass jumping people crap" Endy shook her head.

She is highly upset YaYa told that lie on her and Niema is following up with her cousin bullshit. Endy loves Niema but she be damn if she's gonna keep defending herself when she know she hasn't done anything wrong.

"Girl these tricks better go on and leave us alone. We don't go out her bothering nobody unless you mess with ours. Taiya know what's good for her she better fall back with contacting Nana for real" Chynna gripes.

"I know girl we can't focus on these ho's we have to be here for our people but they will not continue to play us pussy because they will get fucked" Endy heads in the kitchen to get Patience

a bottle because she is beginning to whine.

"Girl I would never hear this small cry she

has with her fat self" Chynna said

"Leave my baby alone she not that fat"

Endy giggles. (Rin g..Ring…Chynna's phone

rings).

"Lord who is it now" she grabs her phone

off Endy's little breakfast nook.

"Lord it's my hubby calling. What's going

on, papi?" Chynna spoke into the phone.

"Nothing I just was checking on you to see

if you spoke to Endy about stuff for the wedding"

he replied.

"Not yet baby we just started getting situated she had to get this ole fat baby fed so she can stop her meowing" Chynna laughed.

"Okay well we need to make sure everyone is on board babe. We got venues and rooms to book and you know Miami gets crowded around April" Reeko says.

"I got you babe let me just get through Roc court stuff and we can get the ball rolling okay."

"Okay, ma ma. How my baby doing?"

"He is good enjoying his cousin he just keeps kissing her cheeks" Chynna giggles.

"Okay well I will see you at home later" Reeko said before hanging up.

"Okay Papi see you later love you"
Chynna said hanging up.

"I just love how he loves you and checks
on you" Endy has a sad look.

"What is going on now I thought you and
Jay was cool" Chynna's confused.

"HELL NO! He is hardly home and when
he is we are arguing or he is on the phone. I'm
about ready to call it quits on this marriage
Chynna for real for real man. This is not what I
signed up for I feel like I'm a single mother he
only gets Patience for a few minutes and then he
puts her down. He begged me to have a baby and
for what? He just sits at the club every night doing
God knows what and I'm sick of it" Endy's voice
gets high which lets Chynna know she is at the
end of her rope.

"Oh my God Endy I had no idea you were harboring all this bullshit. Fuck that you need to tell him that he needs to get his shit together or get the hell on. We know our worth and will not tolerate disrespect you know this Endy. We made this promise four years ago so don't you dare start settling for shit" Chynna snarls.

"Well you're really not gonna like this" Endy says getting Chynna full attention.

"What? What is it?"

"I'm pregnant again and I haven't told him yet. I'm eight weeks" Endy started to cry.

"Oh my goodness! Endy what are you going to do? When did you find out?"

"I found out last week when I went to get my birth control. I don't know what to do because Patience is already a lot on me" Endy exclaims.

"I know baby but you have to talk to Jay about this Endy. You have to do it fast your already two months. I will but I just want to get through the holidays and this court shit in peace and I will tell him" Endy assured her.

"Okay but please keep me posted on what's going on because you know I don't like this we are the only sister each other has" Chynna reminds her.

"I know I love you for always having my back" Endy grabs Chynna hand.

"Whatever big head well let me see what you're wearing to Ari's party tomorrow. I knew

your ass wasn't getting fat for nothing" Chynna
laughed.

"Forget you bitch my booty always been
fat" Endy shoots back laughing.

Chapter 15

The Christmas Eve party at Ari and Tylon's house is jumping and everyone is enjoying themselves drinking, eating, smoking, singing, and dancing.

"What's good girlie? Why you not drinking or dancing? You don't seem like your enjoying yourself" Ari asked.

"I'm good boo just a little tired I was up with Patience most of the night and been running all day" Endy replies.

"Well how the New Year's fashion show coming along? I know it's going to be real nice" Ari smiled trying to get a reaction out of her but Endy face is void.

"Why are you looking so down Endy? What's going on I know you like a book?" Ari questioned again with more concern.

"Nothing boo go enjoy yourself we will have plenty of time to talk I just have a lot on my mind and we have the trial next week. Just a lot going on sis that's all" Endy said trying to perk up so Ari can let it go.

"You you know that shit not going to fly with me but I will let it go for now" Ari hugs her while going off to mingle with the crowd.

Endy knows she mean it too that's one thing about Ari she will harass you until she figures out what's going on. Endy held back a lot and was there for everybody else but who was there for her. She wasn't blaming them because she knew she hid things inside and whenever they do try to pry she just play it off like they are the one that's crazy. Deep down inside she knew it was time for her to come clean with them because she knew something was going on in her marriage but she just doesn't have any proof yet. She hears some chatter in the background and when she look toward the door she see that Rocky and Niema have arrived and that was the last thing she needed was some drama with them. They head straight toward her and she doesn't know how Niema is about to act because she hasn't talk to her since the whole situation with YaYa.

"Well hello you guys" Endy spoke anyway noticing Niema had a sour look on her face.

"What's good cousin?" Rocky hugged and gave Endy a kiss on her cheek.

"What's going on Niema?" Endy spoke dryly since she didn't speak.

"What's going on E?" she replied back just as dry.

"Are we good or are we beefing?" Endy folds her arms.

"I am not up for no drama with you. I'm just trying to have a good time. We can talk about any other irrelevant shit later." Niema ignored the question and walked off.

"Yo, I don't' know what the fuck your bitch problem is but I haven't done shit to her or that mouthy ass cousin of hers" Endy spas on Rocky.

"Look I'm deadass, I don't know what the hell y'all got going on and I'm not trying to get in between y'all nonsense. Y'all need to figure that shit out. This shit petty as hell, E, for real, yo" Rocky responded.

"I don't know what the hell her problem is last time we spoke she texted me on some bullshit about me and Ari supposedly had tried to jump on YaYa which was a damn lie."

"Like I said y'all need to figure this shit out she not gonna be stressing my baby with y'all nonsense" he repeated and walked away.

"Lord I'm trying to be a different person but this cunt is pushing my buttons" Endy whispers to herself and go to find Niema.

Niema heads to the bar room where most of the guests are just eating and drinking. She sees Karishma and Asia

"Ny!" They yelled as she tries to make a break for it.

"Niema come here girl! Where are you rushing off too?" Asia yelled again.

"What's up y'all? I was just going to find Rocky" Niema spoke.

"Oh okay your glowing like hell with your pregnancy Ma!" Asia slurs because she's had a few too many drinks.

"You do look so pretty pregnant Ny" Karishma said rolling her eyes at Asia.

"Thanks you guys I don't feel like it" Niema replied.

"Well you Niema we need to talk." Niema heard the voice and realize its Endy and Ari coming up behind her.

"Okay I see I'm not going to escape y'all ass so let's do it" Niema gave up. "Come on y'all let's go up to the bedroom for some privacy" Ari said.

They all head up the back stairs so they can get this mess settled. When they reach the bedroom they thought they heard something so they all stopped in their tracks but assumes it was nothing and went on into Ari's bedroom.

"Girl you know I always loved your bedroom and this fireplace" Endy stated. "Girl this entire house is just more shit to clean and more rooms to buy shit for" Ari laughs.

Niema on the other hand, is still just quiet and ready to get this conversation over with.

"So Ny I see you're not fucking with us right about now so you mind telling us what's your beef?" Ari began.

"Let me start off by saying I don't have no beef. I do have an issue with how I am being treated by Endy all of sudden" Niema counters.

"Ny I have no beef or issue with you but I did not appreciate you accusing us of jumping your cousin without talking to us about it" Endy snapped.

"I was wrong for that but I was going to speak to you on Thanksgiving about that, but then Jay come out his mouth disrespectful. I felt like I ruined dinner by showing up and when I hadn't heard from you it just made me feel worse" Niema hurtfully expressed.

"Ny you know me and you go head to head all the time but at the end of the day I love you. I dare anybody to fuck with you especially now that you're carrying my nephew. I need us to pull together right now we all have had one hell of a year and right now we need to just be thankful that we are all still here and still friends" Ari told her. That's made Niema very emotional.

"I just feel like everything has changed because I was being selfish with my actions. I want y'all to know that I'm deeply sorry and that I thank y'all for being here with me despite my negligence in this whole situation" Niema voice shivers.

"We know you acted out of hurt babe we get that, but just don't take your frustrations out on us. We are here for you Ny you know that" Endy sits down next to Ny on the white leather love seat that is facing the fireplace in Ari's bedroom.

"I know that you guys and it didn't help that me and YaYa got into it right before I came to Nana's" Niema continued.

"What? Why?" Ari shot up from the chair.

"Girl she is just plain out jealous of me and Endy's relationship. My Aunt Sally can play that sympathy role with her ass but I will not. She is obsessed with me and Endy friendship. I apologize to y'all if I came off like I was taking her side but I really was just trying to see what was going on. She made it like y'all came at her ready to throw blows only to find out it was all a lie" Niema described the scenario she was given.

"Okay now let me tell you the real story. Girl we were minding our own damn business trying to grub. YaYa ass came over being fake as usual and you know me Ny, I'm going to speak on fake shit. So when I did she didn't like it and next thing you know we were face to face and Endy stopped it. So whatever she told you was a damn lie. I hate for someone to lie on me" Ari's livid by YaYa the lies.

"Girl it's all good I just been dealing with the fact that I'm going to be a mother soon. I do want y'all to know that I love Rocko very much. I'm in the all the way. I would never hurt him over no damn Caine" Niema assured them

"I just don't want my cousin hurt you have to understand that. I don't want y'all to be the rebounds for each other. Y'all both are fresh out of long term relationships and now we all have to adjust to it and the new baby coming and not to mention Rae. She is about to have a new brother and sister coming with no real explanation of what is going on with her mommy. It is a lot that has changed and I need you and Rodney to realize it doesn't just involve y'all. Rae is going to need some real therapy with all she been through" Endy suggested.

"I know Endy and I promise you whatever I can do to make it right I will because I should have been more mindful of my decisions" Niema agreed.

"Well Endy don't you have something you need to tell Niema" Ari pushed Endy to talk. Endy shoots her a disapproving look but Ari doesn't care.

"I was going to talk to her Ari damn."

"It's no better time than the present because we are here and we already airing shit out so she needs to be brought to speed so no one is holding anything" Ari Convinced her.

"What's going Endy?" Niema asked puzzled.

"Well I mind as well tell you since Ari done aired me out" Endy grumbles.

"Why? Is it something bad?" Niema questioned

"No it's not bad but it's not good either it's complicated" Ari chimes in.

"Ari I got this DAMN! Can I speak for myself please?" Endy freaks out.

"Okay your right I'm sorry let me shut up."

"Y'all both are scaring the hell out of me. What is going on?" Niema said anxious to know.

"Girl are you ready for this? I'M PREGNANT BITCH" Endy finally spat out.

"WHAT!" Niema replied surprised.

"Yes girl twelve weeks. I'm not happy about it" Endy has a crushed look on her face.

"Why E this might be your boy?" Niema tried to make her see the bright side of it.

"Girl…boy or not, me and Jay are just not in a great place right now. I'm already worn out with Patience. I just don't think we need to have another baby until I know where our marriage stands" Endy stated her concern.

"Girl I'm so sorry I thought y'all were doing great and here I am being selfish thinking of myself. I'm so sorry E" Niema gave her friend a tight embrace.

"It's all good sis this is why I sort of was falling back because I have been going through hell too. It was nothing against you but with all that's been going on with everyone I just didn't want to burden y'all with my problems" Endy said with all sincerity.

"And just to set the record straight I just found out myself. Please don't think it's nothing against you Ny. You know this bitch will suffer in silence in a minute" Ari chuckles.

The door opened and in comes Chynna and Egypt. "What are y'all doing up here? Having a sentimental session because if so why wasn't I invited" Chynna questioned.

"No girl I was telling Ny about my dilemma with Jay and being pregnant again" Endy replied.

"Well you're pregnant by your husband who loves you very much so what's the dilemma might I ask" Egypt said sarcastically.

"Honey it's a lot you don't know and this isn't the time to talk about it. Ny and I been having communication problems and we're just chopping it up to get some clarity on what's really going on with us that's all."

"Well y'all asses are wearing me out with y'all emotional mess just kiss, make up and let's enjoy this beautiful party I am having downstairs" Ari shouts.

"Yeah let's go because I can definitely use another drink well I guess we have two Prego women now" Egypt smiled.

"Yeah I guess so" Endy replied not too sure.

"Well yes ladies we have a lot to celebrate" Chynna adds as they all head out the room to go downstairs and join the others at the party.

◆◆◆NewSouth™◆◆◆

"Taiya I really wish you would chill with the pacing you're making me nervous" Keosha complained as Taiya impatiently paced the floor.

"Lynasia should have been here hours ago. I need to know where my baby girl is going to be tonight. I'm pissed these bastards won't let me see my child for Christmas" Taiya groans.

"Taiya you have to calm down you're going to make that baby nerves bad as hell. I'm telling you stop and let the shit play out" Keosha forewarns her.

"Fuck it then they won't let me see her no way. Maybe I need to go crazy on these bitches so they know I'm not playing with them about my damn child."

"Girl you do that and you're going to regret it. Now I know your upset but you have to think clearly right now Tai don't lose your baby over a nothing ass nigga. Your beautiful get over this court shit, have your baby, and move the fuck on. Don't let this dude tear you down believe me I know how your feeling right now but don't let it break you. I know I'm the last one to talk but I'm maturing now I have my baby girl to look after. I can't let these dudes and these streets take me away from her" Keosha communicates some realness to her.

Taiya seems to finally get a little calmer (Ding…Dong.. the doorbell rings)

"Can you get that for me?" Taiya asked Keosha as she snuggled on the couch with her favorite throw cover watching *This Christmas* with Loretta Devine and Chris Brown. When Keosha opens the door, she is pleasantly surprised.

"What's up y'all it's been a long time?" Taiya heard the familiar voice and turns around to see her other bestie Tiffany. She is the one of the other dancers who messed with Jasean before until her and Endy had a run in. She left town to get herself together and off the pole. The three women along with Lynasia met at the strip club and even though they tried to get it together that life follow them.

"Oh my God when you get here?" Keosha hugged her so tight.

"Oh my goodness" Taiya jumped up running to hug her too.

"Girl I said y'all tail was going to be surprised" Tiffany chuckled.

"Yes I am girl but I must say I'm happy for you to be here I need all the support I can get right now" Taiya stated sadly.

"I heard some of what's going on from Lynasia. Now what is this I hear that Niema and Rocko are messing around?" Tiffany is outraged.

"Yes girl and she's pregnant by him too. He had the nerve to tell me that he wants to be with her and he will continue taking care of the kids" Taiya voice trembled.

"Gurl…Are you freaking serious right now? As much as them bitches called us ho's and sluts she did that?" Tiffany's confused by all the tea she is getting from her girls.

"I was so hurt and pissed off at the fact this jerk cheated on me with her and then got her pregnant on top of that. I just snapped Tiff and when he came to get his shit to move out I shot him. I should have just let his ass go" Taiya's remorseful.

"Awe baby girl I'm so sorry all this has happened to you. So what you can't see Rachelle at all?" Tiffany asked.

"Girl he put a restraining order on her and they granted him custody because they are saying Rachelle could have gotten hurt" Keosha further explains.

"Well where Lynasia stands in all this because I know she loves J.J. and she also loves you" Tiffany questioned because she see this is a very sticky situation.

"Girl I feel like she's playing both sides and soon it's going to be a blow up between everyone. I know she can't go against J.J. family I understand that but she can at least tell them to let her see her child tomorrow is Christmas day she hasn't seen her in over three months" Keosha spazzed.

"Although I understand her not picking sides, she still should tell them how she feels. They are basically like her family now so we have to understand she is not going to say too much to keep the peace in her household. But Gurl…all the shit them bitches talked about us stripping and being ho's and now Niema is the one being a whore. I'm just really lost for words right now because they always play like they're higher than somebody else" Tiffany complained frustrated by the whole ordeal.

"Exactly come the only difference is us and them we got paid for our hoeing" Keosha laughed.

"Y'all bitches sick so what are we doing to bring in Christmas tonight because it's already ten o'clock" Tiffany gets off the subject.

"I'm just glad y'all are here with me because I don't know what I was going to do if I had to be here alone with a house arrest bracelet on" Taiya told her friends.

"Honey we are here through thick and thin. We been down together since day one and even though we would like Lynasia here we have to understand she has a life and a family now. So we are going to enjoy our time together and hopefully she finds time to come by tomorrow. I think she will because she knows I'm here. So snap out of this somber mood and let's enjoy the moment we only live once" Tiffany demands her friends.

Right away Keosha goes in the kitchen to bring them some hot chocolate, Tiffany whips up some snacks, and Taiya puts on some music. The girls changed the setting which changed their moods and they brought in Christmas laughing and enjoying each other. It made Taiya forget about all her troubles and enjoy the holiday cheer for a few.

♦♦♦NewSouth™♦♦♦

"Look, please let that girl see her baby it's Christmas for God's sake Rocko. Don't do something that you will regret later" Luella begged her grandson.

"Nana I'm not letting her go over there with that crazy chic. If my baby gets there and she tries some bullshit then I am going to regret it and I'm definitely going to jail. She already has been texting crazy shit she doesn't care about the law, restraining order or anything" Rocko counters back.

"Okay well how about I take her over there and make you a promise to get her back here in one piece. She just wants to see her child it's Christmas Rodney come on" Luella tried to plead with him.

"Ma I just don't trust it Taiya is out of control right now. Come on you forgot about me being shot and Ari tires being slashed!" he states getting Rachelle presents set up before he wakes Rachelle up.

"I don't remember all that being her fault Rodney Hinton. Now do this for me, let that girl see her baby at least for a few minutes. I promise I will take her and sit there the whole time but don't make Rachelle suffer she miss her mother baby."

When Rocko seen the unhappy look on his grandmother's face he knew he had to make a decision because he couldn't take her being mad at him right now. "Okay Ma I'm going to do this for you because I love you. I don't like seeing you sad on the holidays but the first time she try some crazy mess please leave and I'm cutting her off completely from my daughter. And when my other daughter born, I'm taking her too" Rocko warns her.

"Oh baby thanks you so much for trusting me. I promise I will get her there and back safe and sound. You know we all love these babies the last thing we will do is let something happen to that baby come on you know she is just like my child because I raised you."

"I know Ma I just don't want anything to happen to my daughters despite everything I love my kids."

"Baby I know you do but please don't make Rachelle grow up resenting you for not letting her see her mommy" Luella tried to get him to understand it will only make her resent him.

"Okay it's on you Ma I told you I am trusting y'all with my child but the first time she try to act crazy Rae is not going back to see her ass again" Rocko said storming away upset.

Luella understood his anger completely but she also knew her grandson brought some of this on himself and the child shouldn't suffer. As much as she disliked Taiya, she wasn't about to let that little girl miss seeing her mother on Christmas day. Luella went upstairs to the room where he is talking to Rachelle to let her know that she was about to go see her mother for a little while but she couldn't stay.

"Daddy is you coming to see Mommy?" Rachelle sadly asked staring up at Rocko with those big beautiful brown eyes.
"No Daddy not coming Nana gonna take you to see Mommy. I will see you when you get back here later. So let's go see what Santa brought you" Rocko smiled ready for Rachelle to open her gifts.

"Okay Daddy" she gave him a tight hug and raced downstairs.

"Please watch my baby girl and you be careful too, I don't trust her" he hugs Luella and walked out the room clearly upset. Deep down he knew she was right.

"Boy you don't know if you want to call me Ma or Nana do you" Luella laughed.

"Yo, you're both to me" he laughed too.

They let Rachelle play with her thing for about an hour and then Luella got her prepared to go. "Okay baby you ready to go?"

"Yes Nana" she replied and they head downstairs to leave.

As they walk to the car Rocko race to the window and as he seen them getting in the car to leave. He then saw Niema pulled up just as Luella pulled off with Rachelle. She doesn't quite know what's going on but she knows her boo called her pretty upset. She gets out walking toward the house when someone pulls up and beeps the horn at her. She look back and see it's Karishma.

"What's up girl? Where Nana headed?"

"She just pulled off as I was coming up. Roc called me sounding upset" Niema told her as they both walk to the door.

"I wonder what's going on I know Nana said she was about to step out for a minute but she didn't say where or why" Karishma says holding a pan of chicken her mom Karim made. They proceed to knock on the door and Rocko buzz them in.

"Roc where you at?" Karishma yelled upstairs.

"I'm in the kitchen" he hollered back.

"What's going on babe?" Niema asked giving him a kiss.

"Babe I'm just kind of worried right now" he replies pacing the floor. "Worried about what?" Karishma asks seeing how bothered he seems to be.

"Yeah Bae what's going on?" Niema asked again.

"Nana took my baby to see that stupid bitch Taiya over Ms. Lorraine house. I just don't trust that bitch she is really disturbed and nobody see it but me. Come on she shot me then been

texting me stupid bipolar shit" he shouts filled
with anger.

"Roc you got to chill Nana isn't gonna let
nothing happen to her you know that. You bet
believe she went over there prepared" Karishma
said confident that her Nana had her .38 on her.
She just wants him to cool him down.

"You know Nana always packing, she
better not play we all know better" Niema giggles
rub his back and shoulders trying to relax him also

"I'm telling she does one more thing and
my ass is going to jail. Especially messing with
my daughter"

"Oh you gonna leave me and your kids out
here. Rocko you gots to chill the hell out we don't
need no more nonsense right now" Niema snarled.

He looks at her seeing that she's serious and gives her a hug. Karishma just stands there smiling at the two of them wondering why they never just got together in the first place.

"Hello everyone" Endy spoke loudly as she enters the house.

"Endy we're in the kitchen" Karishma responded back.

Endy walks in the kitchen and feels the energy is off.

"What's going on why everybody looks so down?" Endy asked.

"Nana and Rae went to see Taiya over her mom's house and I just don't want her crazy ass trying nothing stupid" Rocko explained bringing Endy up to speed with the situation.

"Why would Nana do that she knows that bitch is unstable?

"What did Nana do?" Chynna asks, walking in with grocery bags filled with things for the dinner.

"She took Rae to see Taiya at Ms. Lorraine house by herself" Endy answered her pissed that her grandmother would do that and to go alone too.

"What! Why would she want to do that? Did Taiya call her or something?" Chynna questioned.

"No Rae has been saying she wants her Mommy and was she going to see her for Christmas so you know Ma she felt bad and begged me to let her go over there for a few and promised to stay there with him and bring her

back" Rocko explained.

"Fuck that she doesn't deserve to see her.

With all the shenanigans she has pulled and

calling being disrespectful I'm surprised Nana

would do that" Chynna's upset now.

"Well let's just start getting some of this

food together because Aunt Tanya, Aunt Lisa,

Uncle Roc, my mom and dad are on their way"

Karishma advised them.

"Yeah let's do that maybe by the time

everything gets situated Nana and Rae will be

back" Endy agrees.

Everybody starts going to work in the

kitchen mixing and cutting, slicing and dicing,

laughing and talking and the mood soften. Rocko

was enjoying this time with the family but best believe he has his daughter on his mind.

◆◆◆NewSouth™◆◆◆

Luella is hesitant about knocking on Lorraine's door who lived in Linden Projects but she knows this is all for her great grandbaby. (Da, da, da…she knocks).

"Who is it?" she hears Lorraine yell.

"It's me Luella."

"LUELLA" she responded.

"Yes Lorraine it's me Luella Hinton." She hears the door unlock and when Lorraine see Rachelle with her the look on her face is priceless.

"Oh goodness Shelly! Me Me's baby is here" Rachelle runs and hugged her grandma so tight and that just warmed Luella's heart. Lorraine calls her grandbaby Shelly since she was a baby.

"Taiya come here somebody is here to see you" Lorraine yelled down the hallway.

"Who is it Mommy I don't want to see nobody today" a very pregnant Taiya came around the corner. When she seen it was her baby girl, her eyes lit up and filled with tears instantly.

"Oh my God, my baby is here!" She shouts and Rachelle raced right to her mommy. Luella gives a slight grin and Lorraine asked her to come in. The four of them go to the living room to sit down and Luella felt out of place but she knew that baby needed to see her mother.

"Where was you at mommy? I wanted to see you Daddy said you were sick but when you

got better I could come" Rachelle said smiling so
hard.

"Mommy was but I'm getting better your
sister will be here soon" Taiya grabbed Rachelle
hand and put it on her belly.

"I'm having a baby brother too!" She said
to Taiya.

"Who cares?" "Taiya shouts which startled
Rachelle.

"Taiya are you crazy? Don't do that"
Luella raised up off the sofa.

"Hold on please Luella sit down.
Rachelle? Mommy didn't mean that okay"
Lorraine told her shooting Taiya a mean look
while grabbing Rachelle by the hand.

"Baby girl, let's go to Grandma Room so you can watch TV okay" Lorraine took her to the bedroom and comes back.

"Okay Taiya I understand you being upset but it's that behavior that's makes Roc not want her over here now. I'm trying to be compassionate and help you but I can't if you keep having these outbursts and scaring her" Luella explains.

"She's right Taiya you need to learn to hold your temper because she didn't have to bring her here at all" Lorraine agrees.

"What? Your taking their side Mommy is you fucking serious? This man got another bitch pregnant, leaves me and I'm supposed to hold my tongue" Taiya sobs loudly.

"Baby calm down you're going to have that baby nerves messed up" her mother tells her.

"You know what fuck this baby. I don't
care if this baby live or die. He broke my heart
Mommy and you're taking their side" she stormed
out the door.

"Taiya did you forget you shot this
woman's grandson and she is willing to forgive
you and let you see your daughter. You have to
take responsibility for your actions Tai" her mom
pleads with her.

"Rachelle come on baby I'm gonna go
now I didn't want to cause any chaos. I just
thought it was only right she see her daughter for
Christmas but I see this was a big mistake" Luella
said grabbing her Alexander McQueen leather and
suede coat with the purse to match that Rocko got
her for Christmas.

"I'm sorry for all this Luella but I do thank you for coming by and bringing Shelly to see us" Lorraine hugged Luella.

"I know she's upset and I can't say I blame her but if she doesn't calm down Roc will not let Rachelle come near her. Please try getting her to calm down" Luella begged Lorraine.

"I will and thanks again:"

"Me Me, when can I stay with you and mommy?"

With tears in her eyes Lorraine squat down to her grandbaby and said "Baby you will be coming soon okay. Go enjoy all your presents and I hope you enjoy all the things we got you too" Lorraine lips quiver as tears streamed her face.

"Me Me, where's my mommy? I want to tell her bye" Rachelle sadly asked.

"I will tell her bye for you okay. I'm gonna walk y'all downstairs" Lorraine kissed Rachelle forehead and close the door to walk them outside the building. When they reach the front of the building just as Luella was about to walk away a distressed Taiya ran up to her holding a gun.

"Taiya are you fucking crazy put that damn gun down this is not the way to go" Lorraine screamed seeing a dark look in Taiya eyes.

"Taiya put the gun down your baby is right here please don't do this in front of her" Luella pleaded and begged.

"Fuck that y'all done turned her against me telling her she has a brother coming erasing me from her life" Taiya cried shaking and holding the .380 caliber handgun that's her mother's.

"Taiya you must be crazy because you're out here in broad daylight holding a gun to your daughter's grandmother. Put the damn gun down" Lorraine yelled again.

"Please baby, don't make matters worse put the damn gun down" Luella begged her again says just inches away from her own pistol in her purse.

"Mommy stop it put it down!" Rachelle cried out to Taiya. Lorraine has enough and charge full speed at Taiya, but when she does Taiya spot Luella picking up Rachelle trying to make a run for it. "NO! DON'T TAKE MY

BABY!" Taiya yelled, as her mother wrestled her for the gun.

"BOOM BOOM" the gun goes off twice. "MOMMY NO!"

Chapter 16

Well everyone is gathered at Brookdale hospital on Christmas day instead of enjoying family. Taiya did shoot herself in the arm and the foot, and grazed her mother's foot but thank God it could have been much worse. The main concern is that the baby is okay. They have police and detectives at the hospital and the family is full of emotion right now.

"Ma this is exactly why I didn't want you to take my daughter over there look at this shit now. Her ass is definitely going to jail this time. This bitch really playing us like some bitches" Rocko screams punching the wall.

"Look you all are going to have to calm down" a little black nurse says.

"Fuck this shit I'm gone. I don't have time for this bullshit. This bitch around her pulling guns and these pigs better take her ass to jail. I'm outta here, Nana" Rocko said grabbing Rachelle from Luella.

"No you're going to sit your ass down and make sure your daughter is okay first. I understand that your upset but we can't just leave like this. We have to make sure that baby inside her is okay too' Luella reminds him.

"Nana you should have known her unstable ass was gonna pull some bullshit. She is still bitter behind the break up and the fact that Rocko has another baby coming. A boy and he's having it with Ny so I don't know if it was the best time to have family meetings" Endy advised her

"Endyia don't raise your voice at me. I said I did it for Rachelle that's still her mother at the end of the day. I didn't think the Ho was this crazy but like I said we are gonna make sure this baby is okay because that's still our blood at the end of the day" Luella walked up pointing sternly in her granddaughter's face.

"I'm sorry Nana but that bitch is gonna feel me. I'm so done with this chic she has caused so much ruckus with the family. I told Rocko a long time ago to leave her ass alone and now look at this mess. She's been cheating on him the whole entire relationship and now she wants to play this victim I'm tired Nana. I'm just fed up she's gonna catch it" Endy said very weary at this point.

We are gonna take a walk Nana call us if anything changes" Chynna grabs her purse to walk with Endy.

"Okay sweetie go calm her down please. You know Endyia is crazy" Luella told her.

Chynna grabs Endy by the hand "let's take a walk, ma ma." The girls walk so they can talk.

"I know your angry E hell I am too I want to beat her ass until I'm tired, but we got to make sure the baby is okay. For Roc and Rae not that bitch" Chynna's told her wrapping her arms around Endy's shoulder. Rocko and Endy are very close like sister and brother.

"What is it gonna take for this chic to disappear Chynna ever since Rocko started dealing with her it's been problems I hate him and

Ny did what they did, but I'm so glad it got his ass away from her" Endy gave a sigh of relief.

"I'm glad he's going to have custody of the babies. This shit with Ny still don't sit well with me I don't want her to hurt my cousin. One thing I will always commend him on and that's being a good father" Chynna replied.

"Thank God because if Rachelle has to depend on her she is going to be one messed up little girl. I told that dude to watch where he plant seeds" Endy shook her head.

(Chynna phone rings…she instantly picked up) "The doctor just came to let us know that Taiya and the baby are okay and so is Ms. Lorraine" Karishma said.

"Okay that's good news we are on our way back up then" Chynna tells her and hang up the phone.

"That was Rizzy she said Taiya and her mom is okay and they said the baby is safe let's head back up there. Then Chynna ask Endy something she wanted to ask all night "by the way where is Jay at? I haven't seen him all day" Chynna's curious as to why he is not there with Endy. He usually is by her side with she is stressing so it's just strange he's been M.I.A. lately.

"I don't know and I don't care" Endy brush off the question.

The two of them both make it to the waiting room where they see all the family getting prepared to leave. "Are you okay Roc?" Endy asked her cousin who is seemingly distraught by the current situation.

"I'm good Cuzzo just ready to get my baby girl home and in the bed" he dryly responded.

"Aren't you going to Nana's?" Chynna asked him.

"Nah, I'm going to Ny's. Auntie and them going over there with her" he told them putting on Rachelle coat who finally fell asleep completely shaken up about the whole ordeal. She just saw her mother pull a gun on her great grandmother and shoots herself and her grandma.

"Okay well I have to go get Patience from Ma Evelyn. Rocko please be careful and get some rest. Don't stress yourself too much okay" Endy hugs him tight.

"I won't I just want all this shit to be over and her ass go ahead to prison where she belongs. Now I have to explain this shit to my daughter" he gripes.

"I know baby but God will take care of it all I just thought I was doing what was right" Luella palms his face with tears streaming her face.

"It's not your fault Ma I know you were only doing what's right for her" He said holding Rachelle in his arms.

"I just didn't think she would go this far baby! I really didn't!" Luella cried and anger swept the whole room.

"I'm going to file papers for full custody of my kids Nana I can't trust her ass. She goes too far" he announced.

"I won't fight you on it no more. Their your children and if you feel it's best they be with you then I have your back" she hugged him.

"I pulled the car around Mommy" Rodney (Rocko's dad) told her.

"Okay well y'all be careful go home and get some sleep we will all get together tomorrow and have dinner. Today has been overwhelming for us all" Luella advised the rest of her grandchildren. Everyone said their goodbyes and head home.

♦♦♦NewSouth™♦♦♦

Taiya just lies in the hospital bed staring out the window wondering how fast her life has turned upside down. She is at the point if she's going to lose her babies by going to prison then she doesn't care about anything else. Rocko has hurt her and she wanted to do all she could to hurt him back.

"Ms. Martin, are ju okay?" The little Hispanic nurse asks but Taiya just sits there in silence as a police officer stood outside her room door. She knew she was wrong but the heartbreak she was feeling has her over the edge.

"Well, if ju need me, just give a buzz" the nurse says, as she exits the room.

"Hello!" a voice says that enters the room. Taiya turns around to see that it's Tiffany and Lynasia with flowers and balloons. She looks them over and turns on her side with her back facing them. A look of confusion sweep across the women face.

"Tai we are only here because we love you. We're not here to argue or judge you baby girl. We simply just want you to know that we are here" Tiffany says rubbing her shoulder as she continues to lay in silence.

"Your Mommy is doing good she is getting discharged and ready to see how you're doing" Lynasia adds.

"Baby the nurse said you haven't eaten and that's not good for the baby. Please just eat something" Tiffany begs but Taiya doesn't' budge not one bit.

"I know so much is going through your head right now but baby you have to stop taking matters in your own hands because all it does is turn into more mayhem" Lynasia continued talking walking over to the other side of the bed to face her.

"Nay we are supposed to be trying to make her feel better not worse" Tiffany snarls.

"I understand that Tiffany but she has to understand she can't continue to keep fighting fire with fire sometimes she has to let karma come at it's own pace" Lynasia groans back.

"Oaky we are here as her friends so why don't you try doing that and stop riding the damn fence" Tiffany shouts.

"Would y'all both just shut the hell up because y'all can leave? I didn't' ask y'all to come here" Taiya sat straight up in the bed and shouts at them.

"Well first of all, nobody is riding a damn fence because if so I wouldn't be here right now. I just want to make sure your hateful ass is okay but you're taking your frustrations out on us and it's not fair. I have been here since all this mess started so don't play me like I'm riding no motherfucking fence Tiffany" Lynasia shouts back.

"Well you're the one talking about what she should and shouldn't have done. It is what it is and what's done is done. She can't do shit about it now" Tiffany said.

"Look both of y'all bitches just leave I just want to be left alone" Taiya tells them.

"See what I mean she is so ungrateful despite how my man is feeling about you right now I still manage to support your black ass and this is how you treat me" Lynasia walked over grabbing her coat and purse.

"Nay don't leave you know she is not in her right mind and on meds why would you take to heart anything she is saying right now" Tiffany question her.

"Look I'm sick of pacifying a grown ass woman. Now she has court in less than two weeks and not to mention when she leaves here she's going to jail for possession of a firearm. Then lastly she has two babies she needs to be thinking about right now it's not just about her Tiff" Lynasia yelled before storming out the room.

"Nay don't leave! NAY!" but Lynasia have already turnt the corner and headed to the elevators.

"Ju okay, Ms. Marten" the Hispanic nurse came back because she heard the commotion with the cop right behind her.

"Yeah everything is fine her and our other friend was arguing" Tiffany explained.

"Fuck her she's not my friend" Taiya laid
back down still pissed off.

"Ju mum is coming now" the nurse says.

"Thanks for letting us know and nurse…."
Tiffany replied looking for her name tag.

"Oh, Ms. Perez, can you please bring
some ginger ale and crackers for her?" Tiffany
asked making herself comfortable despite Taiya
making it clear she doesn't want them there.

"There goes my baby" Lorraine entered
the room with crutches. Taiya looked at her mom
and her eyes fill with tears because she knows it's
all behind what she has done.

"Taiya I'm good baby don't cry Mommy a
trooper you can't get rid of me that easy."

Lorraine jokes not wanting Taiya to feel worse than she already does.

"Hi Mommy you okay" Tiffany stands up so she can sit in the recliner chair.

"I'm great baby I was worried about my babies more though" Lorraine exclaims smiling at her daughter who she see is so broken.

"Baby girl how are you holding up in here?"

"I'm okay Ma I want to see Rae so bad but I know that is not happening right about now" Taiya cried.

"Baby I know your hurt but you have to find peace in this situation before you kill someone or hurt yourself or even the baby. I don't know what pushed you over the edge but I thought it was very sweet of Luella to bring

Rachelle over even with Rocko saying no"

Lorraine explained to her daughter.

"Mommy I'm tired. I give up. I no longer

have any more fight in me. I have to go right back

to jail when I leave here because I let my

emotions outweigh my rational thinking. I brought

all this on myself. I cheated on Roc ever since we

been together and I got too comfortable. In the

end, he got tired and moved on and I just can't

handle it especially since it's Ny out of all people"

Taiya cried harder.

"I know baby and yes you have done him

wrong in the past but nobody deserves this"

Lorraine holds her.

"No Ma Lynasia is right y'all can't pacify

me be real I fucked up and I guess karma came

back to bite me in the ass. That's the thing when it

comes you never know in which form it will show up" Taiya sobs so loud. Lorraine walks over to the other side of the bed and sit next to her daughter.

"I know baby but Mommy is here and I'm not going anywhere" Lorraine assures her hugging her daughter.

"Mommy please promise me one thing"

"What's that baby? Just say it and it's done" Lorraine told her

"That you will make sure you see the girls as much as you can and make sure they know who I am" Taiya laid her head on her mom and lets out a loud cry.

The officer rush in but when he see how Lorraine shoot him a mean look and see she's crying he eased back out and closed the door.

"I promise baby."

◆◆◆NewSouth™◆◆◆

"Endy what's going on with you babe?"
Egypt asked her cousin who seems more quiet
than usual.

"Girl I can't believe the year we have had
and I'm so ready for it to be the New Year" she
replied.

"I feel you on that our family has had
some crazy ass up and downs I will tell you that"
Egypt chuckles which made Endy smile.

"You know what though I'm happy for Ny
and Rocko because they seem genuinely happy
together. I think once all the court stuff over and
the babies get here they will figure it out. We all

know Niema Mason is a strong woman" Egypt adds.

"Yeah I'm not too fond of how it came about but I'm ready to meet the little Prince and spoil him something terrible" Endy tried to look on the bright side.

"What y'all out here talking about?" Asia walks in the kitchen.

"What's going on with you and Jasean y'all seem so distant" Egypt questions.

"Girl we are not in the best space right now and I had something I wanted to talk to the family about when we all got together but Hurricane Taiya happen yet again" Endy her head.

"What is it?" Asia chimes in.

"None of your business nosey I will tell everyone together" Endy snaps.

"Okay, Okay you don't have to get stink about it. I was just concerned" Asia gave a sarcastic look.

"Well Nana wants all of us to come in the family room right now she said" Asia told them grabbing a piece of upside down Pineapple cake Luella made.

"Your ass always eating and don't gain a damn pound" Egypt laughs. They all head to the family room where the rest of the family is at.

"I need you girls to sit down because I have something to say and I don't want to have to repeat it" Luella informed them.

"So do you want us to leave Nana" James

asked.

"You can leave or stay it really don't

matter but this is the only time I think I got all the

women in my family under one roof so I need to

say this now" Luella stated them. Endy and

Chynna has a concern look on their faces.

"Babies don't worry it's nothing bad it's

just something I need for all y'all to do" Luella

assures them.

"Mommy is everything okay?" Tanya asks

her mother. Luella just sits quiet and waits for

every one of her granddaughters to have a seat.

"Now I'm glad you all here because we

need to get some peace with everything going on.

Now I remember a time when we were all close

but somewhere down the line we got distant and

started arguing and fighting each other. I don't know what's going on but I refuse to the let the devil take my family. I need all of you to start coming together and being there for each other. I mean it Rocko is going to need us to be strong when he goes to court so all this bickering and mess you girls got going on I want it to stop. We need to start being open with each other and stop holding secrets because all it does is destroy us. If we have something to say then we need to say it, deal with it, and move on" Luella express concern to her family.

"Well I have something to say" Endy stands up. Chynna gives her a look like, what are you doing?

"What is it baby? What do you have to say?" Tanya asked her daughter.

"Well everybody should know that I am three months pregnant and Jasean doesn't know yet" Endy blurts out.

"What? Oh my God Endyia! Why haven't you said anything sooner?" Luella face lit up.

"It's just been so much going on and I didn't know what I was gonna do."

"What the hell you mean you didn't know what you were going to do" Tanya shot up off the loveseat.

"I'm just saying Mommy, me and Jay haven't been really getting along. I just don't want to be stuck with two kids on my own" Endy face saddens.

"Baby I don't see Jasean leaving you with two kids" Tanya walked over to hug her daughter.

(Da…Da...Da…Da…There's a knock at the door). Karishma race to the door to look and see who it is

"It's Jasean" she turns to tell them.

"Well open the door child" Luella whispers ready to face her grandson in law. Karishma opens the door and gives him a quick hug.

"What's going on family? I figured I would find my wife here" Jasean jokes but he see the room full of women seems kind of tense.

"What did I just walk into?" he frowns.

"Nothing much but I do think you and your wife need to talk" Tanya sternly stated with her hands on her hips.

"What you talking about Ma I talk to my

wife everyday" Jasean looks at Endy.

"Well obviously y'all not talking enough"

she shoots back.

"Yo E what's going on" he turned to her.

"We'll talk when we get home Jay" she

murmurs.

"No you need to tell him right here right

now" Tanya advise her.

"Tanya let her handle it the way she see fit

stop trying to run her life. This is the reason why

she pushes everyone away" Luella hollered at her

daughter frustrated with her pushiness toward

Endy.

"Aunt Tanya is right Grandma would you please just let queen Endy do this so we all can have some peace" Asia sarcastically intervenes.

"Bitch you better shut the hell up before I put my hands on you" Endy scream at Asia.

"I wish you would put your hands on me you better worry about why your man out all times of the night" Asia shoots back.

"You li'l Bitch" Endy charges her.

"Endy No" Luella shouts while Tanya, Chynna, and Egypt jump between the two.

"E what the hell is going on Ma" Jasean grabs his distraught wife.

"I'M PREGNANT DAMN IT! Now are y'all happy it's out there you go.

Everyone in the room just stare at her because she is the one who is always so strong so to see her break down is very shocking to the family.

"Baby that's why you been so ill with me" Jasean tries to comfort her.

"FUCK YOU JAY YOU DON'T GIVE A DAMN ABOUT ME!" she grabs her purse and dash out the door.

"I will go check on her Jay. Asia you know what, your mouth is gonna get your ass in trouble" Egypt tells her sister. Asia just looks at how disappointed her family looks at her but she was just tired of everyone treating Endy like she was special.

"I'm sorry okay."

"Y'all should have just let her do what she wanted to do at her own pace damn" Keisha jumps up.

"I just want her to feel comfortable talking to us we're her family. She needs to know she can come to us about anything" Tanya explained why she intervened.

"I understand that sis but sometimes you have to let her be" Karim hugs Tanya who is clearly upset.

"I know you meant well sis but you know Endyia is independent and likes to hand things on her own" Keisha says also walking over to join her sisters.

"I just don't like seeing her this upset the family is going through so much right now I just want us to stick together that's all" Tanya expressed sadly.

"I know sis but you have to let it be, what's going to be, these girls are grown now. We can't tell them how to live their lives any more our jobs are done. All we can do is be there as their mothers and support them" Keisha adds.

Egypt enters back in the house and shoots Jasean a very sad look.

"How she doing Egypt I want to go talk to her" Jasean has a distress look on his face.

"Yeah Jay please go talk to your wife she needs to know that you're here for her?" Keisha persuades him.

"I know Auntie I love Endy she knows that. Nothing comes before her and Patience." He heads to the door to go check on her.

Luella and Asia comes back to the Living room from talking.

"Where is Endyia?" Luella asks.

"She is outside Jay went out there to talk to her. Hopefully some sense can be made of this whole mess. I don't want Endy to even think about getting rid of her baby" Tanya said.

"She's not auntie I know my mouth is terrible but I love my cousin and I want to apologize to all of you for this we already have enough going on with Taiya and Rocko situation" Asia is feeling bad for her actions.

"Aye I don't know what the hell is going on with you and Endy but you better get that shit together and start being supportive of your cousin" Keisha walked up pointing her finger in Asia's face.

"I know Mommy I said I'm sorry" Asia tears up.

"I don't know what's going on. I do know I want to have a conversation with Jasean because if he is up to some file shit I'm going to find out and if it's true he will have a whole lot to deal with because Endy has put too much on hold for his ass" Chynna forewarns her family.

"Hell yeah he will have a lot to deal with because I told him if he wasn't ready then don't pursue her when he pulled his last unfaithful act" Tanya joined in.

"Look this is Endy's life we can't go involving ourselves I said let her handle it" Luella shouts fed up with her family.

The door opens and the room quickly gets quiet. It's Endy but she's alone "are you okay?" Tanya walks over and grabs her daughter hand.

"Yeah I'm good, I'm sorry Ma I didn't mean to come off disrespectful" Endy apologizes.

"I know baby but if your butt wasn't pregnant I would have slapped the shit out of you. Where is Jay at anyway?" Tanya laughs.

"He had to shoot to the house and change clothes for work," Endy tells them and everyone just looks at each other.

"We just want you to know we are here for you cousin whatever you decide but you have to stop holding shit in. Call us just like you did with Niema I know that's your best friend but we are your friends too" Egypt grills her.

"I know that I just hate to burden y'all with my problems but from now on I will open up more. I just wish I could beat Taiya's ass for pointing a gun at my grandmother. I'm just frustrated on so many level y'all" Endy admits to the family.

"I know Endy but we have to do shit right we can't be messing up the case for Roc" Chynna replied.

"Well if we all start being open and honest with each other then we wouldn't feel the need to hide things from each point taken, Mommy could of told us that she wanted to take Rachelle to see her family" Lisa says.

"Your right then we could of made sure she was safe because this bitch on some psycho delusional shit. She better be glad we can't go to that damn room and I love my cousin" Chynna says.

Luella just looks around at her family happy that they are talking about sticking together more. She has always wanted them to get along but when the grandkids got grown and her mother got sick family time became a war zone.

"Well I just want to tell Endy something while we all are here and being honest. It's about Jasean" Asia spat out in front of everyone.

"Jasean what about him" Endy questions noticing Asia is a little reluctant.

"Okay Asia if it's not something good maybe you and Endy should go chat alone" Egypt told her sister.

"No we said we are going to be open and honest so whatever it is she can say in front of y'all" Endy turns her attention to Asia.

"Well maybe we should talk by ourselves" Asia agrees with Egypt.

"No I'm tired of hiding what's going on so if it's something you need to say then say it."

"Well before I say this I want you to promise me you won't act up" Asia begged her cousin.

"What, is he messing with another chic? Is that it?"

"No Endy but I did see him leaving the Crowne Plaza Hotel one morning when I was coming out about a month ago" Asia quickly spat out.

"WHAT AND YOU'RE JUST NOW TELLING ME?" Endy yells at Asia.

"I didn't want to say anything until I had facts this is y'all marriage Endy so I couldn't come at you with no bullshit. Plus the next day was Thanksgiving and all that shit happen" Asia explains to an agitated Endy.

"What the fuck you mean you wanted to wait until you had facts. The fact was he was at a hotel early in the morning and he wasn't with me. I remember that night because he left Nana house that night because him and Roc go into it" Endy recalls back to that night.

"No wonder that motherfucker was so quick to get away from me that night."

"Endy baby don't jump to no conclusions maybe he has a reason. Please promise me your gonna talk to him first don't go at this situation angry" Luella begs Endy.

"I'm not gonna go at him angry. I will say this I'm going to get to the bottom of this hotel shit" she said.

"Whatever's done in the dark will come to the light. I just pray this was some business shit and no infidelity mess is going on" Chynna groans.

"Y'all know what let's turn on some music and enjoy the rest of the night it's only ten o'clock we done hung out later then this" Endy tries perking up she don't like her family to see her in a vulnerable state.

"You sure you're okay baby" Tanya asks.

"Yeah Ma I'm with y'all. I will be having a new baby soon it's time to celebrate. I will handle Jay later it's Christmas" Endy convincingly states. Asia rush over to turn on the music, Chynna started to mix up some drinks in the blender, and the rest of the ladies started getting food prepared. The mood softens and the family is finally trying to have a good time.

"Cuzin, you good?" Karishma asked Endy.

"Yeah I'm good I'm finally enjoying time with my family all that other drama I will get to the bottom of it just not right now" Endy said with a smile on her face. "Okay I love you Endy."

"I love you too Rizzy but don't worry

cousin have this."

Chapter 17

"Are you gonna at least bring in the new year with me?" Endy stands with her arms folded with a scarf and bath robe on.

"E I told you I'm gonna be there I just need to make sure the club straight and everything is together for the guests we have coming through. I got to make sure the celebrity VIP is right and secure babe come on we talked about this" Jasean reminds her.

"No you talked about it but I said I rather spend a quiet evening at home. All you do is live at that got damn club I'm sick of it" Endy storms off to the bathroom and slams the hell out the door.

"This damn girl always with some bullshit man" Jasean mumbles to himself as he continues to get dressed with towel gracing his waist showing just the right amount about pubic hair. A few minutes later Endy comes out the bathroom and she's dressed in a beautiful black velour dress with small window back out and her curls pinned up in a bun. Her pregnancy glow was definitely showing. However Jasean is donned in Gucci from his hat all the way down to his sneakers. When they catch eye contact both are weakened at the sight of each other. The love they have for each other is indescribable but they just can't seem to get it together.

"Babe look I know you got to work but sometimes I just want you to spend some time with me. I feel like you're not even happy I'm pregnant. It makes me feel like I may need to get an abortion" she tells him.

"Ma don't even think like that I'm happy we having another baby I just wish Patience was at least a year old before we had another one. Well we can't stop what God has planned for us if it's meant for us to have another baby than we are having a baby don't let no abortion shit cross your lips no more. I love you E and I'm happy about my baby" Jasean said giving her a warn kiss which made Endy feel at ease.

♦♦♦NewSouth™♦♦♦

The family decides since it's been so much disruption going on lately that will have a house party with the family at Luella's.

"When is Endy supposed to get here?" Asia asked her grandmother.

"I don't know but she needs to come on it's already getting late" Egypt chimes in.

"Y'all chill out she's coming she text me about a half hour ago saying she was getting dressed and on her way" Luella said.

"Okay Nana you're trying to be down. What you mean chill?" Asia laughs.

"Hell I'm just as hip as y'all are" Luella also laughs.

"Well she needs to hurry up it's already nine o'clock and she supposed to bring the rest of the food" Egypt add grabbing her cell to call her.

"ROC WHAT ARE YOU DOING? COME DO THE MUSIC FOR US!" Luella yelled upstairs.

"I'm coming down Ma" he yells back down.

"Bae, don't leave everything is going to be just fine. Endy is just in her feelings because Jay on his ass hole shit. You know how she do babe come y'all will be good tomorrow" Rocko assures her.

"But I been calling her and she hasn't answered and it's just so much going on that I need to talk to her about" Niema complained.

"Baby just come on down stairs and let's enjoys bringing in the New Year like a family. All that nonsense with y'all can wait. We not doing this bullshit tonight man" Rocko demands pulling her up off the bed in his bedroom he has at Luella's.

"Okay babe I'm sorry your right we should be excited about the new year and in three more months our prince will be here" Niema smiles

"So are we good? Can we go downstairs now?" he asks. "Yeah we good" she smirks and plants a kiss right on his soft lips. She never thought she could love someone as much as she loved Caine but Rocko has been a breath of fresh air and the meaning of true love. Rocko wasn't as chocolate as Caine but he was her tall slender brown sugar. The two go downstairs to join the rest of the family and bring in the new year.

The doorbell rings and there's a few knocks at the door. "Somebody answer the door it should be Endy!" Luella shout.

"I got it Mommy" Tanya race to the door and when she opens it she is shocked.

"Hi Tanya how you been?" Lorraine spoke with a crutch under her right arm.

"What the hell are you doing here?" Tanya groaned.

"I'm only here to check on your mother and to see Rachelle for a minute that's all. I'm not here to cause no problems dear" Lorraine explained.

"We are trying to have a peaceful night with just family and I don't want my mother upset tonight" Tanya snapped.

"Look I completely understand y'all being upset. Taiya is getting an evaluation and she will be locked up until the court date. I just want to extend my apologies to Luella I'm not trying to mess up y'all family time or make any excuses for my daughters behavior" Lorraine plead with Tanya.

"Fuck y'all apology when I see that bitch I'm going to kick her ass" Asia yelled as she see its Lorraine at the door. A few of the family members hear Asia and come rushing to the front door.

"Lorraine your best bet is to leave my mother's house before shit gets crazy" Lisa warned her.

"I'm going to say this again I apologize and I was only making sure Luella was okay and to see if I could see my grandbaby that's it" Lorraine again pleads.

"Are you freaking kidding me? Your bitch ass daughter has shot at my mom and shot you and her damn self and you thought it was okay for you to bring your ass here?" Keisha charged at her, but Lisa grabbed her before she got close.

Lisa is trying to hold her while calling Khalil (Keisha's Husband) to come get her.

"Key stop it damn it, this is your mother's house" Khalil pinned her against the wall but she's still fighting to get loose.

"Marlo why are you just standing there" Lisa yelled at her husband.

"Khalil got her I'm just trying to make sure y'all okay before Mommy get down here" Marlo told them.

"It's too damn late what the hell is going on?" Luella screams as she sees the uproar happening.

"Mommy she needs to go why is she even here" Keisha screams.

"First of all, lower your damn voice in my house before I slap the shit out of you. Lorraine didn't do shit it was Taiya so I'm gonna tell you one more time to calm your ass down. Regardless of what she is still family because she is Rae's grandmother so y'all better show her some damn respect" Luella told her family while a sobbing Lorraine remained in the door way.

"I'm sorry Luella I just wanted to come by and check on you and see Rachelle for a minute but I don't want to cause any trouble so I'm going to leave" Lorraine cried.

"Yo y'all tripping Ms. Lorraine don't have shit to do with this" Rocko spits. "Yeah I think that's best" Tanya intervened.

"Aunt Tanya come on man" Rocko asked her.

"No you won't just leave we all have to get through this now she did all she could to get Taiya the help she needs but we can't blame her for that child's actions" Luella said.

The family all give each other disapproving looks but deep down they knew Luella was right Taiya always had anger problems. No one ever thought she would go as far as she has now.

"Okay y'all Nana is right, we can't take our anger out on Ms. Lorraine she can't help what Taiya has done nor can she change it. All we can do is pray justice is served and she gets the help she needs for the babies' sake" Chynna agreed.

Everyone starts to relax and realize that Luella and Chynna are right. "Well I just can't, I can't" Keisha yank away from Khalil and stormed off with Lisa, Egypt and Asia behind her.

"Lorraine baby come in so you can see Rachelle. Rocko, go get her so she can see her me me," Luella said. Rocko kissed Lorraine on the cheek and goes to get Rachelle so she can see her.

"Thank you Luella. Thank you Rocko for this I love y'all and I have nobody else my child is sick mentally and it's my fault. I should have gotten her some help years ago" Lorraine cried and Luella embraced her while Tanya and Karim empathized with her pain.

"It's okay we will all get through this baby" Luella says as she has her in a tight embrace.

Endy finally arrive at her Nana house she is hesitant to go in because Karishma has already informed her on what has happened. Jasean not bringing the New Year in with her and not being able to drink just put a damper on her mood so she sits in the truck getting herself together.

"Let me take my ass in here and bring in the New Year with my family since they will be who I'll be relying on" Endy said to herself. She gets out the truck and goes to grab her bag of party favors out the trunk but she see it's lifted where the spare tire goes. Her curiosity gets the best of her and she puts that bags down to see why but when she opens it her eyes damn near pop out because it looks to be packages of cocaine and stacks of money in her truck.

"What…the…fuck?" Endy mumbled. There's a big yellow envelope sitting in the corner and she's hesitant to look in it but this is her truck so she feels she has every right to. She grabs the envelope and open it, she see pictures, two USB drives, and a set of keys. Endy is stunned and confused because Jasean supposed to have left that life alone once they started the businesses.

"This dude is on some straight bullshit" Endy shook her head.

"Yo you need some help" J.J. asked her. She quickly covered up the stuff and closes the trunk.

"No I'm coming up right now" she threw on a fake smile although her blood is boiling right now she doesn't want to ruin the rest of the night. She decides to put it to the back of her mind for right now and bring in the New Year with her family.

"What's good cuzzo?" J.J. plants a kiss on Endy cheek.

"What's good baby I'm ready to bring in this new year of change" Endy said.

They enter the living room and she speaks to everyone and puts on a happy face even though her mind is going. The family is having a good time and everyone is dancing and singing oldies from the O'Jays to the Gap Band, to Earth Wind and Fire, and many more. It was good times again everyone was enjoying themselves even Lorraine and that itself made Endy at ease. She hates to see her family at odds especially with everything that's going on with all of them. At this time she feels they all need to be there for Rocko.

"Endy why are you over here all quiet?" Asia came and snuggled beside her.

"I'm good baby just can't imagine in about seven months, I will be having another baby if the good Lord willing" she replied.

"Speaking of which, where is Patience at anyway?" Asia questioned noticing Endy didn't bring her.

"She with Ma Ev tonight she said she wants me to sleep in tomorrow she's excited about the baby" Endy smiled thinking about how excited she was when she told her she was expecting again.

"Yeah you need to start getting some rest boo I know I'm always challenging you and Chy but I love y'all and would kill a motherfucker behind my cousins. I hope y'all know that" Asia said.

"Girl I know that I love you too" Endy laid her head on her shoulder. "Come on y'all it's time" Luella told everyone as they gather in front of the big television in the family room.

"Everybody come on and get y'all a glass of Champaign" Chynna shout walking around with two bottles of Rose.

"I want a small glass damn it I deserve it" Endy jokes.

"Okay just a small glass now I want my grandbaby to have all his fingers and toes" Eddie said.

"How you know it's a boy daddy?"

"Because God knows what I want" Eddie laughed. (The doorbell rings) "Would y'all get the door" Keisha said to Egypt and Asia who are closer.

"4…3…2…1…HAPPY NEW YEAR" the crowd roars and everyone is hugging and kissing each other. Endy feels someone grab her from the back "what the hell?" she spun around to face Jasean.

"Happy New Year's baby I love you I wouldn't have missed this for nothing" he grabbed her face and throws his tongue down her throat. Shocked by his arrival she hugs him tight just glad he made it home safe. Especially with everything she's found in the truck.

"Baby I didn't think you would make it" she's so filled with joy.

"I had to I don't ever want you to think I'm gonna to leave you and my kids. I love y'all more than anything in this world E" he kissed her again.

"I think I owe Ny and Roc an apology at the end of the day that baby is our family and Ny has always been a good girl" Jasean told her.

He walks over whispers in Rocko ear and the both go out the room. Niema shoots Endy a worried look and Endy smiles to let her know it's okay.

"I bet you were surprised huh" Chynna asked Endy.

"Girl yes I felt so bad because I cursed him out before we left the house" Endy chuckled.

"Girl that's your raging hormones talking he got to know that."

"Yeah Chynna but me and Jay got more problems than I can handle at this time but I won't ruin New Years with it but we got to link up and talk soon okay." "E you sure everything is okay?" "Yeah Chy everything is good."

"Okay now don't make me kick some ass messing with my E Pooh."

"Ewe stop it I haven't heard that in years" Endy frowned giving her cousin a hug.

"Well cousin it's 2013 now it's time to start fresh."

"Yes it is cuzzo, yes it is" Endy said and they toast each other.

"Yo man I just want to apologize for all the shit I said. I don't agree with how shit went down I do understand it" Jasean told Rocko.

"Well I apologize too I never meant to break the code but I always loved Ny since we were kids. To see her go through so much hurt with Caine just made me love her more. She's a good woman Jay."

"I know she is man I just was trying to be there for my cousin but he made his bed. I think he is cool with everything now. I told him to focus on his baby girl and let this shit go" Jasean told Rocko.

"Yeah we good and he came to see me at the hospital I think he more upset with Ny but I can't let him disrespect her man not as my woman" Rocko informed him.

"I respect that Rocko and he won't that's my word B" Jasean and him shake on it.

"Well are y'all going to come join the party its cold out here" Endy asks them with Niema behind her.

"Y'all just coming to be nosey we cool E" Rocko told her.

"Y'all better be because we are a family whether y'all like it or not" she replied. (Boom…boom…boom).

"Well that's Brooklyn for you gun shots on New Year's Eve" Niema laughed.

"Well let's go inside with the rest of the family" Endy told them and they all head back in the house.

The family is singing "Auld Lang Syne" and everything just felt right for the first time in a while for Endy. She loved her family but she knows she has to have a conversation with Jasean really soon.

◆◆◆NewSouth™◆◆◆

"So are you going with Rocko to court today?" Aunt Sally asked Niema.

"I don't know Auntie I just don't want to make shit worse for him."

"Well I can understand that but what does Rocko say."

"He wants me there but I just don't think it's a good idea to do that Auntie I just think it's too much."

"Well baby in the next three months you will be having a baby in the Hinton family so you have already done too much. You can't tuck and run now baby get it together and be there for your man or is it something you need to tell me" Aunt Sally asked.

"No we good he's such a gentleman to me and always puts me and Rachelle first. I just wish things could have been different like I wish I would have chosen him back in high school but I was blinded by love" Niema snarled.

"Baby, you have no time for should of, could of, would of's; this baby is coming, and he's coming now. I know the situation is not the greatest but you have to be there for Rodney baby." Aunt Sally wanted Niema to understand that she has to show Rocko her loyalty.

"I get it Auntie I will think about it okay. Where is YaYa at?"

"She got her an apartment on the upper east side on E. 92nd Street." "What? Manhattan! How the hell she pulled that off?"

"I don't know she said she got some new Executive position at her job and they are helping her with the apartment" Aunt Sally said washing the dishes but Niema is not buying it. Something is going on and she's gonna find out.

"Well I'm about to meet Roc at Nana house and I will call you later to let you know how everything goes" Niema kissed her on the cheek and grab her purse to head out the door. She gets to the car and her mind is racing on how the hell YaYa can afford a $7000 a month apartment. (Ring…ring) Niema phone rings she see it's Rocko calling her.

"What's up babe?"

"What's good Ma? Are you on your way?" Rocko spoke loud into the phone.

"Yeah I'm on my way now babe just left from talking to Aunt Sally" She responded back fastening up her seat belt.

"Okay babe I'm waiting on you I need you more than anything right now. I'm at Ma house now" he said.

"I'm on my way now I promise I'm here for you Bae" she convinced him. "Okay see you when you get here Ma and thank you" he tenderly replied. He was soft for her and she enjoyed every minute of it. All the doubt she had about not going to the trial had disappeared she definitely need to be there for her man. She was going to be there for her man no matter what because he's shown her nothing but support. She cranks up her Benz and head over to Luella's so they won't be late.

They arrive at Kings County court house and Niema stomach is full of flutters she didn't know if it was the baby or her nerves. It's also very cold outside and the wind is whistling.

"Ny you okay?" Rocko asks sensing her nervousness.

"I'm good baby I just want to make sure your good" Niema smiled concealing how she really is feeling.

"Y'all come on its ten till" Luella said walking up the steps to the court building. Rocko lets out a sigh and they follow her up the steps. When they get to the courtroom they are going be in, Niema stomach becomes terribly upset and she run off to the bathroom. Rocko wants to see what's going on but he need to get in the court room so he sends his Aunt Tanya to check on her.

"I got her baby you go ahead and sit down we're coming" Tanya reassured him and head off to check on Niema. When Rocko enters the courtroom he feels a chill across his whole body but shakes it off and keep walking to the front to sit down. He sees all his cousins, aunt and uncles on the right side of the room and he starts to relax a little.

"ALL RISE!" the bailiff yells. Everybody stands Rocko looks back and see his Aunt and Niema haven't come in yet. Judge Matthew Curry enters the court room. He handled all the big cases in New York. Rocko is getting worried but he has to stay focused.

"This is the case of the state of NY versus N'Taiya Martin, in the shooting of Rodney Hinton," the bailiff yelled. He hears the door finally open and its Niema and Tanya tip toeing their way to sit next to Endy.

The lawyers have made their opening statements and the prosecution is up to call their first witness. "I would like to call Rodney Hinton to the stand" Joel Becton (Rocko Lawyer) says.

Rocko walked up the stand his forehead sweating and butterflies in his stomach but he knew he had to get up there and tell the truth if he wanted to get custody of his daughters. It was no looking back now. So he calmly walked and sat looking straight ahead everyone could tell he was nervous.

"Do you solemnly swear to tell the truth, the whole truth, and nothing but the truth so help you God" the bailiff said as Rocko place his right hand on the bible.

"I do" he said and sat down ready to go to fight this case to the end.

The witnesses had all been heard from the prosecution and defense or that's what the family thought but when the defense attorney asked can they call one more witness on the stand the family becomes nervous. Who could be this witness? The family is now concerned and confused.

"Your Honor, I would like to call Ni'yana Bradley to the stand." Taiya's attorney, David Ratliffe, said, smirking at Rocko. Everyone is in shock especially Niema because she doesn't know what's her point in even testifying.

"What the hell? Your cousin is fucking snake Ny for real" Ari mumbled. "I swear y'all I don't know where none of this shit is coming from" Niema assured them.

"I hope not because this is some straight BS" Tanya said. YaYa walked to the stand with a smile on her face because she knew that everyone was shocked to see that she's there on Taiya's behalf.

"Do you solemnly swear to tell the truth, the whole truth, and nothing but the truth so help you God."

"I do" YaYa said positively and Niema is froze in her seat.

"Ms. Bradley can you please tell us your name and address?" Ratliffe asked and she told him. The questions in the beginning were pretty standard but then they started getting deeper.

"Can you tell us how you know Ms. Martin" Ratliffe asks YaYa.

"I met her through my cousin Ny" YaYa looked at Niema and smile. "Can you tell us who Ny is?" he asked.

"Niema Mason my cousin she's pregnant by Rodney Hinton" YaYa said openly.

"So your cousin who is sitting over there is pregnant by Rodney Hinton too just like the defendant N'Taiya Martin is also pregnant"

Ratliffe displayed. "Yeah my cousin with another guy when I got here which is Rodney's cousin Endy husband cousin so it's like everybody messing with everybody and I'm quite confused myself" YaYa said smiling.

"This bitch" Endy yelled out.

"Order in the court" Judge Curry yells.

"Endy chill out baby we don't need to be getting put out" Tanya grabbed her hand.

"Precede counselor" the judge instructed.

"So all these people are somehow connected" Ratliffe proceeds to question YaYa.

"Yes I mean my cousin introduced the Hinton family as her family she knew Rocko, I mean Rodney was with Taiya for some years. I didn't even know they were messing around at first but she told me later" YaYa said truthfully.

"Bitch is you serious? You don't even know this bitch" Niema stood up and yelled.

"Order in the court if you have one more outburst I'm removing that whole row" Curry shout.

"Bitch your treacherous you will go against your family for someone you don't even know" Endy stood up beside Niema.

"Order in the court remove that whole row out my court room now" Curry yelled to the bailiff. The bailiff walked over and asks all them to stand and leave the court room.

"Bitch you're going to get what's coming to you I told you don't mess with my family" Endy yelled. Tanya grab her damn near dragging her out the court room. They go down stairs to lobby to let Endy gets some air because if not she is going to kill YaYa.

"Baby you have got to calm down" Tanya told her daughter.

"Mommy these bitches are really testing us and I'm tired of it" Endy yelled and everyone looks at her.

"E calm down babe you are going to put stress on that baby" Chynna begged her and she immediately complied and chill out.

"Well let's just waste some time and take a walk" Niema insisted.

"I tell y'all one thing that bitch gonna get what's coming to her if my cousin don't get no justice today" Endy groaned.

Chapter 18

The family is in the lobby area now, waiting to hear the jury verdict since Judge Curry had them removed from the court room for their outburst while YaYa was on the stand. Endy and Chynna is furious and Niema is just shocked that YaYa would betray her to this extent.

"I really can't believe YaYa pulled that bullshit in court" Endy paced back and forth trying to call Jasean but as usual he's not answering.

"This man never answers the phone" Endy shakes her head.

"What the hell is going on with y' all Endy I never seen y'all this distant before" Ari asked.

"He is always working and I don't know Ari but I told him if he doesn't start treating me like a wife again we're going to have some real problems" Endy told\ her.

"Well do you think it's another woman?"

"I don't know Ari but if I was to find out this bastard cheated on me again it's not going to be pretty for him because I'm going to take his ass down in every way I can. I told him if he wasn't finish playing he could have left me out the game" Endy said.

"You know his ass went crazy when you were dealing with Sincere he thought you were playing with his ass. If Ny would have showed Caine that treatment, maybe she would have gotten better results" Ari laughs.

"Stop it stupid here she comes" Endy giggles shaking her head.

About an hour later they start seeing the family coming out the elevator and Luella looks pissed. "Nana what's the matter?" Chynna asks but Luella just keeps walking towards the front door.

"They gave her involuntary manslaughter because the state of mind she was in when she committed the act. They didn't even consider the recent shooting and all of the shit she has been doing to taunt us their saying that's a separate matter. Plus I think her being pregnant played a big part too and it sure didn't help that YaYa went her ass up there and went against us" Lisa adds.

"This is exactly why I'm going to kick that bitch ass. She playing with me and messing with my family" Endy shouts.

"Endyia calm down let's go outside and check on Mommy" Tanya told her. She pulls Endy outside to check on Luella with Niema tagging close behind them.

"I'm just ready to eat it's over now. Roc better be done with that chic and get my nieces as soon as he can" Keisha grits.

"Let's just calm down y'all how is Rocko taking it?" Chynna asks but as soon as Keisha and Lisa were about to tell her. The stairwell door opens and it's him, his dad Rodney, and J.J.

"Roc are you okay babe?" Chynna runs and hug him.

"I'm good cuz I just wanted her to pay for what she did and for me to be able to get full custody of my daughters. The courts played me with the charges but I knew they would sympathize with her a little more. She still gonna be charged for the gun she had on Christmas Day too and for shooting her mother. All I want is my babies to be safe and we get the hell out of New York" Rocko says.

"Don't let this bitch run you away from your home" Keisha snaps.

"I'm not auntie but my only concern is getting them out of here and to a new environment which the judge says he doesn't see a problem with. Being that I took blame for my actions and showed good character I should be able to get full custody with no problem. I just want to get my family out of New York." Rocko express to his family. He is over the drama with everyone. He just wants him, Ny, and their children to start fresh down south.

"Well I don't want you to go Roc, but I do understand it" Chynna told him.

"Where's Ny at?" Rocko asks seeing she's not in the lobby.

"They went to check on Mommy and calm your cousin down" Lisa told him. "Lord who Endy!" He laughs knowing how Endy is very overprotective of him.

"You know it B, you know she thinks you're a damn baby" J.J. laughs with him.

"Man let me get out of here and calm her down" he said.

"We all need to go grab something to eat and just thank God she is going to do some time" Rodney (Rocko dad) told his family.

"Yeah let's go because Niema and Endy needs to feed my babies" Rocko said as he puts his arms around his two aunts.

◆◆◆NewSouth™◆◆◆

"Where is Endy? She loves Peter Luger Steakhouse thought she was coming" Egypt whispers to Chynna.

"I don't know but you know when her and Jay is going through she doesn't talk she just handles it and then shit comes out later" Chynna mumbled.

"Okay I just want her to know we're here for her" Egypt says.

"Where's Ms. Endyia at?" Lisa asks her daughter.

570

"I don't know Ma maybe she met up with Jay" Niema butted in.

"Well text and asks her why she didn't join the rest of us for dinner" Luella tells her granddaughters.

"Okay Nana I will." Chynna gets out her phone to do just that but her calls are going straight to voicemail and she is not replying to her texts.

"We can go by there when we leave here" Egypt says.

Chynna mind is racing because no matter what is going on her and Endy pretty much communicate more than their other cousins. Although the last few months have been hectic Endy has become very distant and Chynna does not understand why but she will find out.

"Well I guess Endy is not going to join us she probably got something to do you know she is always making moves" Chynna blabs trying to throw her family off.

"So Roc you're leaving Nana huh?" Luella said to her grandson.

"I need a new start for me and my kids" he replied.

"Well I already told your aunt Linda that you were going to be down there and she's excited to see y'all" Luella tells him while cutting her steak.

"I know I'm ready to see what the south has to offer. I'm about tired of this fast life I'm ready to settle down and move on with Niema. I know how shit got started with us is messed up but we do love each other" Rocko express wanting his family to be embracing of their relationship.

"We all love Niema very much and I hope y'all do make it but y'all can't deny the fact that this whole thing has fucked shit up for everyone" Keisha says. "Keesh!" Khalil snarls at her.

"Don't Keesh me! Rocko and Niema we love y'all but truth be told this shit got way more out of hand because of what y'all did. Now the whole family has to suffer the consequences. So I'm sorry if I can't just laugh and kumbaya the situation with the rest of y'all" Keisha jumped up.

"KEISHA SHUT UP! The situation is done what's done is done we can't turn back time" Luella spoke loud enough to get the attention of the other people eating at the restaurant.

"You know what I'm just going to go because I'm not gonna sit here and be fake. Our lives has been turned upside down because of their fucking negligence and y'all gonna sweep it under the rug hell no" Keisha jumps up grabbing her coat.

"Why you always got to keep drama going? We supposed to be boding as a family right now hasn't all this shit taught you a lesson" Tanya shoots at her.

"Y'all can sit here and act like this shit is alright with this bitch shooting Roc and pointing a gun at my mother but it's not okay with me. I see why Endy didn't want to come and join this fake ass shit. Since when the Hinton's are okay with motherfuckers coming for us" Keisha shouts.

"Mommy we gonna go" Khalil stands up.
"Yeah that's the best thing I heard all day let's go" Keisha stormed off.

"Mommy I'm sorry about this" Khalil kiss Luella on the cheek and grabs Keisha purse.

"Family I love y'all but let me take this woman home it's been a long day. Roc it's all love man and keep ya head up" Khalil slaps him five and kiss Niema on the cheek. Poor Niema just sits with tears streaming her face because she feels like everything the family is saying is true and it just makes her feel worse about the baby she has growing inside her.

"Niema don't do that baby we love you" Luella assures her.

"I think I need to go it's just too much right now" Niema starts to cry.

"Baby that's auntie you been around us long enough to know how she is" Rocko wraps his arm around her.

"Yeah Ny you know we love you regardless of how things went down you are about to have a member of our family" Chynna adds.

"I think we gonna head out y'all this has been an emotional and stressful day" Rocko sense Ny is ready to go.

"I'm sorry for everything I love y'all like my own family. I would have never done this intentionally y'all got to know that" Niema cries as she seen Asia look at Chynna and Egypt rolling her eyes.

"Ny it doesn't matter now the baby is coming and we are all gonna have to find a way to move past all this" Tanya says.

"Well we bout to be out I love y'all but today has been exhausting" Rocko jumps up grabbing Niema by the hand and kissing everyone on his way out.

"Y'all be careful okay and regardless of the matter son we love y'all" Rodney told them.

"We know that Dad" Rocko pounds his dad and they head on out the restaurant. Just as they head out Chynna phone rings "Its Endy! Now she calls back" Chynna shakes her head.

"Where you at?" She said in the phone.

"Yo I need you to come to my crib asap. I need you to come now but don't upset the family. Please hurry Chy" Endy speaks loudly in the phone.

"What?" Chynna shouts which makes the whole family look up.

"Is something wrong with her?" Tanya asks worried.

"No Auntie she is just feeling sick and want me to bring her something to eat so I'm gonna call it a night" Chynna said getting her purse and coat.

"Are you sure everything is okay Chy?" Lisa asked her daughter.

"Yeah Ma I'm just going to check on my cousin is that okay" Chynna snarls.

"Look chic don't get smart with me" Lisa points at her.

"I'm not Ma" Chynna laughs giving her mother a hug.

"Well I'm going with you I'm tired of being left out" Asia stands up and so does Egypt.

"Y'all no chill she just hungry that's all" Chynna tried to say without making them suspicious.

"Well we want to go is it a problem with us coming along" Asia smirks knowing damn well something is up.

"No come on." Chynna reluctantly agreed but she knows Endy won't be happy.

"Okay girls keep y'all secrets we always find out" Luella told her granddaughters as she watches them walk out the door.

"Something going on and we're gonna hear about it soon enough just watch" Luella tells the rest of the family.

Chynna is speeding down the parkway trying to get to Endy's because the urgency in her voice has her worried. "Chynna are you going to tell us what the hell is going on?" Asia asked.

Chynna remains silent and continue driving. "Well is she okay at least?" Egypt continue to pry.

"Look y'all that's my word, I don't know what's going on but the shit sounds urgent" Chynna tells them.

"I wonder if her ass flipped on Jay about the telly situation" Asia pries trying to get Chynna to say something but she continue driving silent. After about forty-five minutes they arrive at Endy's and they are all stunned when they see the house surrounded with the police swat team and a

swat van sitting in front.

"WHAT THE FUCK?" Chy stop the car

Asia yells damn near making Chynna hit a police

car.

"OH SHIT WHAT THE HELL THIS

NIGGA GOT MY COUSIN INTO NOW!"

Chynna screams.

"Y 'all calm down just park so we can see

what the hell is happening" Egypt says. She stops

and they jump out the car leaving the doors open

and all. They see Endy all hysterical by the front

door with her cordless phone.

"E what the fuck is going on?" Chynna

yells.

"This has some shit to do with Jay don't it" Asia adds going into the house.

"Asia come here don't go make shit worse" Endy screams at her but she goes in the house anyway.

" I don't know what the fuck is going on but Jay is not answering the phone and no one is picking up at the club either. They said it has something to do with extortion, assault, and money laundering." Endy shouts pacing back and forth.

"Did you try calling CJ?" Egypt asks her.

"Yeah but he is not answering either. All I know is that I was getting ready to come meet y'all at the steakhouse and I heard the doorbell ring. When I go to answer the door it's police at

the door with a warrant to search the house" Endy
cried.

"Okay what I need you to do is calm down
we gonna get to the bottom of this shit" Chynna
hugs her.

"What the hell are they looking for their
tearing up the damn house" Asia questions after
checking out the scene inside the house.
(Ring…Ring) Endy phone rings when she looks
down its Marilyn calling her.

"I can't right now Chynna please get it"
she passes the phone to Chynna.

"Hello" Chynna shouts in the phone.

"Yo Endy this is Caine."

"Caine what the fuck is going and why are you calling from your mom's house?" Chynna asked which alerts Endy.

"What's up Chynna? I'm still trying to find out what the hell happen myself but let Endy know the cops came and raided the club, E-Class, and they just took Jay to jail. They looking for me and Uncle Jack right now tell her to stay calm and don't say shit" Caine said giving her the run down.

"What the hell you mean Jay is locked up and tell her don't say shit? Does he know that they just raided the house too? She doesn't even know what the hell is going on somebody need to say something" Chynna snaps on his ass.

"WHAT! THE HOUSE TOO! Yo Jay got caught up with some bullshit I can't say much right now but tell E to stay calm and I will hit y'all back" Caine hangs up.

"I know this son of a bitch didn't just hang up on me damn it" Chynna groans.

"What he say Chy?" Endy's ready to hear.

"Jay is locked up and they looking for him and Uncle Jack too."

"WHAT? Locked up for what?" Endy yells.

"I don't know babe but that's not it they raided E-Class and the club" Chynna says.

"My fucking store this is some bullshit. I didn't do anything to deserve none of this bullshit." Endy started crying again which makes her cousins even more upset. "E we have no time to hide this shit from the family we have to get them on board because whatever Jay has going on it must be big and we can't have you tied up in this bullshit" Chynna advises her.

"Chynna okay damn let me get my thoughts together before y'all go telling shit."

"We need to go see why your husband is locked up and why they closed the store. You got to put your game face on because we don't know what the hell we about to find out" Chynna tried prepares her.

"Ms. Newman I'm Officer Clay we're gonna need you to come down to the station for questioning" a tall white slender cop tells her.

"Come to the station for what? I haven't done shit fuck y'all" Endy spat.

"Ms. Newman you're going to have to come with us willingly or by force but you are going down to the station" he sternly stated.

"What the hell you mean by force? I didn't do shit so I'm not going nowhere" she shouts.

He looks back to give the other officers a queue that she's not cooperating. "Endy chill we will go with you just cooperate with them you know you didn't do shit so don't make them think your guilty of shit" Asia grabs Endy by the arm.

"Yes just go we got you don't make a scene" Egypt chimes in.

"But this shit is stupid why I'm being questioned about something I don't know shit about" Endy snarls.

"I know babe but your husband must know something or they wouldn't have arrested him so let's just go and see what is really going on" Chynna begs her.

Endy eventually come to her senses and agree to go down to the station. "Okay I'm going but I'm riding with my cousin" she told the officer.

"Fair enough we will give you time to lock up the house and grab you belongings and meet us there" he confirmed and walked away.

"Y'all call Nana and my mom but let's wait until we know exactly what's going on before we tell everyone else please" Endy directs them and she goes in the house to grab her purse and keys.

"This is about to be a long night" Chynna shakes her head.

"Okay, baby, did you want me to come with you?" Niema asked Rocko, after learning the news of what's going on with Endy.

"Nah I'm good you need to rest I'm sure it's nothing big like that."

"Okay well please keep me posted." She hangs up her phone and flops down on the couch across from Aunt Sally.

"What's going on now?" she asks seeing how disturbed Niema expression looks.

"Well it's seemed Jay done got in some shit and Endy has got caught in the middle yet again."

"Trouble? What kind of trouble?" Aunt Sally asks concerned.

"I don't know the details but I know he said the feds closed the club and her store. He said Endy had to go Downtown for some type of questioning."

"Well I told you Jay is no angel he has secrets just like the rest of these men" YaYa buds in walking in on them.

"Aunt Sally I told you I'm not dealing with this bitch she crossed me for the last time" Niema barks. " Ny look I didn't come here to argue auntie asked me to come over so I did" YaYa stated.

"Auntie why would you do this right now? I'm going home I don't want to be under the same roof with her" Niema jumped up grabbing her bags.

"Y'all are going to sit y'all ass down and listen to me" Aunt Sally yells at them both.

"Niema this is your family and I know she hasn't been doing everything right but we have to find a way to get pass this mess life is too short."

"Now about Endy I can't believe all this is happening I know Tanya and Luella is pitching a bitch" Aunt Sally sighs.

"You telling me I just hate that Endy tied up in his mess she doesn't deserve it" Niema grumbles.

"I know but sometimes we have to pay attention to the red flags come on all the shit they got isn't coming from no promoting, club, and E-

Class. That's just bullshit Ny and you know it"
YaYa exclaims.

"You need to mind your fucking business and stop worrying about me and my friends." Niema screams again at YaYa this time walking toward her. As much as Niema wants to believe Endy doesn't know anything she also knows how much she loves Jasean.

"Well if she knows anything it will show she's my best friend so I know when she's hiding something" Niema assured YaYa.

"Okay not trying to upset you Ny I just want you to know I love you and didn't want to hurt you" YaYa says sincere but Niema is not buying it.

"Why would you go against my unborn child's father like what was that about?" Niema questions her.

"I just think they feel like their better than everyone else Ny I hate the way they treat you. They all knew about the shit Caine was doing but still continued to smile in your face like shit was good Ny. Can't you see I have your back more than any of them bitches you're my blood."

"Really Ni'yana you took shit I told you and used it against my child's father in court how can we come back from that. I'm tired and my emotions are on ten right now so I'm going to get some rest good night" Niema storms off upstairs to her old room.

"That child is so stubborn but I'm glad you came anyway baby" Aunt Sally hugs YaYa.

"I don't know why she hates me so much but worship the ground Endy walks on. I would never do anything to hurt her" YaYa replied hurt.

"Baby you knew better than to go on that stand against Rocko. Although I understand why you did it, I still don't think it was right especially with him being shot in the matter. But I always told y'all to be honest even if it means hurting someone we love. Just give her time baby she will come around she just has so much going on with her pregnancy, court, the move, Endy being pregnant and now she hears this. Just be there for her and let her know you love her" Aunt Sally told YaYa.

"Okay auntie your right I'm about to go meet up with some coworkers in Downtown, Manhattan" she says grabbing her gold and black

Michael Kors purse to match her boots and pea coat.

"I see you been looking real New Yorkish here lately" Aunt Sally laughs and watch her walk to her car. When YaYa gets in, she waves to let her know she good and Aunt Sally close and locks the door. YaYa sits there for a moment sucking in everything that just happened.

"So Endy is pregnant and the plot thickens so I see now" YaYa smiles to herself shaking her head.

Chapter 19

It's been three days since Jasean has been released from jail and Endy has been giving him the cold shoulder. He knows he really messed us but he is putting something really dope together for their one year anniversary which is in another week. He goes in the kitchen and sees her feeding Patience in her high chair.

"Hi Daddy's princess" he says which makes Patience giggle. However Endy just looks at him in disgust and rolls her eyes.

"Hi beautiful" he kiss her on the cheek but she doesn't flinch not one bit. "You know I thought the New Year would bring us better things to look forward to for our family but shit is just getting worse" Endy gripes.

"Bae I know I fucked up big time but you haven't let me explain. I'm trying to be open and honest with you all the way no bullshit" he tells her.

"I don't want to hear shit you have to say. It's already bad enough that you were doing illegal shit at the club but then you involved my fucking store in this bullshit and had my own cousin Karishma lying to me about it. Not to mention you're extorting a congressman and James Carter at that" She screams furiously and throws a glass in the sink so hard it shatters.

"E calm down you're going to stress the baby" he grabs her by the arm.

"Get the fuck off me don't you touch me right now you sorry bastard. Why the hell would you involve my business I worked hard for, in some money laundering and drug bullshit? I knew you were lying when I found that shit in the truck talking about it was your Uncle Jack's stuff. You knew the shit was yours the whole time" she yells and run off to the living room. She doesn't like arguing in front of the baby or for her to see her upset.

"Endy damn at least let me talk how the hell you're going to know what's going on if you don't let me explain" he yells back. "EXPLAIN! Explain what Jay? What's done is done. Now, the cat is out the fucking bag, so talk about what?" she screamed, which startled Patience

."Waaaahh!"She runs and grabs her out the high chair.

"Jasean Newman you can get your shit and go because right about now I don't know if I even want to be married anymore" Endy sobs.

"Baby don't say shit like that look I know I messed up. I have a lot of making up to do, but don't give up on us. I will do anything Endy just please don't leave me right now" he begged her.

"Jay I thought we said no matter how bad, hard or ugly shit is we would always be honest with each other" she says with tears just streaming her face as Patience just stares at her.

"Baby please just give me one more chance I swear I will never hurt you again" he gets on his knees in front of her.

"I'm so hurt and embarrassed right now. I feel like a fool and just need some time to think" She says and walks away with the baby.

"WAIT! What that mean?"

"It means I'm going down south with Ny and Roc I had enough of New York and enough of your ass." Endy walk to the bedroom and slams the door leaving a regretful Jasean speechless.

♦♦♦NewSouth™♦♦♦

"What the hell is going on Caine? And Why are you calling me private" Keosha yells in her cell phone.

"Keosha I told you to chill stop trying to involve yourself in shit that doesn't involve you. Just get my baby, get the twenty bands out the safe and y'all go to my mom house" he told her.

"I know something is up why Jay got arrested? I heard it's some shit to do with him pushing drugs out the club" she continue to pry.

"See what I'm talking about? Stop listening to shit you heard out in the streets it isn't shit like that" Caine argues.

"I don't want to go to Ms. Marilyn house she don't care for me so why would I go there. Well take my daughter there and you do what you want but get the hell out the crib ASAP!" he shouts and hangs up the phone.

"I know he did not just hang up on me" she throws the phone down on the sofa. (Da,da,da,da, da…a knock at the door)

"Who the hell can that be?" Keosha says as she throws some items in a duffle bag and race to open the door. To her surprise it's Marilyn standing there with a stink look on her face.

"Where is my grandbaby?" she asks brushing past Keosha.

"Well hello to you, too she in the room. I'm packing our things now" Keosha reluctantly answers.

"Did I just hear you say our?"

"Yeah Caine said for me and Cadence to go to your house until he calls" Keosha answers with her hands on her hips.

"Well I guess that's only right, could you just come on please" Marilyn goes on to the back to get the baby.

"Lord I don't know if I'm going to be able to do this" Keosha shakes her head.

"I'm not fond of you coming with me either but I will go to hell and back for my grandbaby" Marilyn said cuddling Cadance.

"Well I'm almost done I need to grab a few more things" Keosha race to the bedroom. (Da, da, da,da, da…another knock at the door)

"I got it you just need to hurry up" Marilyn says sitting Cadence down on the floor. (Da, da, da, da…the knock gets harder)

"Okay I'm coming damn it" she yells rushing to the door. When she opens the door a piece of gold steel is pointed at her face. "WHAT THE FUCK?" Marilyn yells as she sees this man that stood about five-nine pointing a gun with two other dudes behind him.

"Bitch move back and put your hands up" he says as the two others follow behind him also holding guns.

"BITCH!" Marilyn repeats to make sure she heard him.

"That's right bitch move back and shut the fuck up before I waste your old ass. I want all the jewelry and money right now. Oh and that fur on the couch I need that too. You try some bullshit and your ass is getting popped." He warned her, as two other men entered the apartment. The tallest one, who stood about 6'6, locked the door.

"Oh my God Please, don't hurt my baby" Keosha yells and Cadence starts crying.

"Bitch shut the fuck up! Both of y'all sit down on the couch now" another man yells who's a little on the chubby side.

"What is this about?" Marilyn asks unfazed by the armed men. "Motherfucking payback and I'm here to collect. Y'all keep an eye on them while I go look for my money" The main guy says heading to the bedrooms he seems to be the leader of the trio. The chubby and tall slender men just follow his orders.

"If I know my child then this has all to do with him" Marilyn says and Keosha gives her a startled look.

"Ms. Marilyn!"

"Ms. Marilyn my ass is this how he's going to live his life putting his woman and baby in danger? Well what y'all gonna do? Kill us, rape us, what?" Marilyn shouts at the two men guarding them.

"Rape y'all nobody want your old ass or this ho" the tall guy says. "Motherfucker do you know who I am because obviously you don't" Marilyn tells him.

"Bitch you better shut up before I pop your ass. Yeah you ran the streets with CJ King in the 70s who gives a fuck" the chubby says and walks up on Marilyn.

"Marilyn please just shut the fuck up" Keosha yells cuddling Cadence closer to her.

"You better listen to your little daughter in law she seems real smart right about now" the tall man says. (Boom…boom…boom) they hear the main guy tearing up the bedrooms.

"What the hell is he looking for?" Keosha asks.

"Don't worry about that just chill and sit there quiet" the chubby guy tells her. "Y'all wouldn't be doing this shit if CJ was here so you must have known he was gone" Marilyn tells the men.

"Caine! Fuck Caine! That motherfucker is as disloyal as they come; especially, if he wifed a stripper bitch over a bad bitch like Niema" the tall guy says, which alarms them.

"So, y'all Ny's people? Y'all here for her?" Marilyn asks.

"Hell no I don't know that bitch but I have seen her with your pussy ass son" the tall guy replied.

"Well it's mighty funny that you would mention her right now" Marilyn shoots.

"I'm gonna tell your ass one more time to shut the fuck up. I'm not fucking playing old lady" the chubby one said putting the gun to her head.

"No please we will do what you say just please don't hurt my baby" Keosha cries.

"Bitch shut up nobody gonna hurt that gorgeous little baby girl of yours. I do a lot of shit but I won't harm a baby" the main guy said coming from the back with the duffle bag which had the twenty thousand in it.

"No please don't take my bag I need that" Keosha jumps up.

"Oh really well I need it too tell your boy thanks and I appreciate the interest. Y'all come on let's be out this bitch" the main guy says heading towards the door.

"I hope it serves you well punk ass motherfuckers" Marilyn yelled.

Before she knows it the chubby guy storms over and points the gun to her head. His hand is shaking and all "Man just let me smoke her old ass" he says.

"Please don't do it! Marilyn chill just let them take that shit it's not worth our lives please Cadence is here" Keosha cries.

"I'm not scared of these pussy ass niggas girl get some balls if these bastards really wanted to hurt us they would of done so already" Marilyn assured Keosha.

"Bitch you better shut the fuck up because if it was up to me I would have been popped your old ass you got too much mouth" the chubby guys says.

"Well this shit isn't over you fat fucker" Marilyn yells.

"You mouthy bitch" he smacks the shit out of Marilyn busting her lip and making Cadence scream.

"Yo Biggs chill" the main guy shouts.

"Shut that fucking baby up. And if y'all dare get the police involved, we will know and it won't be pretty when we come back. Because, we will come back" the tall one says.

"We won't call the police. Ms. Marilyn, please, just shut up." Keosha cried, pleading with the men.

"Yeah, you better listen to your daughter-in-law" the guy who seems to be the main guy said.

"She's not my damn daughter in law."
Marilyn snaps with blood dripping from her
mouth.

"Look y'all can have whatever y'all want I
won't call the cops just please go on I swear"
Keosha sobs.

The two men just look at her and laugh.
After ransacking the house and grabbing some
more items, the trio decides it's time to finally
leave.

"You tell that punk-ass son of yours
thanks for paying up, and don't take so long next
time" the main guy laughed. He pointed the gun
in Marilyn's face, which infuriates her even more.
The two women sit quiet until they know the men
are completely out of sight. Marilyn jumps up and
race to the door to lock it and to make sure their
gone.

"Keosha get your ass up, grab your shit and let's get the fuck out of here. We have to find CJ now. I tell you one thing this shit isn't over" Marilyn growls.

♦♦♦NewSouth™♦♦♦

Endy is getting prepared to go over Evelyn's house to talk to her about everything that's going on with her and Jasean. (Ding…dong…her doorbell rings) She knew she wasn't expecting nobody and no one have called her so who could it be. With all that's going on with Jasean and these charges you never know who is lurking around. She grabs her little 9mm Jasean brought her for her birthday and walks slowly to the door. She looks out the peephole but she sees nobody there. She snatch open the door to find a big yellow envelope taped to her door.

"What the hell is this?" she looks to the right and left but no one is in sight. Endy rips open the envelope and sees a note and a picture attached. She grabs the note and the picture of what looks to be a sonogram and become immediately puzzled.

"What the hell? I haven't had my ultrasound done yet?" Endy then begins reading the note:

"Hello Endyia, I just thought you should know that I have been dealing with your husband for about six months. I'm currently five months pregnant and yes it's by him. I'm not trying to break up y'all family or what y'all have going on. I do want him to take responsibility with taking care of this baby because I hate to take this to the courts. Oh I'm sorry your man is not what you thought he was but hey these niggas for

everybody. Tell Patience and the new baby they are about to have a little brother or sister.

Sincerely Soon to be Revealed

"What the fuck? This got to be a complete fucking joke" Endy body instantly becomes steamed. She searched the room for her phone and sees it sitting on the end table. She quickly dials Niema number but she gets no answer so she dials Chynna next.

"What's good baby mama?" Chynna jokes with her.

"Bitch you won't believe what the hell I just got at my front door?" Endy screams.

"Endy what is it? Are you crying?" she replies back.

"Chy I just got a letter with a fucking ultrasound attached saying I been with your husband for several months and that she's five months pregnant too."

"Who the fuck is it Endy?" Chynna asks.

"I don't know but I'm about to fucking find out. I haven't called him yet but I'm about to see where he's at and get to the bottom of this shit right now. I just want you to know what's going on. I'm about to get Patience ready and take her to Ma Evelyn house so I will hit you so we can meet up?" Endy tells her.

"Hell no E you're not about to leave with that baby by yourself" she shouts at Endy.

"I got my piece I'm sure whoever it is probably is long gone."

"Probably my ass I'm on my way to you now. Don't leave because best believe I got my shit" Chynna says.

"Okay, bitch, hurry up. I'm on go mode right now" Endy says, getting Patience's bag ready. She calls Jasean next, but he doesn't answer. She tries two more times and sees he still doesn't answer so she sends him a text:

"This your wife you need to get in touch with me ASAP"

She then calls Evelyn to let her know she is on her way. "Hi I just want you to know that I'm still coming."

"Okay baby some shit went down with my sister and Keosha. We will talk when you get here though. Is everything okay Endy?" Evelyn asks.

"Yeah everything is okay Ma I will see you in a few" she replies.

"You sure? I know my son been an ass lately, but I'm still Ma Ev" Evelyn reminds her.

"I know Ma" Endy giggles and wrap up the phone conversation because she see she has a text and Niema is calling.

"Hello" Endy answers. "What's going on boo?" Niema speaks back.

"Well I just received a damn envelope at my door with a sonogram and note inside. The note is basically saying Jay been messing with some chic and now she's five months pregnant. She knows I'm pregnant and my daughter's fucking name." "What? Endy are you messing with me right now" Niema asks unsure.

"Why would I lie about something like that? Ny if there is any truth to this bullshit at all him and that bitch is gonna die" she spat.

"Endy now let's not get ahead of ourselves and jump to conclusions just get in touch with Jay now" Niema advised her.

"I did he supposed to meet me at Ma Ev house. I'm about to head to Ma Ev's house in a minute to talk to her about all this shit Jay has going on. Girl this is just too much to be processing right now I'm trying my best to stay stress free but these motherfuckers are pushing me to the limit. I need you to meet me there" Endy voice quivers

"I know but you have to stay strong because you have a long road ahead of you. With Jay having this extortion charge against Carter on top of drugs and money laundering you really need to save your strength babe. I'm gonna meet

you and Chynna at Aunt Ev's house. Just, please,

remain calm" Niema begged her.

"I will boo see you there" Endy says

before hanging up. She continues putting on

Patience coat and hat and putting her in her car

seat Chynna text that she's ten minutes away.

(Ding…dings…the doorbell rings) She straps her

baby in her seat and grabs her gun again. She

walks to the door and peep out to see it is Chynna

at the door.

"Girl I had to be cautious."

"Bitch put that gun away around my damn

cousin. Hi, Pay Day," Chynna says to the baby

who is just smiling up something.

"That right there is what keeps my days

bright I swear yo" Endy smiles at her baby.

"I know babe where is this letter" Chynna asks.

"Well, chica, you're going to have to read that shit in the car because I told Ma Ev I would be there about 30 minutes ago" Endy tells her, grabbing the car seat, as Chynna grab the baby bag. They go out the door and to Endy's truck to head to Evelyn house.

"Endy are you sure this shit don't have something to do with all this mess that's going on. Maybe Carter got someone to do it."

"Chynna maybe so I'm just saying if it's any truth to it I'm done with that bastard and he's going to pay me very well I mean that shit" Endy's so serious too.

"Well it just doesn't make sense why would she wait until now to say something it's

just too much of a coincidence for me cuz"
Chynna doubts Jasean has cheated.

"It better be Chy because this bastard got
me all the way fucked up if he thinks he is going
to just throw away all I have built for this family.
He better pray it's a coincidence because if it's
any truth to this shit I'm taking that ass for
everything. I didn't build this family to be treated
like shit. I'm so serious right now" Endy says
with this raging look on her face.

"I know it sounds bad right now but you
have to give him a chance to explain please don't
go jumping to conclusions right away. Promise
me you will go in with an open mind about this".

"I will Chynna but I'm just warning you if
it's any funny shit his ass is mine" Endy tells her.

After they finally arrive at Evelyn's house in Queens in close proximity of JFK Airport they see Marilyn's car parked out front. "Oh Auntie is here too" Chynna informs her.

"Yeah I know Ma already told me she was here I don't give a fuck I know she already knows what's going on anyway grab Pay bag for me" Endy said jumping out the car to get the baby. They walk up to the door and hear some type of commotion going on but it's muffled.

"You hear that?" Chynna asks Endy.

"No but I'm sure whatever it is we're going to find out" Endy says and ring the door bell. The house gets quiet "who is it?" Evelyn yells through the intercom.

"It's Endy, Ma. Come on. It's cold out here and your granddaughter is heavy as hell," Endy yells back in the speaker. Evelyn buzz them in and has a surprised look on her face when she sees she has Chynna with her.

"Oh, hi, my beautiful babies. Y'all too fancy for Ma Ev" Evelyn jokes.

"I love that outfit daughter" Evelyn tells Endy who's wearing a Gucci jacket with the stretch jeans to match.

"That is hot" another voice says and when Endy looks she see its Keosha standing beside Marilyn.

"Mommy, I didn't know you had company. I could have come another time." Endy's reluctant to talk since Keosha is there.

"Now, I know Keosha is not y'all favorite person, but she is family. So, as bad as we hate each other, I need y'all to get a long for me today. So please y'all do this for me because right now CJ and Jay has gotten themselves in something so deep that they have dragged all of us in with them" Evelyn tells them.

"Well I'm about to be removed from all this chaos. They can have these streets, the money and the ho's" Endy shoots Keosha a hateful look and has a seat on the sofa. Chynna is still standing opposed to having this pow wow with them.

"Chynna baby please have a seat" Evelyn begs her.

"Okay but I'm telling you now I'm not biting my tongue."

"We know y'all don't but tonight have been a very crazy night for us and we all need to be sticking together right now" Marilyn is pissed.

The doorbell rings "Oh shit." Endy blurts.

"What?" Chynna asks.

"That must be Ny but I didn't know Keosha and Auntie were going to be here" Endy informs Chynna.

"I don't know who this can be" Evelyn runs off to open the door. When she returns, she shoots Endy a crazy look.

"I tried to get here fast as I could so I can see what the hell is going on" Niema said but as she reaches the living room she stops.

"Hello baby girl you look so beautiful carrying that baby" Marilyn jumps up to hug her which agitates the hell out of Keosha.

"Hi Ma I didn't know you were going to be here" Niema responds surprised. Endy shoots her 'I didn't know look'.

"Hi Ny I didn't know either but we're here" Endy and Chynna greets her with a hug.

"Well if it's okay with Marilyn I can just go so y'all can have y'all talk" Keosha tells them.

"Hell no you're not be leaving because I need to talk to all of you. I wish Lynasia, Taiya, and Ari was here too because I need to tell y'all girls something about men and life" Evelyn states.

"Well I know they don't want me here so why would I stay" Keosha shoots. "Bitch nobody thinking about you I'm here for my damn friend.

Your ass is irrelevant" Niema shot back.

"Look I don't give a damn who did or said

what. I'm talking right now and y'all are going to

listen" Evelyn yelled which silence the room.

"Okay, Aunt Ev, you're right. You have

the floor. I'm sorry" Niema calms down and have

a seat.

"First of all, I hate to say this but y'all

have let these men ruin y'all and now y'all are full

of disappointment. You have no one to blame but

yourselves for this self-destruction. Never let a

man disrespect you because once he does it, and

get away with it, he will continue doing it.

Women sit here going against each other instead

of checking these men and frankly I'm sick of it.

My son is no angel but I bet he knows better to try

Endy again. Now CJ has gotten himself in a world

of mess and my sister and Keosha were robbed at gun point tonight at CJ's house. So yes shit is getting real and y'all better try to stick together instead of going against each other. Whoever is after them will be coming for us," Evelyn informed them.

"What the hell are CJ and Jay doing? Ma oh my goodness is y'all okay?" Niema jumps up to hug a sobbing Marilyn.

"Yes I'm okay but I thank God they didn't hurt my grand baby. I don't know what I would have done" Marilyn cried harder.

"I'm so sorry all this is going on. They are going out here getting into bullshit and not thinking about the people who they're involving. I'm going to ask you this, are you sure he won't cheat again? Because I'm not so sure Ma" Endy said with her eyes filling with tears.

"Yes I'm sure baby he's not that stupid to mess up again."

"Well how do you explain this?" Endy slaps the envelope on the coffee table.

"What is it Endy?" Evelyn asks and Endy burst into tears. Everyone is confused but Chynna, who cradles her cousin while Evelyn goes thru the envelope reading the letter and looking at the ultrasound picture. Marilyn and Niema race over to look at what has her so upset.

"You see that shit Ma and for some odd fucking reason I feel like there is some truth to it" Endy cried.

"Endy now I know Jay haven't lost his damn mind. He knows better I expect this foul shit out of CJ but not him" Marilyn said walking over to comfort Endy. Keosha sits there in shock because the way Jasean portrays his love for Endy

like no other female can deter him from her so

this is quite a surprise.

"Endyia this has got to be some bullshit.

Have you talked to him yet?" Evelyn asks.

"Yes but I haven't told him anything yet. I

tell you one thing if he has done some shit like

this to me after all I have done for him. I promise

I will make him regret this bullshit I mean it"

Endy warns her.

Niema is also in shock because despite

everything she never really seen Jasean as the

cheating type. He always showed Endy respect

and made her feel special.

"If I can say one thing" Keosha asks and

everyone fell silent. Niema shoots her a hell no

look.

"Please you two I know you all don't get along but let her speak please. You might need to hear what she has to say" Evelyn asks.

Endy sighs. "What do you possibly have to say?" Endy asks Keosha.

"I just want to say that I know Jasean loves you. I never saw him disrespect you. Just look at tonight. Ms. Marilyn and I went through a traumatic situation, but do you think Caine cares? His daughter could have been killed and he is not here yet. However Jasean has called constantly to check on you and let you know he's on the way. His main concern was if you and his child were okay I was sitting here when he called his mom four times. It wasn't until Ms. Marilyn called Caine and explained everything that he became concerned" Keosha is now tearing up and despite it all the girls felt bad for her.

(Ding…dings…ding...the door bed rings)

"Who is it" Evelyn shouts into the intercom.

"It's me, Mommy" Jasean shouts back.

"Endy please chill don't fly off the handle babe" Chynna grabs her hand.

Jasean enters the home and is surprised to see all the women in one room especially Niema and Keosha.

"Can someone tell me what is going on?"

"Well first of all, I don't know what the hell your cousin has gotten himself into, but three men robbed me and Keosha at gunpoint with Cadence right there in his house" Marilyn screams.

"Auntie what you mean robbed y'all? Who the hell was it?" Jasean whole facial expression went straight vicious.

"Jasean I need you to calm down where is CJ" his mother asks.

"I don't know Ma. I thought he was here with y'all. Yo E what's the matter?" he walks over to hug her. She pushes him away

"Don't you fucking touch me you sorry bastard." Endy snarls at him.

"What you talking about?" Jasean's now confused why she's upset.

"Let me take a walk before I slap the motherfucking taste out your mouth. I'm too angry right now to deal with this bullshit" Endy said and walked to the kitchen.

"I will go check on her" Chynna darts evil eyes at Jasean.

"Well son I don't know what y'all men be thinking about but here you go" Evelyn passed him the envelope.

"What the hell? This must be some type of joke" he yells as he reads the letter.

"Mommy you can't possibly believe I would jeopardize my family this way. Somebody is setting me up y'all got to know this right? It's probably Carter or someone in his camp" Jasean continues explain.

Although Evelyn knows her son loves Endy she has a feeling he may have been dipping his pipe in the wrong plumbing. "Well Jay baby if it's not true it will blow over but until then I suggest you go talk to your wife she's the one you need to convince" Evelyn kiss him on the cheek. Jasean immediately goes after her.

(Ring…Ring...Marilyn cell phone rings) Oh now he want to calls back. "WHERE THE HELL IS YOU AT?" Marilyn yelled in the phone. "Mommy, I'm sorry. I'm about to pull up to Aunt Ev's house. Y'all just have the door open" he said and hung up.

"This boy is going to give me a heart attack I'm telling you" Marilyn shakes her head.

"What he say?" Keosha asks.

"He should be here in a minute." As soon as she asks, the door opens and he comes rushing in the house straight to Keosha and Cadence kissing them both. Niema have never seen him so affectionate so it took her by surprise.

"Y'all okay" he palms her face and turns around to kiss Marilyn.

"What the hell is she doing here?" he groans.

"Let's make this shit clear this is my damn house. She is like family we can't help that shit went down. I can tell you this, all the shit that is happening to you has been a result of your behavior. You chose to cheat and have a baby so don't come calling her no names. So you better start living and treating people better or you will be running for the rest of your life Caine" Evelyn points her finger letting him know she meant what she said.

"Okay, Aunt Ev. I'm sorry. Ny I apologize to you too" he said through his teeth.

Endy and Jasean walk back in the living room hand and hand and she seem calm now. "Is everything alright?" Evelyn asks them.

"Yeah Ma I'm going to take his word that somebody playing games but it just still seems crazy. I'm going to trust my husband this time" Endy said.

"E come on I love you and my kids I don't have time for these ho's out here. Someone is setting me up I can promise you that. I would not hurt you like that. You're my life Endy" he kissed her.

"Awe" everyone said at the same time beside Niema who feels something isn't right.

"Y'all know that dude is soft; but yo, we have to go and find out who these cats was that robbed my shit" Caine reminds them.

"Yeah well I'm asking y'all to please be careful, don't hurt anybody, and don't get caught" Marilyn tells them.

"Yes please be careful y'all have kids to make it home to" Evelyn adds.

"Yeah Ma won't get caught" Caine said and kissed his baby girl and Jasean kissed Patience.

"Ma I'm not going to be stupid I'm gotta make it home to them" he kiss Endy too. Jasean phone rings its Reeko cousins who they get their guns from.

"Alright talk to y'all later" Jasean said and they rush out the house.

"I hope whoever did this has a good explanation for it because you know they are not letting it slide" Marilyn says shaking her head.

"Well Marilyn I pray that's it's handled peacefully but knowing our boys I seriously doubt it." Evelyn sighs.

Chapter 20

Jasean and Caine are on their way to a spot out in Brownsville to meet Reeko Uncle Juan and his crew. They heard the dudes who robbed Caine is out that way and Juan use to date Marilyn so he doesn't play when it comes to her or her family.

"I just don't think Carter sent them to do this bullshit to me that just not his style. It had to be someone who thought I was gonna to be slipping. They better thank God they didn't hurt my daughter but they did violate my mom's so they are definitely going to be handled" Caine groans.

"I feel you bruh like what the fuck were they thinking going to your crib. They better be glad you weren't there because shit would of gotten real ugly real quick. Out of all times, Aunt Marilyn left her gun in the car. You know any other time she would have had the heat on her."

"That was God because they probably would have had to kill her you know moms ain't going down without a fight" Caine replied.

"Yeah, Auntie would have hit 'em up. She's known to be the sharp shooter" Jasean laughs.

"Yo for real what is this shit about a baby and some letter left at your crib?" Caine is curious to know.

"I don't know what that shit is about, but I'm not about to let no bullshit fuck up my family. Me and Endy been through enough I won't let her down again" he gripes. For some reason Caine feel like it's more to it but he won't pressure him,

when he's ready to tell him he will.

"Pull over right here. He said they at the

garage on Junius Street, across from Food

Bazaar" Caine tells Jasean. He pulls over and they

see the gate is open a little at the bottom of the

garage.

"Yo hit Raul and Thiago to see if they're

here yet" Jasean tells him. Caine calls but gets no

answer so they wait a few minutes. Next thing

they know, the gate flies open, startling them.

When they look, and it's Raul and Thiago: two of

Reeko's cousins.

"What's up? I been hitting y'all for like

the last ten minutes what's the plan? Is Unc down

with us" Caine daps them up.

"What up come inside. Uncle Juan is here and will explain how everything is going to go down. We love your family like our own and you know he doesn't play when anybody fucks with y'all moms" Raul tells them.

"Yeah I hear that, everyone loves the Newman sisters" Jasean laughs.

"Hell yeah my Uncle said they use to put in work back in the day. They are very well respected around New York" Thiago adds. "Yeah and they wonder why me and this dude so damn crazy" Caine spits.

They walk in the garage which is quite dark with little light from the outside and reeks of oil, tires, and gas. They can hear someone talking in Spanish in the back office. Caine and Jasean know the Perez family very well, but they're always cautious of their surroundings.

"Hola amigos lon tine no see" Uncle Juan speaks with a Hispanic accent. He gets up to shake their hands. There's like three other men dressed in suits surrounding him.

"What's good Uncle Juan how you been doing?" Caine asks. "Estoy bien I good so wha bing chu here? Sit down" Uncle Juan told them seated at his big desk. The office looks totally different than the rest of the garage; it's much cleaner and surrounded with bullet proof glass.

"Some niggas from Brownsville ran up in my crib took my dough and put guns to my moms and girl head with my baby girl right there" Caine explained still enraged as a motherfucker.

"We want them dealt with but we're not trying to get our hands dirty you feel me. Did y'all find out any info in the streets" Jasean asks him.

"Yeah, Uncle Juan said one of the motherfucker's lil chic told one of his guys, Cheddar, out in Queens about the hit" Thiago says.

The bitch dropped dime as soon as the nigga offered her a stack. She said their names are Serious, Chubb, and Seven. They're from Fort Greene projects. Sound familiar at all?" Raul asks.

"Nah but I know one thing they were careless as hell with covering up their tracks that's for sure" Jasean adds.

"Wa chu jus let me hanal it and I wul jek wit chu lata" Uncle Juan says and nods to the men standing beside him who all exit the office. They all know that it's done the dudes that ran up in Caine crib better go ahead and tell their mothers to buy that black dress..

All the girls are meeting up at Endy's to help her get ready for her long overdue getaway to Miami for her Anniversary. She is not supposed to leave for the next couple of days, but she is going to surprise Jasean early. He is already down there laying low on business closing a deal on a new club while Uncle Juan handles those creeps. She has Asia and Karishma running her store until she gets back. The feds finally agreed to let her open her doors to E-Class since she had no dealings with Jasean side shit. She has consulted with her mother and Evelyn with watching Patience so she is all set to go. Jasean has federal court in April, so they are trying to spend as much time together as they can. They don't know what the future holds for them and their family.

"Endy, let me see the outfit, girl that bustier showing them juicy breast, Honey." Ari chuckles.

"I know, girl. I'm going to feed my man these things tonight. Like, Happy Anniversary, Baby" Endy said grabbing a hold of both her breast rubbing them up in Niema's face laughing. They are so happy to see Endy in good spirits these days especially now that everything is getting back on track with her Jasean.

"Well what y'all think?" Endy asks the girls. She prances out the dressing room with a mauve colored pants suit fitting her thick ass to a tee. Then she's wearing is a black strapless, sheer, see-through bustier with heart shape mauve color lace in the front. It's holding her juicy tits up right nice.

"Girl that man gonna tear your ass up something serious" Chynna slaps her five.

"Girl I'm gonna be having his ass hollering" Endy says twerking her big ole booty up and down while Niema slaps it.

"I'm going to miss y'all so much man." Niema get emotional as she enjoys her girls laughing and joking. This is something they haven't done with each other in a while.

"We gonna miss you too Grandma Turn homewrecker" Ari jokes.

"Ari stop it I'm not a home wrecker!" Niema yells.

"You know I'm just joking with you. I'm ready to see my nephew come into this world. I just don't see you being no mommy this is gonna

be new" Ari wrap her arm around to her.

"Do you realize we have had a rough ass

year with these men of ours?" Niema says to

Endy.

"Girl it has been crazy with all the shit that

has went on, but you know what God makes no

mistakes. We went through all this for a reason"

Endy tells her. "Y'all just don't understand how

ready I am to get away from New York and start

over" Niema sighs a breath of relief.

"I know you are girl I wish I was coming

with y'all I know Auntie gonna be cooking up

something" Chynna says rubbing her stomach.

"We have had our ups and downs but I

want y'all to know I love you all so very much.

Now let's stop with the mushy shit and help Endy

finish getting ready for her man" Ari said

breaking up their sentimental moment. She was

never very affectionate until she got around Endy

and Chynna.

"Yes my bags are packed and I'm ready

for MIAMI!" Endy yells.

The other women just laugh at her but they

know how much she needs this break and time

away with her husband. They help her get her

bags in the car and take her straight to JFK

Airport. She is so ready to get to Miami and

surprise her baby she has butterflies in her

stomach. "FLIGHT 5057 LEAVING KENNEDY

TO MIAMI" the rep says over the speaker. Endy

grabs her bags and get in line.

♦♦♦NewSouth™♦♦♦

"I hope Endy has a good time babe she really deserves it, hell we all need to get away from New York right about now. I just hope I can find some women to get along with down south. I am going to miss my girls, the food, and shopping" Ny say to Rocko whose rubbing her feet.

"Yeah baby we will be gone in two days to go search for our new home. Are you really ready for this big change from New York to North Carolina" he questions. "Yes baby my mind has not changed about that believe me we need to get away. I'm just saying I'm going to miss everybody that's all this is our home. We were born and raised here so it's just crazy that we are actually moving away" she explained stroking his head full of curls.

"I just want you to know that I got us baby. It's going to be a big change but we gonna need it to raise our beautiful family. It's going to be a lot with Rae and the new babies but we're gonna make it work babe" Rocko tells her.

"I know baby and the way you love your children just lets me know that I chose the right man to be with" Niema kisses him so gently.

"You better stop it before you start something up" Rocko says gripping a handful of her booty.

"Stop grabbing my butt" she giggles.

"Call Endy to check and see if she got to Florida safe I'm about to get me another plate of the shrimp Alfredo." he kiss her and goes to the kitchen. She calls Endy twice but there is no answer so she calls Tanya to see if she heard from her.

"Hi Ny what's going on baby?" "Hi Ma have you spoke to Ny at all?" she asks.

"No is everything okay" Tanya becomes concerned.

"No everything is fine I just thought she would of called someone by now that's all" Niema clearly states.

"Oh okay well I'm sure she is okay she probably too busy enjoying her man and being free from the baby. You know her only time she has away from Patience is when she is at that damn store. I was ready for me baby to slow down" Tanya said with relief.

"I know she really needed this, my bestie had a rough year. We all have, that's why I'm so ready to see what the south is about" Niema sighs.

"It's going to be a great place for you and Roc to start over. Y'all going to need it with all y'all have been through. Hell I am considering relocating myself New York isn't getting any better" Tanya laughs.

"You got that right Ma well let me get back to my man but if talk to Endy tell her to check in please" Niema laughs. She immediately wraps up the call with Tanya but when she turns around Rocko is standing there naked with his hard dick out.

"Well, well, well I see someone miss me huh" Niema walks seductively towards Rocko.

"I want to be inside you so bad right now. You think we can make that happen?" He says.

He then slips his hands under her night gown and touches her clit which instantly gets her moist. She murmurs out a low moan which makes him rub her clit even more. This time she moans even louder and grips his dick.

"I can't take it bae I want you so bad right now" he whispers in her ear.

He picks her up and carries her to the bedroom and gently lays her on the bed removing her robe she has on.

"I love you so much Rodney" she whispers back to him.

"I love you too Ma." He replied.

He then stands up and rub her belly in amazement that he finally found someone who he cannot live without and she felt the same about him. He dives his face in her neatly manicured pussy and sticks his tongue so deep inside that he made her cum in seconds. All she could do was grip the sheets on her bed tight as she could. Once she took all the licking she could she was so ready for some sticking.

"I'm going to ride you until my juices cover this big juicy dick baby" she moans getting up to do just what she said. Niema gets up and hops on his dick and ride that shit like she was on a bull. All he could do was suck on her nipples to keep from screaming out.

"Damn Ny this pussy is so fucking good and wet baby" he grab her ass just to get in deeper.

"Ahhh…ahhh…ahhh….Roc…Roc" she screams and moans as her pussy gets wetter.

As his dick pounds this juicy pussy he feels himself about to let go but he doesn't want to cum before her so he holds back. He feels her pussy getting tighter and wetter that's when he knew she was about to lets out the warm cream he loves so much. She could no longer take it the thrust became harder and faster.

"Baby I'm about to cum" she groans. "Cum on this dick baby it's yours." He groans back. "Ahhh…baby…I'm about to cum" she groans more.

Rocko just keeps giving her that dick like she likes it harder. Niema feels her body tensing and her pussy gets tighter until she can't take it anymore. She loved making love to him because it was always just like it was their first time.

"Ahhh...I'm cumming...I'm cumming baby...Ahhh" she screams out in sweet agony.

"Ahhh... baby, I'm cumming too .Damn, this pussy is so good. I can never get tired of making love to you baby" Rocko says gripping her face as they suck on each other's lips. "Ahhh... shit, baby that was so fucking good" Rocko mumbles, still holding Niema tight. They just laid there until they both fell quickly asleep. It was just like the first time they made love his body was in tune with hers as hers was with his.

♦♦♦NewSouth™♦♦♦

Endy gets to Miami to the Condo they are staying at around 8 pm and it seems Jasean is still not there yet so she begins to put her plan in motion to have the room romantically ready for him when he gets there. She undresses all the way down to her bustier, a black thong and some mauve pumps. She lights candles all around the living room and pours two glasses of champagne. She see its several glasses in the sink and shakes her head because his ass just feel like dishes are a woman's job.

"This boy knows he something else leaving dirty dishes in these people sink." She mumbles to herself.

She sits down on the couch and picks up the phone to see where he's at but she hears a noise. (Boom…Boom…Boom). It sounds like it's coming from upstairs so she grab a knife and takes off her heels to walk quietly up the stairs. But as she gets closer, she hears what appears to be a woman moaning and she thinks she hears Jasean voice too. So she continues walking toward a bedroom with the door cracked. It seemed to be dark with only little light shining from the television.

"Ahhh... Jay! Ahhh... baby, go deeper" Endy hears the female voice says. Endy stomach was in knots she could not believe what she was hearing but she had to see who this female was. She continued walking slowing to the bedroom. When she gets to the bedroom door, she tried to peep through the crack of the door but she really couldn't see anything so she pushed it open a little more.

"Ahhh... baby. Damn, this dick is so good" the woman moans.

All Endy can see is some woman legs up in the air and Jasean fucking the hell out of her. She walks closer but they are fucking so hard they didn't even see or hear her at the door. She pushed the door completely open and stood in the door

way watching them have sex before her very eyes.

"Oh shit baby get up" The woman pushed

Jasean off her and jumped to the side of the bed

with a pregnant belly.

"Endy? Baby please let me explain this"

Jasean's in shock.

"So this is why I couldn't come with you?

This is what you left early to do? So you do have

a fucking baby on the way? You pussy

motherfuckers" Endy screamed and charged

toward them with the knife in her hand.

"Baby let me explain this!" Jasean jumped

back as the woman grabbed her clothes. Endy

darts across the room to attack the bitch but

Jasean caught her and the knife just in time

because she cut him across the arm. He was able

to wrestle her enough to drop the knife. Endy couldn't quite get to the chic but she knew exactly who it was.

"You're defending this ho? Are you fucking serious? Let me go Jay I can't believe you did this shit to me, to our family you fucking bastard" she yelled to the top of her lungs with tears flooding her face.

Jasean let her go once he got tired of being smacked, bitten, and kicked and the woman was in the clear to run for it. He had hoped she took her ass far away from there as she could. He didn't know what to do but he knew his best bet was to stay away from her from her and out of her way.

Endy always thought if she caught him cheating she would probably kill him and the girl. Although she wanted to, Endy knew she had to be

smart so she calmed herself down, turn around
and walk back downstairs distraught with a
million thoughts going through her head. It seems
like everything is going in slow motion. She put
her clothes back on and tears streamed her face
but she knew she had to get out of there fast as
she could before she went to prison in Florida.
She knew she couldn't put her family through
that.

She walks outside dazed and confused she
is trying to gather her thoughts to understand what
the hell he was thinking. The more she thought
about it the angrier she became.

"Hello could I have a cigarette" she asked
an older lady she seen smoking outside.

"Are you okay hun?" the woman asked.

"Yes I'm okay thanks for asking" Endy replied and walked off with cigarette and the woman's lighter. The woman was gonna say something but she just let her have it.

She walks to Jasean's Lexus that was parked out front and anticipates what she should do. Endy cries her heart out but not before she spots a shirt and towel Jasean had in the car. She checks to see if the doors are open and they were. She set it on fire to the shirt since it cost him $300 threw it in the car. She watch it burn until the whole car is on fire.

"Endy please don't do this baby, I'm sorry" he said as he ran to his car that's quickly filling with flames He got close enough that she slaps the dog shit out of him.

"I want a fucking divorce you sorry son of a bitch oh and I won't be having this bastard ass baby. You and her go ahead" tears flood her face.

"Endy please baby let me talk to you don't take my baby away from me" Jasean now in tears.

She starts to walk up the street but stops "Oh and tell YaYa her ass is mine I'm nowhere near done with her yet." She spat and turned around to walk up the street because she can hear the sirens.

"ENDY, ENDY!" Jasean yells but she doesn't stop. "What the fuck have I done?" he yells grabbing his head.

◆◆◆NewSouth™◆◆◆

Endy finds a bar to have a drink and finally gets the nerve to call someone. She decides to call Niema. (Ring...ring...The phone wakes Niema up). She sees its Endy calling her

"Hello." A groggy Niema answers the phone.

"That ho ass cousin of yours ass is mine Niema I'm fucking her up on sight" Endy screams.

"What you talking about Endy? What happen?" Niema jump up half sleep and confused.

"I just caught her and my sorry ass husband fucking in the Condo down here in Miami. The one he supposedly gotten for our anniversary" Endy cried.

"Oh my God Endy I wanted to tell you I swear I didn't know it was going that far." Niema confessed.

"WHAT THE FUCK YOU MEAN YOU WANTED TO TELL ME? SO YOUR SHIESTY ASS KNEW THIS SHIT" ENDY VOICE SCREECHED.

"Endy hold up let me explain"

"FUCK YOU! Don't worry about it call my family tell them to get my bail money up because I'm gonna kill all y'all bitches" she said and hung up.

"Endy wait, Endy" Niema yells but she already hung up. "What is it Ny? What the fuck going on with Endy" Rocko is woke now.

"Endy caught Jay and YaYa fucking out in Miami. I wanted to tell her" Niema cried.

"WHAT? Is this motherfucker serious?" Rocko jumped up. He tried calling Endy but there's no answer so he tried Jasean he doesn't answer either. He calls them a few more times and decided to call the rest of the family.

"Fuck this get dress we are going to my nana house now. I can't believe this bullshit. " Rocko throws on his clothes

"Roc I need to tell you something" Niema said getting dressed too.

"NY COME THE HELL ON! WE CAN TALK IN THE CAR!" He yelled.

About an hour later everyone gathered at Luella's house still trying to reach Endy or Jasean but still no answer from neither of them. Finally Chynna phone rings "Hello" she quickly answered.

"It's me Jay."

"Where the fuck is my cousin at?" Chynna shouts in the phone about to cry. Tanya grabbed the phone from her because Chynna is just too upset.

"Hello Jasean where is my daughter and what the hell is going on?" Tanya spoke loudly.

"Ma I don't know where she's at she's not answering the phone the police are here about to take me to jail. Please tell her I love her and I'm sorry man. I'm sorry Ma please I'm sorry" Jasean yelled as the cops take the phone from him.

"Jasean wait what's going on? I don't give a fuck about you and YaYa where's my child" Tanya yells.

"Hello Mam?" one of the cops answer the phone.

"Yes hello can someone please tell me what's going on?" Tanya is now in tears confused about what the hell is going on.

"It seems there was an altercation at the resort, a vehicle was set on fire, and we're taking Jasean Newman in for questioning" the lady cop explains.

What the hell is going on? Where's my baby? Where's Endy?" Tanya drops the phone.

"What is going on? Where is she?" Luella grabs and shakes Tanya but she is just too upset to answer.

"I just want my baby girl back home Mommy. Niema ever since you entered this family it's been nothing but turmoil and chaos. I just want my baby home" she cried louder.

"I'm sorry Ma, I'm sorry I didn't think she was telling the truth. I just didn't think Jay would do that y'all I didn't" Niema cried.

"So you knew about this bullshit you fucking snake" Chynna yelled.

"You and that lil bitch better hope I find my daughter" Tanya stormed out the living room.

Everyone is standing in silence confused and pissed by the whole ordeal all they want to know is WHERE'S ENDY?

TO BE CONTINUED

PART II AFTER THE BETRAYAL

COMING SOON